Hits
Different

Hits Different

Tasha Ghouri
& Lizzie Huxley-Jones

HOT
KEY
BOOKS

First published in Great Britain in 2024 by
HOT KEY BOOKS
4th Floor, Victoria House, Bloomsbury Square, London WC1B 4DA
Owned by Bonnier Books, Sveavägen 56, Stockholm, Sweden
bonnierbooks.co.uk/HotKeyBooks

ISBN: 978-1-4714-1509-8
Signed edition ISBN: 978-1-4714-1732-0
Also available as an ebook and in audio

1

This book is typeset by Envy Publishing Ltd
Printed and bound in Great Britain by Clays Ltd, Elcograf S.p.A.

Hot Key Books is an imprint of Bonnier Books UK
bonnierbooks.co.uk

For you all out there, you are beautiful
in every way – remember that!
T. G.

For all my disabled friends who live harder,
louder and brighter; this one's for you.
L. H-J.

Chapter One

I've been dancing my whole life.

There's nothing like the rush of nailing every step, every flick of a hand in a new dance routine. I can lose myself in the movement of my body, in the way the beat feels in my chest, the satisfaction I get from every perfectly timed move. In that moment, everything else in life falls away.

When my body is in motion, I feel free.

I feel *me*.

But it's all a secret from the rest of the world. It's just for me.

My phone is precariously propped against the window frame which just about gets the right angles for filming my routines. It doesn't have to be perfectly shot anyway, because I never show anyone.

I flop onto the bed and watch back the video. It took me all morning to get the choreography down for SHINee's track 'Lucifer', and I actually look pretty good. Sure, dancing routines solo when they're usually performed by a group of five people is a totally different vibe, but I think I did a good job of adapting the choreography. My arms could snap

1

sharper, and I spy one of my feet lagging a bit as the beat changes, but I style it out enough that I don't think anyone but me would even notice.

I'm a perfectionist. There's always room for improvement. But it's good enough for now.

Inevitably, I'll do a few more takes before I move on to a new routine in a few days. That's how it's been since I was a little girl. Pick a song, dissect the choreography until I can play it back in my head with my eyes closed, and perform it to my phone camera. Sometimes I get creative and mix some things up, like I did today with 'Lucifer'.

But that's it. It never goes further than that.

They never get posted anywhere, but I save them all to my Cloud, which I've had to upgrade a few times over the years to get enough storage. They're like my diary, in a way. All the dances are tied to memories and moments in my life, like how I learned a routine to 'XO' by Beyoncé because Pen was playing it the day I went on my first date with Mason. Or the routine for 'Bye Bye' by Rosa Cordova that I made Pen learn with me the week we finished high school. It's my life, and I don't want to share them with anyone else.

Once the video is stored safely, I delete it off my phone. That's another one locked down.

I should hurry up and get ready for dinner, but instead, I do my semi-regular browse through the new job adverts on *Entertainers International*, a website that collates all the available jobs for dancers, singers and lots of other performers. Most of the jobs are for cruise ships or hotels or even the occasional corporate event. They don't tend to deviate from that, so I usually just lie here thinking about the possibilities of living in another country, dancing in a fancy hotel.

I don't know why I do it, if I'm honest. It's not like I'd ever apply for any of them. It's more like window-shopping. Imagining a different life. There's just something kind of comforting to me about seeing all these dancing jobs all over the world, and knowing that people are out there applying for them. I know Mason thinks it's weird though, so I don't do it when he's around. Dancing is just a hobby, after all.

But as I'm scrolling, something catches my eye.

Agency seeks new and unique dancers for understudy roles on international tour with major recording artist.

An international tour? Imagine that. That's the sort of thing I used to dream about when I was a teenager and I'd rope Pen into doing routines with me in front of the huge mirror of Mum's built-in wardrobes. Dancing every day and being paid for it . . . that must be really cool. But still, it's not realistic, is it? It's not a career that a normal person like me can have. It's probably the sort of thing you have to be posh to do, or you'd have to know someone in the industry already. Maybe all dancers are nepo babies? I don't really know.

My phone buzzes with a text from Mason, which brings me back to the real world. He's taking me out to dinner tonight to celebrate his promotion at work.

Mason

> Sorry babe, running late.
> Do you want to meet me at
> the restaurant instead?

We're going to this cute little Italian place on the Shambles where we had our first date, almost a year ago. I always feel so fancy when we go there, even though it's not like there's a dress code or it's super expensive. It just feels special, I guess. I feel special there.

Mason and I met on a dating app, and I knew straight away that he was a bit of me. The dark blond hair, the bright blue eyes. He looks like he could play a very English version of the boy next door. And when we met, I realised just how smart and driven he is. I wasn't sure he'd really go for me, because it's not like I'm as career-minded as he is, but we had the cutest date followed by cocktails in one of the nice outdoor bars in town.

We keep things casual between us, not putting any labels on anything. It works. We're young, after all, and it's not like I'm ready to be his wife. Imagine. I know that he cares about me, and in our own way we're committed to each other. He's not met my parents, and I've not met his yet either but that's fine. They live down in Devon where he grew up, so it would be a long trip to go see them. Mine are only twenty minutes away, so I figure when we get round to that stage, we'll start with them. I still can't quite believe it's almost been a year. Life's funny like that. You always think you'll get round to something, but time can go by in a blink.

Meeting at the restaurant means he must have forgotten

that he was going to pick me up, but that's OK. There's enough time to get a bus. I might even have time for one more take before I go . . .

Before I can set my phone back up, Pen bursts into my bedroom and I leap out of my skin. They've walked in on me dancing before; they know it's what I'm always doing up here, after all. As usual, they're a riot of colour in an orange-and-pink heart-patterned jumpsuit over a stripy T-shirt.

'Have you seen this?' asks Pen, shoving their phone practically under my nose. Their auburn curls bounce excitedly.

'What? Your phone? Constantly in your hand,' I say.

'Har har,' they say. 'Very funny. Obviously I mean the *thing* on the phone. Take it, will you? It's an article about Rosa Cordova's European tour.'

I take the phone. I'm still gutted I couldn't get tickets to see Rosa Cordova perform, but the restaurant where I work barely pays me enough to cover my rent, eat and pay the bills. If I'm really lucky, I can occasionally stretch to a slightly nicer bottle of wine, rather than the supermarket's own brand.

But I've watched a ton of Rosa's shows from this US tour on TikTok and it all looks amazing. Huge sets, costumes that change every few songs, and some of the best backup dancers I've ever seen performing choreography that I'm dying to learn, if I can find a full-length video anywhere. So far it's just thirty-second clips that cut back to people screaming 'I love her' and, during the chair routine, 'I wish I was a chair.'

'All her dancers left the tour,' Pen says wide-eyed, before I even start reading.

'What?!'

'Yeah, there's been a huge leak about it. They've all been hired out from under her for the Payton Rey tour.'

Rosa and Payton were huge rivals in the early 2010s, two teen singers who were always pitted against each other. Obviously, I was just a baby then, but there's been loads of deep dives on YouTube recently about their long-running feud, especially now that they're both on enormous tours. For Payton it's a comeback tour. Rosa, queen that she is, never left.

It wasn't clear whether their rivalry was real or manufactured for the publicity, but this seems like *real* drama. I scroll down the article, hungry for more details.

'What are they going to do on the Payton tour?' I scoff, thinking of the last few performances Payton has done at awards shows. They never excite me. The movement seems obvious, and there's so little consideration for different audience view. 'They're just going to end up holding props and wiggling. It will never be choreographed as well or as much as Rosa's shows. Why would you leave for second best?'

'All right, we get it. You're a nerd about dancing,' Pen says, bumping my shoulder and giving me a warm smile.

'This is so bad though. Some of Rosa's dancers have been with her for years and years. What's she going to do? It's awful.'

'I know, it's terrible, isn't it.' They say this with far too much enthusiasm for someone who usually only loves a bit of drama when it's fictional. Pen is hardly reading DeuxMoi or Popbitch on the regular. I'm not even sure they'd know what those are. And yet, they're practically vibrating with excitement.

Clearly, I'm missing something.

'Why exactly are you telling me this, Pen?' I say, frowning.

They gently take the phone from me, and scroll to the bottom of the page, before returning it to my open hands.

'They're basically starting again and redesigning her entire show before the European tour, at her compound in Ibiza. Like building new sets, making new costumes and training up new dancers.'

'That's huge? I'm not sure anyone's ever done that before.'

'Hello? Did you miss the part where I said *new dancers*? Look. They're doing an open-call audition.'

'Oh, that must be the job I was looking at just now,' I say, trying to sound casual about it.

'Daydreaming again?' they say, which I choose to ignore.

'I was wondering who the artist was. Rosa Cordova . . . Wow.'

My mind flashes to the many, many (possibly too many) TikToks I've seen, the impressive and brilliant routines. The way the dancers move as one, like a flock of starlings against the night sky. The artistry and spectacle of the show they create *with* and around Rosa. There's just really nothing else like it.

'They're hiring new understudies,' I say, 'so I guess only the main cast got poached, and they promoted all their current understudies. It's a big cast . . . they must have so many people on standby in case someone can't perform.'

'You've thought about this a lot, haven't you?'

'Not really. It's just how it works, isn't it?' I say, looking through my wardrobe for an outfit for dinner. 'I'm just interested, as a fan of Rosa, in what that'll mean for her next tour. It could be a disaster. Or amazing. It's wild.'

'Right.' Pen is staring at me.

I sigh. 'What?'

'Do you not think it's more interesting that this understudy job, dancing with one of your favourite musicians, arguably your dream job, is right there in your hands?'

I frown. 'What are you on about, Pen?'

'Sweet thing,' they say gently, their big green eyes softening. 'That could be you if you just apply.'

'What?' I say, not quite believing what Pen is saying to me. 'Are you having a laugh?'

'I would never joke about an opportunity for your dream to come true, Cass.'

Even though they're talking nonsense, I kind of love them for how seriously they say this. But they are being completely ridiculous. As if I'm going to apply to be an understudy for Rosa Cordova. The hiring people would be laughing at my CV. What am I going to put on there? Washes dishes for a living and has a passable sense of rhythm?!

Pen looks at me as though they can hear my thoughts, which, to be fair, they know me well enough to basically do. 'You should read through the info on the advert and have a proper think about it.'

'Which I guess you've already done?' I deadpan.

'Naturally, darling. I'm nosey,' they say, and I laugh despite myself. 'But really, have a look. There's a bit in it about how they're encouraging applications from dancers from underrepresented backgrounds.'

'Pen, I don't think they need any more slim white girls,' I laugh.

'You know that's not what I mean.'

'Hm,' I say, staring at the article again, and running my finger along my hairline to my cochlear implant.

If it was anyone else saying this to me, I would feel weird. But Pen's known me so long, and they know what it's like to be visibly different from everyone else.

'Just do an application,' they insist. 'What's the worst that can happen?'

'I embarrass myself?' I say seriously.

'OK? That doesn't sound too bad in the grand scheme of things, does it?'

A voice in my mind says *it would be worse to not try and never find out*. My stomach is filled with butterflies and I don't even know why. I'm not really seriously considering this, am I?

Sure, when I was a little kid I dreamed of being a dancer. But it's not like I've kept up going to dance classes, though the fact I work a minimum-wage job has something to do with that. I've not been to an actual dance class since my first cochlear implant broke, and I couldn't face trying when I couldn't hear anything.

And it's about more than just filling out one application. I'm worried it would open a Pandora's box of questions about my future.

Besides, I love my life in York with Pen, and Mason.

And being a kitchen porter is easy for me – every day is the same and I'm a hard worker, so I get the job done, even if its sticky and smelly and often gross. No one bothers me back there, and I don't have to talk to customers. Sure, it might not be what I want to do long term, but the fact that the chefs will prepare whatever I want for lunch makes up for it a little bit. I'll work out something realistic I want to do eventually. It's fine for now.

Mason always talks about the importance of coming up with a career plan. But he would; that's his job talking. Plus, there's a bit of an age difference between us. I'm only twenty. He's twenty-six. I still have time to work out what I'm doing with my life, right?

What I don't want to do is start filling my head with silly ideas about futures that will never happen. That's a direct route to heartbreak.

'Cassie? I know you're thinking about it, deep down,' Pen prods.

'I . . . I don't know,' I say and it comes out as a whisper. 'I don't think I'm qualified.'

'They're not asking for qualifications or previous experience. Look, there's this whole section about new talent.'

They try to show me on the phone, but I bat them away. 'Pen, I've got to get ready for my date or I'm going to miss the bus.'

'I thought Mason was picking you up?'

'He's running late,' I say as I dig through my jewellery drawer for a cute necklace to wear, hoping that turning away will end the conversation.

Typically, it doesn't. When I turn around, they ask, 'Just tell me you'll think about it?'

'OK,' I say. 'I'll think about it.'

Done. Thought about it. Case closed, I think.

'A bit more than that, please, Cass,' they add, before disappearing into their room.

Most of the time, I love that they know me so well. The rest of the time that familiarity has a habit of biting me on the butt.

We've been best friends since we were twelve and realised that our shared love of romcoms, the cheesier the better, made us compatible. Plus, we were the different kids. I wear a cochlear implant; they are non-binary. That difference in how we experience the world connected us.

But our friendship really solidified when Pen's parents decided to get divorced. When it got too much, they'd come stay at my house and we'd pyjama up and put on whatever show they liked. I just wanted them to be OK.

And then when we were sixteen and sitting our big exams at school, my cochlear implant started acting up. I'd had it fitted when I was six and they're supposed to last for pretty much your lifetime, or so I'd hoped. But mine straight-up broke, which meant I couldn't hear anything at all. Like, literally nothing. People think that cochlear implants are some perfect quick fix that mean you can immediately hear perfectly, but it's a piece of technology you have to train yourself to use. And technology can break, even after all that. And there was a long wait for a new one to get ordered and fitted. It was a really lonely, scary time. But Pen made sure that I was keeping up with classes and revision by taking the most detailed notes possible for me. They even started taking a course in BSL from their phone so that they could talk to me that way. They just are my rock.

When we left school, not really sure what we were doing with our lives, we moved into a tiny little flat on the outskirts of York. Everything we've done since, we've done together. I love that about us.

And if I applied for that job, well, it would be me alone, wouldn't it? Not that I'm actually going to apply. Even if the link is right there, on the page that's still open on my phone.

There's no time to do my hair properly, so I just dry-shampoo the roots and hope that I've not used so much that it turns my blonde hair white. In the end, I look a little like I've put my finger in an electrical socket, but it kind of works.

I hurriedly do my makeup and hope that using my fingers instead of my brushes which are still in the bathroom waiting to be cleaned won't make it look too textured. I can never get an eyeliner wing quite right, so I go for smokey eyes instead. Smudged accidentally, or on purpose? Who can say?

I decided on a cute little matching white top and miniskirt co-ord. Not too dressy but not too casual either, and the bright white brings out the warm tones in my skin.

But it doesn't take long for my mind to drift again. That kind of lifestyle probably wouldn't suit me, anyway. Tours go on forever, and you're always moving. Plus it sounds like you'd have to go out to Ibiza to rehearse for weeks and weeks beforehand. I'd be away from home for a long time. Away from Pen, and Mason.

I could really do with not daydreaming when I need to hurry up and leave the house. There's only two buses an hour, and I don't want to walk or I'll end up all sweaty and gross. I slick on some lip gloss and hope for the best.

I bundle my keys, phone, purse and spare CI batteries into that tiny bag all the influencers are obsessed with, the one that's secretly huge inside, and rush out to the hall to throw on my platform trainers.

Which, typically, are in Pen's hands.

'Did you think any more?'

'Pen, give me the shoes, or I'll miss the bus.'

I swear their eyebrow twitches upwards, but they don't give up the trainers. 'The deadline is Tuesday. Oh no, tomorrow, I think. I just want to make sure you have time to apply . . . if you want to.'

I groan and throw my hands in the air in frustration before heading back to my room, where I slip my feet into a pair of sky-high tan heels that make my legs look even longer than they are. Mason likes it when I wear heels, so this is probably the better choice anyway.

'What are you doing?' Pen asks, when I come back through. 'You'll fall on the cobbles.'

'I'll be careful.'

They hold out the trainers to me. 'Just wear these. I don't want you to hurt yourself like last time. Remember how blue your ankle went? It was gross.'

'I'll be fine. Look, I have to go.'

'We can work on it together tonight when you get back if that would help,' Pen says and I can see how much they're trying. 'We can stay up late! It'll be like a study session.'

That does sound nice. But . . . I can't think about this. And maybe the best thing would be to just let the deadline pass so that Pen will drop it.

'I might stay at Mason's.'

Hopefully he'll invite me back, and then I won't have to deal with this interrogation.

'You never stay at Mason's on a weeknight.'

'It's a date night. It doesn't count.'

'You don't have any of your bits with you. I know those bags are roomy –'

'I have things there.'

Both of us know that I don't really have anything at Mason's. It took months for me to leave a toothbrush there. I have a tiny section of a drawer for batteries and a spare pair of knickers. He just doesn't have a lot of space in his flat, and I live super nearby anyway so there's no point really.

'Look, it's not a big deal!' I say when Pen raises their eyebrow.

I'm halfway out of the door when they grab me gently by the elbow and turn me round. 'Sorry. Are you angry with me?'

'No, but I don't have time for this!'

'I'll help you. You know I will.'

'Argh, Pen,' I say, grabbing their hands and making them look at me. 'I love you. But I don't have time. It's not going to happen for me.'

And with that, I rush out of the front door.

Chapter Two

Mason is already there when I get to the restaurant, probably because I walked at half the speed I normally do in these shoes. At least I'm not a sweaty mess, even if I feel frazzled inside from that weird conversation with Pen. Oh well. I just hope I look nice for him.

The waiter greets me at the door as I fight through a bit of a queue, and shows me to our usual table. It's busier than normal, and there's a big group of people who must have finished work and gone straight to dinner on the other side of the room making loads of noise.

'Sorry I'm late,' I say, kissing him on the cheek.

The waiter pulls out the chair for me, and I sit down opposite him.

'Not at all,' he says. 'I've only been here a few minutes.'

Phew. I hate being late, especially when it's for a fancy occasion. I never want to leave anyone sitting there wondering if I'm going to show up.

He looks so good, still in his work clothes from the office. He always looks good in a suit. Today, it's the navy blue one, my favourite. The blazer is fitted so nicely against his

15

body, but doesn't strain when he moves.

'Sorry if I'm out of it. I've kind of had a bit of a weird one,' I say, laughing awkwardly.

'Oh yeah? Mine was completely hectic,' he says.

'What happened?' I ask, as he pours me a glass of white wine. It's his night, after all. 'Wait, we should toast your promotion first!'

'With white wine? Maybe we should get something bubblier,' he says, craning his neck for the waiter.

'We can do that later. It's just for good luck.'

We clink glasses, and I take a sip. It's cold and crisp and a little tart for my taste but I like it.

'So anyway, urgh, it was just totally bananas. Ton of client meetings this morning. We're really in a tech boom, you know, so everyone is looking to onboard new talent.'

'Does that mean more work for you, then?'

'Pretty much, especially thanks to the promotion, but it also means more commissions. Means I can bring you out to nice places like this.' He raises his eyebrows over his wine glass at me.

'Thank you,' I say, blushing.

'You don't need to thank me, Cassie. I like to treat you. You deserve to be wined and dined and shown off. Speaking of, you look seriously hot tonight.'

The blush creeps further over my cheeks. I love that he can still make me feel as enchanted as when we first met.

'Mase,' I giggle. 'You look good too.'

'I'd hope so. I went to woo a new client this afternoon – that's why I was a little later getting back than I hoped – and it always helps to look smart. They take you seriously if you look the part, even if you're still faking the confidence.'

'That makes sense. Actually, speaking of confidence –'

'Do you know what you want?' he says this while reading the menu, and then looks up at me expectantly.

'Oh! No, I haven't looked yet.'

Maybe now isn't the right time to bring up the job. After all, it was just a silly whim . . .

It's so loud in here from the big group and the sound of plates and glasses and people moving around that I've been worried I'll miss something Mason says if I look away, so I've been paying close attention and semiconsciously lip-reading the whole time we've been here. If I look down, I'm not going to be able to keep up with the conversation.

'I'm starving.' He puts the menu down on the table. 'I think I'll get the pork ragu. Maybe start with some arancini.'

'OK, I'll just look now,' I say, hoping he knows that I'm concentrating on something else for a moment. He's not rude about it, but sometimes he just doesn't quite get what being deaf and using a cochlear implant means, in practice.

I skim the menu as fast as I can, and settle on seabass with sautéed clams and some fresh vegetables. I never really eat fish at home because it's so expensive and I'm always worried about messing it up, so I usually get it when we eat out. It feels like an extra treat. Plus it'll go nicely with the white wine Mason chose.

'I'm ready,' I say, and he calls over the waiter for us to order.

We've been here enough times that the staff all know me,

and none of them do that weird overly loud speaking voice that people sometimes do when they find out I'm deaf. But they take their time with me, which is nice.

The same waiter brings us over some bread, oil and vinegar after taking our order. Mason dives in immediately, and carries on talking about the intricacies of his promotion. It sounds like he'll be working late more often. His office is in Leeds, so he commutes from his flat on the river here every day. He's always had to go out to schmooze clients, but it sounds like that'll be even more of his role now, so I guess there'll be less time for us to hang out. I'm really proud of him though. Maybe I can get the train in to meet him for lunch once or twice a month.

That sparks a thought I had earlier, and when there's a big enough gap in the conversation, I say, while hoping I'm not interrupting, 'Hey, I was thinking –'

'Uh-oh,' he says with a laugh, and I giggle with him.

'I was *thinking* that maybe we should meet up with my parents soon? It would be so nice for you to meet them. I know you've met Vics briefly before, but maybe we could see the rest of my family one weekend. We could always visit theirs if you wanted.'

'Oh. Yeah, if that's what you'd like?' he says, and looks away. 'It's just things really are busy at work right now so I'm not sure I can promise the time to stay with them for a weekend.'

'No, no!' I say, waving my hands so much that I nearly knock over the glass of wine. 'I wasn't thinking anything intense like staying over the first time you meet them.'

'That's good to hear,' he laughs and I join in a little awkwardly.

A staying-over trip is definitely unnecessary seeing as they live so nearby. I thought I'd mentioned that to him before but I must not have.

I decide to backtrack a little. I don't want to freak him out and make him think I'm asking for a big commitment or anything. After all, it's not like we're official or anything.

'No, I want it to be casual. I thought perhaps we could go to dinner? I know evenings are tricky, so maybe we could pick a Sunday afternoon? Go for a roast?'

The group of office workers on the table next to us laugh loudly just as he speaks, meaning I can't hear what he says in response, and it's so romantically low lit that I can't reliably lip-read either.

'Sorry, what did you say?' I ask, wincing at the ache in my brain as I try to concentrate on him. I'm definitely going to have a killer migraine later if the noise levels keep up. Processing sound the way I do takes so much mental energy.

'I said I'll need to look at my work calendar. Maybe something later this summer.'

It's already June now. Does he mean later this month, or July? But what if he means August? Surely not. Maybe I missed something he said.

Either way, I suppose we'll just make a plan in the future when it works for both of us.

'That sounds great,' I say, beaming as widely as possible so he knows it's OK.

'I'm sorry,' he says, taking my hand. 'I'm sure you'd love it to be sooner, but we'll make it work, won't we?'

'Yeah, of course.'

He always works so hard for me, and is so kind and nice.

The arancini arrive and we agree to split them between us. I realise that if he's been so busy today, he probably skipped lunch. I take one, and when he offers me more I turn it down.

'Thank you,' he says, as though I've just given him the keys to the city. 'I've been running off just coffee today. Tell me about your day?'

'Well, not much happened, but I did have this funny conversation with Pen earlier,' I say, fiddling with the napkin on my lap.

'Oh yeah? Funny how?'

'Well, not like *funny ha ha* or anything. Just kind of strange.'

He gives me a questioning look. 'What mischief is Pen getting you into now?'

'Nothing bad!' I insist with a laugh.

I don't know why I feel nervous bringing this up with him. After all, it wasn't that deep anyway.

'Did you hear about the Rosa Cordova thing? Wait, no, of course you didn't if you've been busy. Basically, a bunch of her dancers got hired out by her rival for a tour at the same time, and so they need replacements. I think they made all the understudies they had left the main cast. It's drama.'

'Are understudies the people who fill in for the proper dancers?'

'The understudies *are* proper dancers.'

'You know what I mean, babe.'

'Yeah, of course. Anyway Pen found the job advert and was trying to get me to apply.'

'For what?'

'To be one of the understudies.'

'Right,' he says slowly. 'And the job is like on tour, travelling the world and stuff?'

'Yeah!'

I can't explain what it is but I can feel something rising in my chest. Like I've taken a deep breath.

'But I'm guessing they'd be looking for people with proper credentials and training for a job like that,' he goes on. 'Theatre school graduates, at the least. A CV full of previous gigs. A creative job like that comes with a huge level of responsibility, so they'd want proven candidates, I imagine. Must be tough hiring that many people so quickly.'

And with that, the feeling is gone.

I'm back down to earth.

Of course they would want people who had experience they could point to. What do I have? A Cloud folder full of dances I recorded in my bedroom.

I give him a big smile. 'Yeah, exactly. I guess it would be really competitive too,' I say casually. 'Anyway, I told you it was silly. They'd probably laugh at my application. "What's your experience?" Videos I never showed anyone.'

Mason pats my hand across the table. 'It would only be the lack of training that would rule you out.'

'Well,' I say, freeing my hand to pick up the wine glass and take a sip. 'Pen said, I think, that there was something about looking for new and undiscovered talent from marginalised groups, so maybe that wouldn't matter so much.'

Mason snorts. 'They always say that, but do they *really* mean it?'

He's the recruitment consultant. Of course he'd know all this stuff.

'Good point.'

Why do I feel so deflated?

'Why don't you look at taking some dance classes here?' he says. 'Get back into it properly now you're an adult with your own income?'

'Oh. I probably can't afford that at the moment.' Heat crawls up my neck. I always get embarrassed about how much more than me he earns.

'I'll help you. Don't worry about that.'

'I can't ask you to do that.' The heat on my neck spreads.

'You don't have to. I just said I would.'

'I can't repay –'

'Cassie. Let me help. I know it'll make you happy, and I want you to be happy.'

'Thank you,' I say, feeling a bit overwhelmed by how nice this is. 'I can't believe I let you have the rest of the arancini and you're essentially giving me dance lessons.'

He flashes me a grin. 'Hmm, now I'd better make sure I'm not being fleeced. What's the market value of an arancini? Do you think it fluctuates depending on what's in them? Maybe we'll have to do a case study on this.'

I giggle. 'I mean, they were *very* good.'

'This is true.'

'And I am very cute.'

'Also correct.'

'So maybe, just on this occasion, it's a fair trade?'

'You drive a hard bargain, Ms Clyne. What about if you make it up to me tonight?' He runs his hand up my leg under the table and I know he's inviting me back to his. I'm instantly relieved: more time with Mason, and no nagging Pen for the night? Bliss.

'I'll take it. Deal.'

We shake hands and cheers our wine glasses, and as the weird feelings in my chest dissipate, the night dissolves into candlelight.

Afterwards we head back to Mason's and I show him just how proud I am of him as we tumble into his bed.

Chapter Three

I swear that Saturday lunch shifts were made to destroy my happiness and my home-done manicure. Thankfully, I got out of having to do a double shift, though I could use the money.

Admittedly, right at this moment I would just spend it on a properly done manicure that I would still ruin at work. Pen does a pretty decent job of them, but I miss having long, glamorous nails. Gels. Patterns! Anything with a bit of flair to it.

My shoulders ache from working as fast as I could so that we had enough clean crockery to keep up with demand. I need a massage. Another thing I can't afford, but it's slightly weirder if I ask Pen for one. Mason is away at a family wedding this weekend, so I can't ask him either. He said there were no plus-ones, and I suppose that would be a pretty intense way to meet his entire family for the first time so I didn't mind not going. I'll just have to settle for a hot bath instead.

I decide to save the few quid on the bus, and walk home. The movement will help stretch my tired muscles out. Luckily, it's a gorgeous afternoon, complete with blue skies – the first real summery day of the year, which feels like a good omen. I love days like this, when the flowers are blooming and everything feels fresh and new and full of possibilities.

I stop to cross the road outside the theatre. There's a big advertisement for a couple of musicals that are touring, and will be doing dates here in the next few months. The posters show not only the leads, but the ensemble dancing cast. I can't help but wonder what it's like to be in a touring production like that, dancing every night. You'd be bone tired, but the adrenaline of it all, the rush of the lights and the audience and the applause, would probably make up for it. Plus, I bet professional dancers don't smell like industrial soap and old food. Or at least, I hope not.

A driver who slows to let me cross clearly notices me sniffing my forearm and gives me a very strange look, but oh well.

I've not really stopped thinking about that job all week, as much as I don't want to admit that to myself. And I absolutely do not want to admit it to Pen, though luckily they never mentioned it again.

The rest of the walk home is down quiet paths where I only have to avoid cyclists, though that's easier said than done. I take my hair out of its low ponytail, which normally conceals my cochlear implant. The nice thing about working in the kitchen is that customers don't really see me, and I've worked there long enough that the chefs know the drill so don't ask about it, but still, I always cover it up. The wind takes my hair and ruffles it in the breeze, and I can feel my work headache start to ease. It's so quiet out here that I can breathe.

If I wasn't walking along a pathway with errant cyclists, I'd be tempted to take it out and get a hit of that real silence, but that'll have to wait until I'm home. I don't have any desire to go out from a cyclist propelling me into the river.

The sun is warm on my cheeks, and I decide to stop on one of the memorial benches for a little while, enjoying the fresh air. The seat is surrounded by wildflowers, which have sprung up all over the city, turning it into a riot of colour.

I decide to let Pen know I'm on my way home.

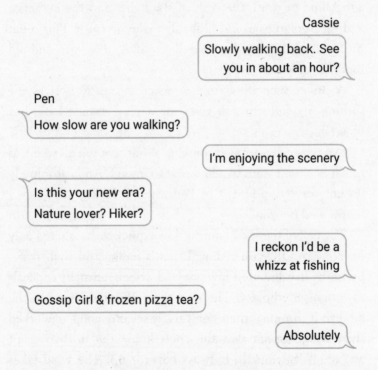

Cassie

Slowly walking back. See you in about an hour?

Pen

How slow are you walking?

I'm enjoying the scenery

Is this your new era? Nature lover? Hiker?

I reckon I'd be a whizz at fishing

Gossip Girl & frozen pizza tea?

Absolutely

Just as I close the chat, I notice something really strange. An icon in the top left of the screen that says I have an email.

Odd – the only people who email me are brands, and all those are set up to go straight into my promotions folder without sending any notifications.

I open up the email app, and am greeted by an unread email marked as a priority, which I didn't even know you could do.

The subject line is *Job Offer: Understudy*.

What on earth? *This must be a mistake*, I think, opening up the email.

But it's not. Somehow it's not.

Dear Cassie Clyne,

We are pleased to offer you the role of Temporary Understudy for Rosa Cordova's tour dates throughout the summer.

I scream so loud that the ducks on the river all fly into the air at once, and a cyclist screeches to a halt next to me.

'Are you all right, love?' he asks.

'Yes,' I pant, but I'm clasping the phone so hard that my knuckles have gone white. 'Just an email! Just a really weird email!'

He stands there, one foot still on the pedal. 'Do you –'

'No, it's OK, you can go!' I cry, leaping to my feet and pacing in the direction of home.

'Oh, righty-ho. Bye!' he cries as he overtakes me.

I start running then, powered by adrenaline and fury and a whole lot of confusion.

Because obviously I did not apply for this job.

But someone did, in my name.

*

'Pen Jones!' I shriek as I race up the stairs to our flat.

I find them in the living room, reclining on the couch in the matching bright orange hoodie and joggers I got them for Christmas. They don't *deserve* quality loungewear.

'Oh, hey,' they say airily, like an innocent person.

'Don't *oh, hey* me,' I snap, flinging off my battered work shoes. I think one flies down the back of the couch but that's later-me's problem. 'Did you apply for that understudy job for me?'

They slowly close their laptop and slide it onto the coffee table. 'Now –'

'You did!' I yell and throw a cushion at their face.

'Maybe I deserved that –'

'I can't believe you! You sent my private videos, my private property, to a bunch of strangers to be judged without asking me. Pen, you know how much my dances mean to me. They're my diary!'

'I know, Cass. But that's why I did it. I know exactly how much dance matters to you, even though you keep hiding it away.'

'I'm not hiding it away. Mase even offered to pay for some classes for me.'

'Oh yeah, and you've already looked them up and booked yourself in, right?'

'Well, no, but I was going to get round to it soon.'

They give me a look that I know means they do not believe this at all.

'I will!'

'OK.'

'I'm going to do it right after we've finished having this argument!' I say, pacing back and forth across our tiny living room.

'I just wanted you to give yourself a chance,' they say, so softly that I very nearly forget to be angry with them.

'That's not up to you! I'd already decided I wasn't going to do it!'

'Had you really though?' they say, reaching for my hand.

I bat them away. 'Don't try to emotionally connect with me when I'm shouting at you.'

Pretty much the first thing Pen learned when they got their job working in a care home was how to connect with the residents through physical contact and empathising, and yes it's an important power that makes them amazing at their job, but right now they are using it for evil!

'You didn't decide anything. You just ran out of the door and said you were staying at Mason's, which is the opposite of making a decision.'

'How is *not* making a decision the opposite of making one?' My head aches from this ridiculous conversation.

'You avoided thinking about it entirely! Avoiding is not doing!'

'That counts as a decision! I decided to not think about it!' I shout, and I hear the petulant tone in my voice, but I don't care.

We avoid each other's eyes. We never really fight, so I guess we're not used to it. All the fire goes out of me, and instead of continuing to wear a hole in the carpet, I slump down on the couch next to Pen, who sits back and sighs deeply.

'I hate fighting,' I say. 'And I may look like I've given in, but I'm just tired and my feet hurt too much. So I'm going to sit and seethe a little instead.'

'That's fair. How did you find out it was me anyway? I'm pretty sure I deleted the Sent emails.'

'There's an almost impressive level of deception going on here.'

'OK, I admit that covering my tracks on purpose was bad. But still . . . My laptop was here. How did you find out? I didn't tell anyone.'

I breathe out angrily, and hand them the phone. It's a bit sweaty from running, but I don't wipe it off. That's how annoyed I am. They can have my sweat.

They're quiet for a moment as they read the email that I left open on the screen before running home to confront them.

'Wait. You got it?!' Pen yells, leaping to their feet. 'Cass, you got it! I knew you'd do it! You're going to be a dancer for Rosa Cordova – this is all you've ever dreamed of!' They look down at me, still slumped on the couch. 'And you're not jumping for joy why exactly? Please say this is not just because you're upset with me, I don't want to steal that from you.'

'It's not you,' I say. 'Or well, not just you.'

'Well, that's a relief. But maybe we could get a little more excited about it?'

I wish I could be excited. Instead, I lean forward and rest my head in my hands.

'Oh no. What is happening here?'

'What am I going to do?' I wail. 'I can't take the job!'

'Why not?' Pen says, kneeling at my feet.

'I just can't,' I mumble into my palms.

'Hey, come on. Tell me what you're thinking.' They peel my hands gently from my face, and I sniff back a snotty sob.

'Stop doing your Nice Health Professional thing with me, I won't have it when I'm still annoyed with you.'

'But I'm *so* good at it.'

I laugh, despite the fact I'm supposed to still be angry with them.

'Plus,' they continue, 'can you really be upset with me when I helped you get the job?'

'I can. Watch me,' I say, laughing as I wipe my eyes. 'I didn't even look at the application package. Did you have to do a lot?'

'Yeah, a big form with your personal details, but luckily I know where your passport and stuff are. Plus an application essay cover letter thing and some footage of you dancing.'

I bite down on my lip. 'What did you send?'

'The "Lucifer" routine.'

'I'd only just finished that!'

'Yeah, and it was perfect. You nailed it.'

I brush off their compliment. They can't sweet talk their way out of this, though really they are right. It was pretty perfect.

'What else? Please tell me you didn't send any routines set to Rosa's music.'

'Don't worry, I didn't. I thought that would look a bit too keen.'

'Well, there's that at least,' I sigh. But then I remember

something from the original advert. 'Wait. They were looking for underrepresented dancers, weren't they?'

'Yeah . . .'

I close my eyes, feeling heat rise in my cheeks. 'Pen, did you write about me being deaf in that application?'

'Yes,' they say and I feel such a mix of emotions. If it was anyone else writing about my experience, I would probably have lost my rag but . . . Pen has been there all the way through. 'But to be clear, I used that essay that you did for the school newspaper so it was pretty much all your own words. I didn't feel comfortable putting words in your mouth.'

OK. I breathe a sigh of relief. That's a bit better.

After all, they do need to know, whether I tell them upfront in the application or afterwards. If I was going to take the job and showed up with an undisclosed cochlear implant, I bet there'd be a lot of questions. A lot of *invasive* questions.

'You better show me what you wrote,' I say.

They bring up a Word document hidden away in folders upon folders and hand me the laptop.

Possibly the worst part of all this is that the application is really good. Like, *really* good. I knew Pen was generally quite good at writing job applications because they're always helping friends of ours, but this is beyond that.

It's full of love. Love for me. And belief that I could do this.

Yes, they took my words, but they spun them out to explain how everything about me adds up to a reliable, hardworking and tenacious person. No one has ever called me tenacious before. I don't think it's something I'd ever call myself either.

It's all so overwhelming that I burst into tears.

'No, no, that's not what's supposed to happen,' they say, wrapping their arms around me. 'Why are you crying?'

'It's too nice! Why are you so nice about me!'

They pull back to look me in the eye. 'Because you're my favourite person and I love you.'

'Gross,' I say and we both laugh. 'I love you too. This is all a bit much. Maybe a lot much.'

'Yeah, it's a lot. And I really am sorry about the going behind your back part of it because it felt like lying to you, but I'm not sorry about the outcome,' they say quietly.

I sniff loudly. 'That's fair enough, I suppose. I accept your apology, but retain the right to be a little peeved for a few more days.'

'Days?!'

'Maybe hours, I don't know.'

'You can be peeved at me as long as you want, but only if we have a proper talk about all this *I can't* business. I don't want to sound like a self-help book, but you did get the job you were dreaming of. And yes, maybe you got it through means you didn't expect, but you still got it on your own merit. I didn't make anything up in that application, and all those videos are you. I think it would be a mistake to turn it down.'

I sigh dramatically and a bit snottily. 'I just can't do it.'

'Can we talk through that thought process?'

'You really do sound like a self-help book now. But fine. I can't take the job for loads of reasons. How many do you want before you'll believe me?'

They spin round to face me on the sofa, and gesture for me to mirror them. I do, reluctantly, and put my hands in theirs.

'All of them. One at a time. Let's go.'

'Fine. Financial. I can't afford the flights to Ibiza for a start.'

'Oh, forget about that. Transport is covered, as is your rent while you're out there. It said in the application documents. They book it all, so you don't have to upfront anything either.'

I blink. I hadn't been expecting that. 'OK, so what happens to this place?'

'We either pay for it until we get back, sublet it, or we get out of our lease and put all our things in storage.'

'Why do you keep saying we?' I ask, wiping a tear from the tip of my nose, because somehow I'm still ever so slightly crying.

'Cass, I'm obviously coming with you. This is your adventure of a lifetime, and I want to be there to support you. And anyway, we're too codependent to be split up, as this whole fiasco demonstrates.'

In a flash I go from silent tears to full-on wailing.

'Only if you want me to!' they cry, waving their hands in panic. 'That was presumptuous –'

'Of course I want you to come with me, you big melon,' I sniff.

'Oh, phew.'

'Where are you going to live though? I'm sure they aren't going to cover both of our rents.'

'Yeah, I don't think I can stay with you, but that's fine.' They tap the side of their nose, and their gold nose stud shines in the light. 'The universe will provide. Or at very least the queer grapevine.'

'The what?'

'You know, like the I-know-a-friend-who-knows-a-friend-who-knows-someone. It's a thing. Trust me.'

'But what if you can't find anything? It is Ibiza in the summer, after all.'

'I have some savings from when Nonna died that I can fall back on.'

'I don't want you using your savings on following me around.'

'Cass, this is basically the first chance I've had to have a holiday in years. Plus, I've been banking that overtime. I want a break. Anyway, next reason.'

'Mason,' I sigh.

'What about him?' Their face is blank.

'He just . . . he didn't seem that thrilled when I told him about it.'

'Oh yeah?'

I sense a growl under there. I don't know what it is with these two, but sometimes they get a bit weird about each other. They both think they're being subtle about it, but it's so draining to be stuck between two people you care about but who don't get along.

I look at my phone. The wedding reception will be well underway, so I can't even tell him what's going on. I mean, I could, but I don't want to interrupt the celebration with my own good news. That would be stealing someone else's limelight, and that makes me feel weird.

'I don't know, he just didn't seem to think I'd get it.'

'Well, you did.'

'I know. I guess he was thinking with his recruitment hat on.'

'But it makes you feel a bit weird that you got it when he didn't think you could?'

'No, that's not it,' I protest. 'I'm just explaining what I think he thought. I would have to leave him behind. I don't know how long it would be until I'd see him again. I bet it'll be really intense.'

'I'm sure he can wait for you for a few months while you follow your dream. Plus he got that fancy promotion, so he can afford to fly out and visit you. You'll get days off!'

'That's true,' I say, nodding. 'And he didn't really know the details so maybe he'll be more excited when I tell him everything. I can talk to him about it tomorrow.'

'I need to ask something you might not like,' Pen says slowly.

'Go on.'

'I just want to check that this decision is not contingent on him being happy about it or saying you can go?'

'No,' I say immediately, and I realise I mean that. But I think he'll support me so I don't even have to worry about the alternative anyway. 'His input matters to me but it's not like I'm tied down, you know?'

We'd had a conversation a few months ago about where things were headed, and now I'm really grateful that Mason suggested we don't get too serious right now. He's got his career to focus on, and I'm still working out who I am,

36

never mind what I want to do. At the time, I felt a bit hurt, like I'd wanted him to throw himself at my feet and beg for my hand in marriage, but now I see that it was the right decision after all.

'So is tomorrow's phone call going to be about talking it through with him, or telling him?'

'You say that like I've changed my mind, which I haven't.'

'OK, what's next on the list?'

We've covered finances, accommodation, leaving Mason behind. But there's one more thing. The big thing. I tap my cochlear implant. 'What about this?'

'I imagine that they have deaf people in Ibiza.'

'Careful,' I say warningly. 'You're on thin ice, remember?'

'OK, sorry,' they say, shaking off silly Pen and going back to serious Pen. 'First off, they know you're deaf because it's in the application and they hired you with that in mind.'

Which means I'll have to be open about my deafness with everyone, I think. Not that I could really hide it, I guess. But still, being in a room full of strangers and telling them I'm deaf is scary.

Pen picks up my phone again and hands it to me.

'I don't know if you saw, but you have another email that's asking about what reasonable adjustments or accommodations you need. And I can help with writing that up, if you want to. I've helped build accessibility plans for work before.'

They're right. There's a list of questions and none of them are too invasive considering it's an email from a HR department.

'I can be like your assistant.'

'What? Following me round with a little notebook and pen?' I giggle but it's hollow. And Pen can see that.

'Almost there. Let it out.'

A heavy sigh rolls out of me. 'I wouldn't just be a dancer, Pen. I'd be a deaf dancer on stage –'

'Only if someone is sick.'

'Don't interrupt me,' I laugh huffily. 'I'm trying to be vulnerable which you know I hate.'

'I do. Sorry.' Pen mimes zipping their mouth shut.

'A deaf dancer potentially on stage, but on stage in front of . . . like thousands of people. Around the world. That's a kind of hyper-visibility I can barely imagine, so it just feels . . . so overwhelming to me. It's scary. And I know it would probably mean a lot for someone deaf to see me up there dancing, but what would the cost be? And it wouldn't just be the concerts themselves. I know how many people are filming and uploading to TikTok all the time. Someone would spot me. What if they made a video about me?'

We're both quiet for a moment. I know they get this. Being a feminine-presenting non-binary person has meant everything from misunderstandings to patients refusing Pen's help, all the way up to scary moments in the street where they've been yelled at or threatened and we've had to run. When you're different, being seen by the whole world can be dangerous.

And even if it's not dangerous, people will still be weird about it. There'll be questions and comments all over the internet. In person too. *Hey, Cassie, what does this sound like to you? Or this?* People are generally well-meaning, but if they aren't familiar with deafness or disability or anything slightly different, they tend to assume things, or ask questions they don't realise are really invasive and personal. It's a lot to manage all that constantly.

To their credit, Pen just gives me a hug. 'I love you. I can't promise any of that won't happen. But I can promise that I'll be there if it does.'

'Thank you.'

'Anything else?'

'What if my cochlear implant breaks again?'

Do I really want to be in another country with a healthcare system I don't understand if my cochlear implant stops working? I mean, I'd hope the job would come with decent healthcare plans but still.

When I had the new one put in via surgery a few years ago, it took weeks, months even, for me to feel comfortable, never mind being able to process any sound with it. In sessions with the audiologist we were constantly retuning, and it took me so much practice to hear with it properly. It was so much work, for such a long time. I know it's unlikely that I'd ever need to have surgery again, but I still get anxiety about something going wrong. Like what if the processor, the external part, breaks? Where would I find a new one in Ibiza? I might have to miss days off work or even quit. I don't know if I could adapt.

I realise I've not said any of this out loud, but I see Pen making a note in a draft email to ask about healthcare.

'Why don't we find out all about what insurance they're offering before you make a decision? I can even find an audiologist on the island for you just in case, and make sure you have enough batteries.'

'I would definitely have to get more to take with me,' I grumble, trying to tot up how many I've got stashed in various bags and drawers in the house.

'Is that everything you can think of?'

'Right now,' I say and then laugh. 'I think there will probably be more though!'

'And they're all valid worries.'

'I know! That's precisely why I didn't apply in the first place.' I side-eye them.

'OK, but –'

'No buts.'

'*But*,' they continue and I roll my eyes. 'You have the opportunity to live your dream. You've wanted this since you were a kid, Cass. Yes, it'll be a challenge and you're going to be outside your comfort zone a lot, but I'll be there in your corner. And you deserve this. You're a hard worker, and you got this job because you're an incredibly talented dancer.'

I sigh heavily. 'Stop –'

'We both know I will not stop being nice to you.' They pat my knee. 'You OK? Need some decompressing time?'

'Probably.'

'Shall I put the pizzas on while you contemplate?'

'I don't need to contemplate,' I say, doing air quotation marks. 'I'm not taking the job.'

I slump further down on the couch, but they're already in the kitchen.

'I'm not,' I say to no one.

It would be silly to think about this seriously. After all, I don't really know anything about it. Like when the job starts, or anything practical like that. I'd have to let the restaurant know too.

I drag Pen's laptop off the coffee table and log into my emails. Somehow reading important emails on the laptop feels more serious than just on my phone.

Everything Pen said about the flights and accommodation was right. The start date for training is in two weeks' time so that the understudy cast are ready for the European leg of the tour, just like Pen told me last week. The job offer stresses that it's a temporary contract for just these European dates. Perhaps they're hoping to get some of the dancers back from Payton. They want a response within forty-eight hours.

Two weeks would probably be just about enough time to wrap up some stuff here, though I'd have to call in a few favours from my parents. The restaurant probably wouldn't mind that much. They could give my hours to someone else.

I could do this. If I wanted to.

If I was brave enough to go.

Lost in my thoughts, I don't even notice time passing, but soon Pen hands me a perfectly cooked and sliced Hawaiian pizza on a plate just for me.

We watch *Gossip Girl* – season two, the flashback episode to the eighties – and I realise at the end of it that I barely took anything in.

'Are you OK?' Pen asks, when they turn off the TV. 'I'll do the washing up and I'll put the leftovers in the fridge for brekkie, so you can go to bed if you want? You must be tired.'

Before they get up, I grab their arm. My mouth goes dry. It sounds like someone else is speaking when I say, 'I'm . . . I'm going to take the job.'

Pen leaps on me excitedly, but as they land on me, they knock the plate in my lap, sending the last few bits of pizza skyward. One slice hits the ceiling . . . and sticks firmly to it, with no sign that it's going to come down.

'We should probably fix that before we leave,' I say with a huge grin.

'Before we leave,' repeats Pen as though they can't quite believe it. They squeeze me tighter, and I can barely breathe. I wriggle in their arms to get some air and look them right in the eye.

'Ibiza, here we come.'

Chapter Four

'There's my superstar!'

Mum yanks me into a hug before I can even say hello and drags me into the house.

It's a few days before I'm due to leave, and my parents insisted they throw me (and by extension, Pen) a going-away party. I'm happy to indulge them because, to be honest, I do kind of love it when they go all out. Plus, they did agree to store all our stuff in their garage, attic, spare room and anywhere else things would fit.

Behind us, Pen closes the door and follows us through the house to the back garden, where my dad is aggressively watering the plants with the hosepipe. Our ancient rescue dog, Hank (my parents were big *Breaking Bad* fans), sits at his feet, occasionally snapping at the water. When he realises I've appeared seemingly from nowhere, he trundles over on his stubby legs for a cuddle. I love him. He's some kind of mix – I think he's got Staffie in him if his enormous seal-like head is anything to go by, but who knows where he got his little legs from. I pick him up and am rewarded with a healthy Dentastix-flavoured face lick and several wags of his tail.

When I put him down, he makes a beeline for Pen, who he is in love with, because they always come over with some illicit treat in their pocket for him. Pen drops down to sit cross-legged on the patio for him to waddle right into their lap, where he proceeds to sniff around for a gift.

'Hello,' signs Dad from across the garden as he coils the hose up neatly.

It's sunny outside today, the first flush of summer in the air. The garden table is laid, with a few blankets slung over the back of the chairs because Mum is so used to me and Vics complaining that we're getting hypothermia the minute the sun goes down.

Mum reappears with a bottle of Prosecco. It looks kind of fancy, probably left over from Christmas.

'Shouldn't we wait for Vics to get here before we open that? She'll have our necks.'

'Don't you fear, I am here!' Vics swans in with all the drama that a Leo sun can muster, dressed in tailored high-waisted tan trousers with a tucked-in shirt.

'Look at you, dressed all fancy,' I say, as she kisses me on the cheek.

'I thought I'd better make an effort for your last memory of me.'

'Seriously, guys. I'm coming back.'

Mum and Vics share a look that I can't decipher.

'What?' I ask, arms folded. They're being so weird.

Mum puts her hands on my elbows, a gentle hold that envelops me in the scent of her lily-of-the-valley hand cream. 'Baby, you're about to go on the most amazing adventure.

We just know you're going to be busy, and we're so excited for you.'

'She's off on tour, off on tour,' chants Vics, clapping with each word.

Mum pours champagne into four flutes. 'Col, do you want some?'

Dad appears at my side and gives me a big squeeze. 'I'm so proud of you,' he says, booping me on the tip of my nose. To Mum he says, 'I'm all right, pet. I need to be at my peak physical focus for this barbecue,' before disappearing back into the house.

'What an alarming sentence,' Vics says. 'Pen, is your first-aid training up to date? We might need you.'

From the floor, Pen laughs awkwardly, burying their face in Hank's fur. There's . . . history between Vics and Pen. I've never quite got to the bottom of it, although I suspect it was just an unreciprocated crush on Pen's side that Vics used to her advantage for all possible attention. It's the one thing that Pen and I haven't really talked about, because I guess it's weird to tell your codependent quasi-sibling friend that you've got the hots for her older sister. I only found out about it because it's extremely obvious from Pen's side – it's the only time they falter in conversation, going from charming, kindly extrovert to blubbering goo in seconds.

'Did the audiologist manage to sort you out a spare processor for travelling?' Mum asks.

'Yeah, all arrived,' I say, sighing with relief. Borrowing a spare part for my cochlear implant has taken a huge weight off me. Obviously there's nothing I can do if the implant breaks again, like it did when I was a teenager, but having a spare processor means at least if that part breaks I can replace it.

'Good, good. Now, I didn't know what your Mason likes to eat, so I made a couple of side salad-type things to go with whatever your father is grilling to death.'

My heart flutters in my chest. This will be the first time he's met my parents.

After I decided I'd take the job, I wanted to find the right way to tell Mason. Over the phone felt weird, so I went over to his with a takeaway at the end of the week. The way to his heart is a beef ho fun. In the end, he was really pleased for me and pleasantly surprised that they really did want undiscovered talent. I think he secretly liked going through all the documents from HR with me, even if he did make a few comments about a lack of long-term stability. And it was nice to see him in work mode.

I did get a bit annoyed with him at one point when he was asking what I was going to do with the flat and stuff before I could even tell him my plans, but I know it came from a good place; he just worries about me. And he got it in the end, though he seemed surprised that Pen was coming along.

I'm not going to lie, it did make me feel kind of happy when he said he'd miss me. We still have to talk about him coming to visit, but I need to work out the logistics of that once I've got there first, so I don't accidentally double-book myself.

In the end, he opened a nice bottle of wine that his work had given him for his promotion, and we drank that curled up on the couch, before a bit of a celebration in the bedroom.

Things have been so hectic since then with packing up the flat that we haven't had a chance to go out and properly celebrate, like we did for his promotion. So in the end, last week I just asked if he thought he might want to come over to my goodbye party instead. After all, it was going to be the last time we would see each other for ages. He didn't seem so sure at first, which I get – it's not like we're official, and meeting the parents feels very like we are. But he said he would come, just to see me.

But since then I've barely had time to text him much other than the usual *good morning* and *goodnight*, and I haven't heard much from him either. He must have had a really busy week too.

'I brought posh crisps,' adds Vics. 'Truffle ones.'

'Truffle? Like a chocolate?' I ask.

'No, like an incredibly expensive mushroom thing that pigs forage for.'

'Weird.'

'It's good, I promise. Like, *fancy* too.'

'I'm honoured that you'd spend money on fancy crisps just for little old me.'

'Anything for my little sister,' Vics signs, and I honest-to-god nearly start crying.

'Stop that,' I sign back, with a watery smile.

Growing up in a hearing family might have been complicated and tough and lonely at times, but having my older sister learn sign language along with me so that I'd have someone to talk to who wasn't my parents meant the world to me. I didn't get my first cochlear implant until I was six, so if we didn't sign as a family, I wouldn't have been able to communicate with anyone easily for years. And even beyond that, because I still had to learn to process sound with my implant, which took a lot of time and practice. Then when my implant broke, we all signed to each other again. Dad had to brush up on his, but Mum works in a school as a SEN worker so had been signing with some of her students, even if she had reverted to English with me for most of my life. No one at school other than Pen signed.

Sign is important to me, as a deaf person. It means I can express myself.

And although we've fallen out of signing together as I've got older, Vics always tries to keep it up, which makes me really happy.

'That reminds me,' she says, and hands me a battered reusable Sainsbury's bag. 'I didn't know if you needed any new dance stuff, and I sized up on my gymwear this year from all my gains, so thought you could use some extra bits.'

Inside are neatly folded leggings, crop tops and a few T-shirts. Many of them in matching colours, like they're full sets. I spy a couple of designer tags, stuff I see on Instagram that I couldn't dream of affording. And I'm pretty sure that some of this isn't actually second hand. Some things look completely new.

'Are you sure?' I sign.

'Of course. Take what you want.'

'Thank you,' I sign and pull her into a hug.

Truth be told, this was something I was really worried about. I've been working at the restaurant since I was a teenager and when you don't have much money, there's not really any opportunity to splurge on new dance clothes. I've been dancing mostly in big T-shirts that I don't mind getting sweaty. And the thing about taking a job like this is that you know you're going to come up against people who have all the new clothes and shoes and really want you to know about it.

'Do you want me to put them in a nice dish?' Mum asks.

'The leggings?' I joke, holding up the bag to show her.

'The crisps, silly.'

'I don't think they'll last long enough to hit the serving dish,' says Vics, nabbing the bag and sauntering off.

'What time is Mason coming?' asks Pen once Vics is out of sight and they return to their normal personality.

'Soon, I think?' I say.

There's no messages from him, but when I scroll up I see that I didn't tell him to arrive for another half an hour or so, just in case Dad had a catering-related incident we needed to fix before outside company arrived.

There's no point texting him now because he'll be getting ready and then driving over, so I just put my phone back into my bag. 'Should be half an hour,' I say. 'I'm going to try one of those crisps before Vics snaffles them all.'

After a brief scuffle over the crisps and a few half-hearted games of fetch with Hank, Dad announces that it's time to eat, and we all gather at the barbecue, plating up cumin- and turmeric-spiced chicken thighs, corn on the cob ready to be buttered, and stacks of aubergine and goat's cheese, threaded onto little cocktail sticks, ready to be slid right into a bun.

'It's vegetarian,' Dad tells Pen, meaning the little stacks, and Pen gives him a thumbs up. For some reason, at some point Dad decided that Pen is a vegetarian and nothing we say will dissuade him from that fact. Pen finds it funny. 'A little gentle stereotyping,' they say. The upside is that Dad really puts in the effort on the vegetarian stuff whenever Pen is coming over, and it's often better than the other food.

The table is heaving, and yet Mum still keeps appearing with dips and marinated artichokes and gleaming peppers stuffed with cheese.

'Will your chap be here soon?' Dad asks.

'Should be,' I say, taking my phone out. 'He's probably got lost.'

He hasn't been here before, and I don't know how familiar with the towns outside of York he actually is.

But there's nothing on the screen. I hate making phone calls because it's so tricky to know what's being said without any visual clues, and sometimes I get interference that makes it even harder to hear, but maybe I should just ring him. Speaking on the phone in general is tough, but I'm used to speaking to Mason and hearing the rise and fall of his voice, so calls with him are generally OK.

Yes, this is a good idea. After all, if he's driving, he'll be able to pick it up in the car and hopefully there won't be so much interference that I can't hear. Worst case, he can just pull over and video call me.

I call him but there's no answer, and it goes to voicemail.

But surprisingly quickly, I get a text back.

Mason

Hey, everything ok?

Cassie

Yeah, just seeing if you need any directions?

To my parents' house?

For the going away BBQ party thing

I add a couple of emojis to signal that I'm being friendly and chill – the meat on the bone, a chef, and the clinking glasses. Hopefully that conveys the right vibe.

But nothing comes back, so I start writing more, just to explain myself.

Sorry, this isn't me nagging, I just wanted to check you were all right because you hadn't sent an ETA or anything and I know sometimes GPS doesn't want to find the house

He's finally typing, I can see that, but nothing happens for so long that Hank comes over to stand next to me, licking my ankle possibly for moral support. It feels like forever till he replies.

I'm really sorry Cassie but I'm not going to make it. Time has got away with me today. I was called into the office to deal with some client stuff asap, and I can't really leave as my bosses are here. Just worried how it would look so soon after a promotion.

But it's my leaving party, I want to say.

And I want to point out how much we celebrated his promotion, whereas we've done nothing for me. Or like, not for me, but for *us*. A nice moment for us to look back on.

It was going to be the first time he met my parents.

I glance back at the table, hoping they're all digging in, and everyone is, except Pen. They sign an 'OK?', their eyebrows raised in question and I give them a shrug back.

It's work. I can't be upset with Mason if work means he can't come. After all, work is taking me to an island in the Mediterranean. I should be understanding. We're just at a busy point in our careers where things are kicking off, I suppose.

I really don't want him to feel bad about this. He can't help it if work called him away.

It's OK, I understand

> In future, it would be nice if you could let me know you're going in on a day off when we're supposed to hang out?

> Just to manage my expectations!

> But it's OK

> Have a good day and schmooze those clients!

I add a row of heart emojis so he knows I'm not going to start something over this. As I send the last one, I see a reply come through.

> Sure, but it's not like you'll be –

I shove the phone in my pocket before I can read the rest of that message. Whatever he was saying, I can think about it later. Right now, I want to enjoy the last afternoon I have with my family before I leave.

'No luck?' asks Vics.

'He got called into work,' I say, and rehash what he said to me. I see Vics' eyebrow twitch, a tell-tale sign of annoyance that she's had since we were kids, but I don't think it's for me. She's just overprotective like that. The same way Pen is. 'I'm sorry, guys, I know you cooked a lot.'

'We did that for you two,' Mum says, patting my hand kindly, and nodding at me and Pen. 'Now dig in, before it gets cold. Or warm? Do salads get warm?'

'We need to do a toast first!' cries Dad.

'With our second glass?' Vics asks.

'The first was just a warm-up.'

'All right, then.' She downs the last bubbles at the bottom of her flute. 'Fill her up.'

Dad tops up, or in Vics' case refills, everyone's glasses and raises his. 'Now,' he begins and immediately his eyes fill with tears. At least I know where I get it from. 'We are so proud of you, Cassie. You've always been a fighter, ever since you were born, and we knew that there would be no stopping you. I keep thinking back to how little you were, learning to dance and speak and hear all at once because you've never done anything by halves.'

The reason I went to dance classes when I was a kid was because my audiologist had suggested it to my parents as a good way for me to expand my hearing skills, and my confidence in speaking with other kids.

'Mum and I had always hoped you'd go back to dancing. You loved it so much, and I know it was such a knock when your implant broke, but to see you putting yourself out there, applying for a job like this –'

'Well, Pen applied,' I say, wanting to give them credit.

'That's because Pen believes in you as much as we do,' says my mum, who I've never seen cry in her entire life but seems to be on the edge of it right now too. 'And we're so proud of you two going off on an adventure together.'

54

'Here's to codependency!' Pen raises their glass and, after catching Vics' eye across the table, almost slops a bit of foam out of the top.

'To us,' I say, and everyone clinks glasses to a chorus of *cheers* and *iechyd da* from Mum. Her granny was Welsh and she insists on keeping the tradition alive, even if it's just as she's about to drink some bubbles.

My heart is full with the love of my family, but I can't stop thinking about that text. Or the part of that text that I saw. Maybe it got better? It probably didn't.

And as much as I love being with my family and Pen and Hank I can't help but glance at the front door every now and then. As though perhaps he'll show up, maybe with a bouquet of flowers to make up for it, because he's explained to his bosses and they all agreed he should go, he's done the work and now he needs to be with his girl.

But there's no flowers, no opening of the door, no Mason. He didn't show up to my leaving party.

Chapter Five

One of Pen's most annoying qualities – not that there are many of them, to be fair – is their insistence that you have to be at the airport three hours before any flight. This works out reasonably OK when your flight is on time, but when there's delays it's not quite so fun.

Which is why, after four hours of sitting at the airport, I feel like I'm going to lose it. Our plane departure time keeps moving later and later. There's no one waiting for me at the other end but it feels like I'm late for my first day at work.

Plus, I'm not the greatest flier at the best of times. While I can take my cochlear implant off, and tune out for the flight, everything else is difficult. I can't afford to fly in decent seats or pay for the meals onboard when it's a long flight, so it's a Boots meal deal out of a carrier bag situation. Not quite the life of luxury I swear I was born for, but somehow was not born into.

And before I even get on the plane, there's all the faff with security. I always have to bring a card explaining why I essentially have a magnet in my head that, yes, will definitely set off the scanners, and yet there's still a lot of awkward dancing around until someone eventually decides that it's actually fine for me to go through. Despite how many people airports see on a daily basis, a lot of the staff have a really limited understanding of disability in general, and definitely deafness. Today I got someone speaking extra slowly to me just to be sure I heard, which funnily enough, did not help.

Everyone else just has to worry about whether they've got a belt on, or making sure they've unpacked their laptop.

Plus I can't stop thinking about how much my life is about to change. It was weird telling everyone, and quitting the job I've had since I was seventeen, though I suspect that might not have been a bad thing for, you know, emotional growth and all that.

And I miss Mason already. Even if we didn't leave on the best of terms.

Cassie

Made it to the airport x

Since the weekend, texting him feels like pulling nails. The text I hadn't wanted to look at read 'Sure, but it's not like you'll be down the road for much longer. It'll all be bigger plans we'll book in.' It wasn't too bad, but still kind of stung? I don't know why. It just felt a bit cold.

There's none of the usual ease and any time I try to reference one of our silly little in-jokes it all falls flat.

I guess he just feels guilty about not being able to come

to the barbecue, but that hasn't made me feel much better. It's a pity we didn't get to see each other face to face before I left because we could have probably nipped this tension in the bud, but oh well. Maybe it'll be easier once I'm actually gone, rather than in this weird limbo where we're close by but not able to see each other. It must be hard to be the one left behind, especially when I've been so excited about it. What if he thought I was excited about leaving him, rather than just the job?

'Stop picking your nails.' Pen slaps my hand away from where I'm at risk of doing major cuticle damage. The only good thing is that we managed to find a quiet bit of the airport to sit in – a waiting room with a closing door which blocks most of the overwhelming airport sound out. The downside is that the other people in here can probably hear Pen berating me.

'No hitting. I'm too on edge.'

'Sorry. They just look too nice to ruin.'

I finally got a manicure, the one I'd been dreaming about while washing dishes. No, you don't need good nails to dance, but I did need them to feel good. Tap into some of that confidence I swear I had once. That *yes I'm hot and cool* I project into the dance videos.

I flex my fingers and hold them up. They do look pretty good. 'Thanks. I probably need something else to destroy though. My nerves are shot.'

'I'm sure they must sell stress balls or something like that somewhere in the airport. They'd make a killing on them.'

I blow out my cheeks.

58

'You could pick my nails?' Pen suggests. 'I would give up my nice soft hands for the cause of keeping Cassie from fighting everyone in the airport.'

'One, ew, gross. I'm not going to pick your nails.'

'It was just a thought.'

'And two, I don't think it'd hit the same. I like you too much to gnaw on your fingers.'

'Woah, who said anything about gnawing?'

I giggle and bare my teeth. In a very terrible Dracula impression I say, 'I vant to chew your fingies.'

Pen flings one hand out towards me dramatically, covering their eyes with the other. 'The sacrifices I make for you! Go on, do it!'

I'm tempted to but we are in a dirty airport where Pen has touched everything vaguely interesting, and somehow that seems grosser than what I actually do, which is stick just the pad of my finger in their nose, pushing up the nostril. They open their eyes, and we look at each other for a solid ten seconds or so, before they sigh and say, 'I'm going to go look around the shops.'

'Don't leave me. I'm needy!'

'Have you heard from Mason yet?'

I shake my head. 'No.'

They sigh. 'I'll bring you back some treats.'

'Thank you.'

Pen gets up to go, and I dig around in my bag for the hand sanitiser. I glance at the people in the seats around us to see if our shenanigans went undetected.

One person clearly noticed, probably because he's sitting

directly opposite me. He looks at me over the top of his paperback with a grin on his face.

I say that like it's not a nice grin. It is. It's loose and relaxed and I instantly know that this man isn't laughing *at* me, but with me.

I awkwardly waggle the hand sanitiser. 'Gotta stay hygienic.'

'Aye,' he says. 'The perils of the old pick-the-nose technique. A classic one though, I have to say.' He speaks quickly like the words are playing with each other, and there's some kind of accent there I can't place. Usually it takes me a while to catch accents, but I hear every word of his deep rumble of a voice in the thankfully quiet seating area.

'You know your close-combat tactics,' I venture, and to my relief he laughs.

'I consider myself somewhat of a connoisseur, especially when it comes to sibling warfare.'

'Oh, Pen's not my sibling, but they may as well be. We grew up together. You have to know someone pretty long to put a finger up their nose.'

'Well, of course,' he says, putting aside his book on the empty seat next to him. 'I'm partial to the old wet finger in the ear myself.'

'That's dirty fighting,' I say.

'It is the worst one, I'll admit. But you know when you've found a good one because it's something you don't want them to do back to you.'

'But what if they do?'

'Casualty of war?'

'I don't think it's worth it.'

'So you're more receptive to a finger in the nose?'

I snort with laughter. 'Not if you say it like that.'

'I said it perfectly innocently,' he protests. 'I'm just a normal man. An innocent man.'

'I think the rest of the people in this waiting area might disagree about either of us being normal or innocent,' I say with a laugh.

'Well, it's nice to meet you, Abnormal and . . .'

'Guilty? Worldly?' I'm briefly thankful for how much me and my parents would watch *Countdown* when I was a kid.

'Oh, I was going to go for Sinful, which I think makes me the worse mind of the pair of us.'

Something about the way he says 'sinful' sends a shiver down my spine, but I'm pretty sure it's just the aggressive air conditioning in here.

'My name's Cassie.'

'Levi.'

'And this is Pen,' I say, as they return, dumping a carrier bag down next to me.

They glance at Levi and then back to me. 'Oh, I forgot about the magazines. I'm going to get some magazines.'

And they leave again, power-walking away before I can say anything.

'Or I guess that *was* Pen.'

I don't want to rifle through their stuff, but I'm almost certain a magazine is already in there from the way the bag has sharp corners poking through it. If I was single, I'd almost think that Pen was trying to quietly wingman me. But I guess

61

they're just feeling as nervous and off-kilter as I am. After all, they quit their job and upended their life too. We're each other's only constant.

When I look back over at Levi, he's moved. To my left, stands a woman using a walking stick, her wheelie suitcase flat on the floor. In one quick swoop, Levi lifts it up and rights it next to her. It's so fast that I half think I didn't really see it.

He and the woman he's helping strike up a little conversation that I can't hear, and I can't help but watch him. His hard jaw and dark eyes would be intense on anyone else, but his manner is so calming. Within seconds she's giggling like he's flirting with her, which he probably is. He strikes me as the type of man who would know how to gently charm someone.

I blink back into consciousness as he spins round to face me. I hope he didn't catch me staring. 'Do you mind watching my stuff while I help this lady to the gate?' he asks.

'Yeah, of course!'

'Thanks. I'll just be a tick, I promise.'

I watch as he holds out an arm for her to take, and lifts her suitcase by the handle rather than wheeling it behind them both.

And you'd think that I'd be sitting here thinking, wow, what a nice man to have leaped up to help her. How charming he is, with soft eyes and a smile that makes you want to trust him.

But really, I just can't stop looking at his arms. The curve of his biceps and the thickness of his shoulders. I hadn't noticed them when he was just holding a book and we were talking about play-fighting. And even though he's now across the waiting lounge, I can't take my eyes off them.

They're just arms, I tell myself.

Which is true. They are just arms. Just arms on a man I met in an airport.

I glance down at my phone hoping that maybe Mason will have texted me back, but there's nothing. No wonder I'm eyeing up strangers at the airport.

'Has he gone?' Pen drops down into the empty seat next to me.

'Temporarily. He's just helping that lady to her gate,' I say, pointing towards their figures disappearing into the crowd.

Pen raises their eyebrows. 'Is he with her?'

'No, he's just being nice,' I say, turning to them so I won't keep looking, as it would be weird if on the way back he caught me gawking. 'Anyway, what was all that about?'

'What?'

'The Disappearing Pen act. You didn't even get another magazine,' I point out, as I realise their hands are empty bar an iced coffee. 'And you didn't get me one.'

'I just thought you were getting on. I didn't want to intrude.'

I screw up my nose in confusion. 'Pen, what are you on about? You don't need to wingman me. I've got Mase at home.'

'So? You're allowed to have a nice time talking to a stranger in an airport. I'm not gonna tell anyone if you were having a little flirt.'

'I was not flirting! I wouldn't do that.' My stomach churns.

'OK. But it doesn't matter if you were. A mild flirt with a stranger is harmless. You just looked like you were having a nice time. You looked relaxed for once.'

What do they mean, for once?

'I said I wasn't flirting!' I hiss.

Typically, this is the exact moment that Levi returns.

'Thanks for guarding my stuff,' he says, sitting back down and flashing a *hello again* smile-nod at Pen.

'No problem,' I say, a little too eagerly, hoping that he didn't hear our argument.

I really wasn't flirting. Yes, I was looking at his arms, sure. And, yes, I was thinking he seemed like a nice guy. But Pen is not psychic as far as I know. It was just a conversation. It doesn't matter that I was daydreaming about what he's like.

'It's so bad that accessibility help in airports is so complicated,' he says, shaking his head. 'Poor woman walked the whole way here from security and no one offered to help her or contact Accessibility.'

'Yeah, and even if you can book them, it's like will they even turn up?' adds Pen. 'And if they do, they're bloody useless and act like they've never met an elderly or disabled person before.'

'Too true. I wish it weren't that way.'

Pen sizes him up for a second, before leaning forward and holding their hand out for him to shake. 'Pen Jones, occasional care worker and magazine hoarder. Nice to meet you.'

He laughs and takes their hand. 'Levi McHugh, itinerant carpenter –'

'And wet-willy specialist,' I add, before immediately

regretting everything I've ever said up to this point but *especially* that final sentence.

My face is on fire as Pen falls apart cry-laughing next to me and I have to take their iced coffee so they don't spill it everywhere.

I should not be allowed out of the house.

What is *wrong* with me?

'Well, I wouldn't have put it quite like that,' he says, that lazy grin widening across his face. 'But I'll take it. Wet-willy specialist. I'd better update my LinkedIn.'

'I didn't –' I splutter but then decide it's better if maybe I never speak again. Perhaps I can just get up and walk out of the airport into some kind of void reserved for disaster people who don't know how to hold a conversation with a handsome stranger.

'Oh, no fear, I'm honoured that my technique has been recognised,' he says, and his grey eyes sparkle with mischief.

'Please . . . stop . . . I'm . . . dying,' gasps Pen between laughs.

'I would like to make it clear that whatever rude thing you're thinking about is not what I meant at all!' I say with a huff.

'I know, and that's what makes it all the funnier.'

'I'll stick my finger in your nose again if you don't stop laughing at me.'

Levi laughs with his whole body, like he has no reservations about giving in to the feeling. He flings his head back, watching as Pen and I bicker, which sets us both off again. My mouth is dry as I watch the rise and fall of his broad chest.

'Well, this is definitely the most entertaining airport meeting I've ever had,' Levi says when we've finally all calmed down. He picks up his carry-on bag – one of those rucksacks that seem to have more pockets than is strictly necessary – and is about to put his book away, when Pen spots it.

'What are you reading?' they ask. Their eyebrows are raised in interest, book fiend that they are.

He holds up the cover. It's *Wild* by Cheryl Strayed. I've not read it, or seen the Reese Witherspoon film. All I know is that she goes for a long walk.

'Have you read it?' Levi says.

Pen nods but I shake my head. 'Do you like it?' I ask.

'She's a great writer. Kind of fearless. You'd have to be, to go on an adventure like that, I suppose. So yeah, it is good.'

I could probably do with some fearlessness. Maybe I'll see if I can find a copy at some point. I'm not a huge reader, not because I don't like reading, but because sometimes when my head aches after a long day of listening, I want to just zone out to TV.

'Planning on going on a really long hike?' I ask.

'Not right now. I've got a flight to catch.'

I snort-laugh, and he grins.

'How far through are you?' asks Pen.

He tilts the book to demonstrate.

'Oh, boy, you're about to have a real bad time.'

'Say no more. So where are you two off to today?'

Just as Pen opens their mouth to tell him, my cochlear implant starts beeping. It's a sound that only I can hear, but it means that my batteries are dying and need to be changed, and it basically won't stop beeping until I do.

'Pen,' I say and point to my ear under my hair.

'What do you need?' they say, giving me their full attention.

'I need to go change the batteries.'

I spring to my feet. Even though I know there's nothing wrong with my cochlear implant when it's low on battery, there's something about it not working perfectly in public that always sends me into a bit of a panic. Usually, I like to go change them in the bathroom – preferably in the disabled bathroom as sometimes there's a little extra space for putting things on and wipes to clean surfaces easily, and also because it's out of sight. I don't love it when I'm fiddling with the batteries and someone comes up to ask what I'm doing, because then I inevitably have to have a conversation with a stranger about being deaf and yes I've always been deaf, no I don't look deaf whatever that means, look, lady, I just wanted to come in here and mind my own business like you should be doing etc. Or worse, I'll drop a battery and have to scurry about looking for where it went, because no way am I losing a full one. Every battery counts.

I rifle through my carry-on bag, and find my zip pouch with spare batteries in it. They usually last me a good two to three days, and it's already been two. I should have just changed them at home before we left so I wouldn't be stressing, but we left so early.

'Do you want me to watch your stuff?' Levi asks, as Pen gets up too.

'Actually, I think our flight will be boarding soon,' Pen says, squinting up at the display in the distance. 'Cass, it's all good. We'll take our stuff and go to the loo and then go straight to the plane, OK?'

I nod. 'OK.' I turn to Levi. 'Sorry!'

'No, it's no problem. I hope you can get it sorted.'

'Yeah, it'll be fine. Just airports, you know.'

He nods like he knows, and I feel much calmer, though the implant is still bleeping away, an alarm just for me.

'It was nice chatting with you,' he says.

'And you,' I say, slinging my bag over my shoulder, and pulling out the wheelie-case handle.

Naturally, the battery change goes simply. I don't drop anything on the gross toilet floor and when my cochlear implant is reattached to the right side of my head, the beeping has stopped. Everything feels normal again.

Or as normal as things can feel when you're about to fly to an island to start a whole new career.

The only thing that feels different is the ache in my stomach when on the way to our gate, we pass the seats we were in only moments before, and I see that Levi has gone.

Chapter Six

I think the universe decided to take pity on us, because after all those delays, our luggage is waiting for us as soon as we get to the carousel.

I had been half expecting we'd have to flag down a taxi ourselves, but in the arrivals hall, we're greeted by a man in a black suit holding a sign with my name on it. His name is Bernard and he explains he's going to be our driver for the next few weeks while we're training in Ibiza. He leads Pen and I outside to a car park, where a huge black car is waiting for us.

Pen and Bernard are already deep in conversation, but my mind is occupied by the fact that this is my life now. And I know I'm here for work, but, man, is it nice to walk out of an airport and feel the Mediterranean sun on my skin. The last time I was on holiday was years ago. Too long. I can practically feel the freckles on my cheeks springing to life like daisies in springtime.

It's so weird to think that when I get back, it'll be the end of autumn, which is my favourite season in the city – yes, I am a pumpkin spice latte girlie and I will not apologise for it.

But I'll be spending my whole summer here. Well, provided I don't blow it.

Bernard lifts our cases into the back for us, and ushers us inside the car, where it's already blasting air conditioning. The windows are tinted, and the seats are so big and comfortable. This is all kinds of fancy I'm not used to.

I'm pretty sure that Pen wasn't supposed to hop in with me, but Bernard didn't question it at all, so I guess we're both getting a ride into town.

That's one of Pen's talents though – pretending they're allowed to be places they're not really supposed to be. Plus, they're so confident and warm, people just go with it. Pen probably knows Bernard's life history, family tree and hopes and dreams by now. It's an amazing skill, really. I've been trying to copy them for . . . well, forever, but my brand of awkward lurking has never translated into casual confidence. Or it hasn't yet. Maybe there's still time.

And so we sit in the aggressively air-conditioned car, looking out of the window at the rich azure sea. All I knew about Ibiza before now was that it was really famous for clubbing. I had quietly worried that we were going to be staying in the middle of the party area, even though Pen pointed out it was unlikely they'd house us on the San Antonio strip if they wanted us to get any work done, and that I didn't have to go out to any of those big clubs if I didn't want to. In the end, the only thing that reassured me was some thorough Google map consultation, when I managed to work out we were staying on the northeast coast of the island.

As we drive, instead of the busy row of bars I had imagined, softly rolling hills sweep past us, dotted with tiny towns of bright white buildings. The roads are lined with thick green trees under a gloriously blue sky. There's hardly a cloud at all. We pass farms edged with low stone walls, with rows and rows of olive trees.

By a stroke of luck – or, I guess, the queer grapevine – Pen has managed to find a little apartment not too far from me. Someone's friend's auntie's partner needed a cat-and-flat-sitter for a few weeks. I swear, the universe is really on our side at the moment.

From the sounds of it, the flat I'm going to be sharing with some of the other dancers is exclusively ours. Hopefully it'll feel like an extended sleepover rather than being trapped with colleagues I'd rather escape.

I hope they like me.

I feel a bit sweaty after all the travelling, so I gather up my hair into a ponytail and enjoy the feeling of cool air on the back of my neck.

I know it's probably silly to be sitting here wondering that when I'm in a taxi on a paid adventure to Ibiza about to start my dream job, but I haven't had to make new friends in a long time. Now I've got to meet a whole cast of dancers, and then there's the choreographers, costume designers, and all the people that make the tour run. Jobs I probably don't even know exist yet.

And Rosa.

I grab Pen's hand. 'What if I meet Rosa?'

'We've talked about this.'

'No, we haven't! What will I wear? What if she *hates* me?'

'You're spiralling again.'

'Shut up.'

They're right. I hate it when they're right.

Every now and then I remember what I'm about to do, and the sheer weight of it all hits me like a series of tour buses. I used to have terrible anxiety when I was younger, and this doesn't feel quite like that, but I'm having to use a lot of the coping mechanisms I learned back then – meditation, breathing, relaxing. And fighting with Pen. That's always a good distraction, even if it doesn't solve the root issue.

We drive for about half an hour, weaving through the rugged landscape, before we turn off into a small town called Altavero. I can see a couple of tall resort hotels in the distance, towering over the rest of the town. They must be down near the beach. I cannot *wait* to check out the beach.

The town is cute. We pass little restaurants and a few supermarkets – always helpful to know I can easily go hunt down new flavours of crisps. And other food, I suppose.

The car pulls up in front of a shiny apartment building that looks so new I could be convinced they built it just for us.

Bernard unloads our bags, hands me an envelope with my building key in it, bids us goodbye and then he's gone and this is really happening.

And that means I have to say goodbye to Pen.

I turn to them, and immediately start crying. I probably need to examine this codependency thing. But not right now. That can wait until after I've finished working for a literal pop idol.

'I'm going to miss you so much,' I snot into their shoulder.

'Cass,' they say, removing me and my various face liquids. They open up their phone and show me the Maps app, with directions from my place to theirs already inputted. 'I am barely twenty minutes away. If you need me, I'll come straight away, or you can come to me.'

'What if the cat hates me?'

'That's actually quite possible. I've been warned that Téresa is a creature who values her own free will, which is cat code for absolute arsehole.'

'She'll like you though.'

'That's a given. Everyone likes me.'

I laugh a snotty laugh.

'But you're going to be great, Cass. Big-girl pants time.'

I nod, unconvinced but trying to be brave about it. 'I've never lived with anyone but you and my parents before. What if they think I'm weird? What if I have some horrible habits that you've just put up with forever?'

'You *are* weird, but they'll love you as much as I do. Go on now.' They give me a squeeze, just as an Uber pulls up next to us, which they hop into and disappear out of my life.

Well, for now.

I'm spiralling again.

Leave the drama for the stage is what my mum always used to say when I was little. But I can't help having a lot of big feelings. Sometimes it feels like I can't keep them all in, even though I try to, most of the time.

I pick up my bags and walk into the ice-cold lobby. Big leafy plants dot the corners of the room, and a receptionist welcomes me and gives me a key. It's so fancy, and they'll

73

even hold parcels for me and all sorts. Not that I know what I'll be ordering to this place, but still, at least if I have to buy some more batteries they'll be looked after rather than left on a doorstep in the sun.

There's even a lift. A lift *inside* my home. No more enormous and slightly dangerous flights of stairs. For now, anyway.

I look at myself in the mirror and my eyes drift straight to my implant. Just as the doors open on my floor, I decide to pull my hair out of its ponytail and wear it down, so that it's covering my ears and framing my face.

My flat is Number 8, right at the top of the building, and I pause outside for a moment, taking it all in. I breathe in deep.

The key is in my hand, and I feel like everything is really happening. Beginning.

But the moment is cut short when the door flies open, and I'm pulled in by what can only be described as a human whirlwind.

'Oh my God, you're here! She's here! We're all here! We're going to have the best time, I'm so happy to meet you.' I catch most of what the girl says and backwards fill in the gaps of what I'm pretty sure she said. She definitely has a strong accent, American, I think, and she speaks at seriously high speed. The last few things she says all run together in a gleeful blur that I hope I don't need to interpret as anything more than 'I'm so excited to meet you.'

I'm pretty sure she invites me to come in, because before I can stop her, she's picked up my bags and is carrying them inside, without stopping to ask me if I need help, which is nice of her.

There's something familiar about her. She's much shorter than me, with a shock of blue hair almost the colour of the sea that's all piled up in a messy bun on the top of her head. The matching blue sports bra and leggings set that she wears is almost the exact colour of her hair and is paired with adorable fluffy white sliders. Her bright blue eyes sparkle against her pale skin, and she has the kind of gymnast's body that's all hard muscle from years of practice. Though I'm not surprised she's so physically fit from how much she's bounced around in the last few seconds since we just met. The girl does not stop moving.

And then she flings her arms around me, hugging me.

'Hello,' I laugh awkwardly, patting her on the back. 'I don't think I've ever been greeted so enthusiastically before.'

'That's my style,' she laughs, and takes a deep breath. To my relief, she slows down a bit. 'Pure enthusiasm. Forcible befriending. I'm Tyra.'

'Cassie,' I say. 'Cassie Clyne.'

'Ooh, that's a stage name. A name to be up in lights!' she says kindly. 'Was your flight long?'

'No, it was just from Leeds in the UK, but it was delayed a while.'

'Oh no, I'm sorry. Are you tired? Let me get you something.' She dashes into the kitchen and pours me a glass of water, topping it up with ice that comes out of a little machine inside the fridge door.

'Wow, thank you,' I say, taking a big cold sip. 'Did you arrive this morning?'

'I got in yesterday on an overnight flight so I do not know which way is up at this point. Jet lag has been kicking my delightful little tush. Did you say Leeds? That's in England, right? Is that where you grew up?'

I know what she's really asking, and I'm used to the question, but also I have to admire how casually and delicately she's asked it. I don't think she knows I'm deaf, but I guess she's picked up on my speech being a little different from most people's. I don't really have an accent, or, well, not a geographical one which is what people mean when they think of accents. Like most people who were born deaf, I have a 'deaf accent'. Because we can't hear the full range of sounds that hearing people can, we can't replicate them easily either. It means that we often sound similar. I've had this question all my life because while Pen has quite a strong Yorkshire accent, I just don't at all. And it confuses people to know we grew up together, for the most part.

'Yeah, born and bred.'

'Like the tea. English people are always telling me our tea is terrible and to drink Yorkshire tea, and my God, that stuff will wake up you and your great-great-grandma.'

As if on cue, a yawn breaks out of me.

'Oh my goodness. Come on, let's get you situated. You can get to know all of us better once you're unpacked and comfortable. I'm sure Sorrel and Veena will be back soon.'

Our bedrooms are all on the same corridor just off the living room and kitchen. It's all white walls and tiled floors, with minimal decoration but just enough furniture for me to be able to put all my things away and feel kind of at home. And there's an *en suite*. It feels like a fancy hotel.

'This is so nice,' I sigh.

'Do you need anything?'

'A shower, for sure. I feel bad that you hugged me before. I'm pretty sure I reek.' I feel so gross, somehow both sticky and crusty from being dehydrated, thanks to many forms of transport mashed with anxiety.

'You got a case of the nervous sweats too?'

'You too?' I'm surprised, because while Tyra seems to exist at a speed unknowable to most humans, she doesn't strike me as nervous.

'Oh, honey, I smelled like I'd been living in the woods when I got here. Don't you worry about it. You get cleaned up. But before you go, let me know how you take your tea.'

That's a question I can answer easily – steeped a bit too long, just a splash of milk, too much sugar. She heads back out to the kitchen.

As much as I like Tyra – which is a relief – I'm also grateful to get a moment alone to take it all in. This is my home.

I take my cochlear implant out to have a shower, leaving it on the dark wooden dresser along with my phone.

The shower looks delicious, a huge waterfall head with decent water pressure, and big wide tiles. It looks as new as the rest of the place. I'm not sure I've ever been the first person to use a shower before.

I decide to take my time and enjoy it. After all, you don't get to christen the shower more than once. And I think the best thing for me right now would be a bit of me time before I meet my other roommates. Tyra is so nice, though I still can't pin down where I recognise her from, but it would feel like possibly too much good luck at once to meet more people I vibe with.

I set out a cute little daisy-print cami sundress on the bed to change into after. Perhaps a little cliché for a holiday destination, but sundresses are a staple for a reason.

My toiletries and makeup have mostly survived the flight, so I take the bags through to the bathroom and dump them on the side, ready to unpack later. Then I strip down and step under the water.

You'd think a hot shower on a hot day was not the vibe, but it really is. In fact, after everything, it's heavenly. I give my hair a really good wash, and while the deep conditioner I slathered on sets in I stand in the heat, letting the rising mist settle on my skin.

My mind finally feels empty after such a weird day. There's so much still to do – two more housemates yet to meet for a start – but this quiet moment alone is sacred.

I wonder if Levi's flight ever left the airport with all the delays. I can't even remember if he said where he was going. I feel like I got so many snippets of who he was as a person – the kind of guy willing to leap up and help an elderly lady through an airport. I wonder what 'itinerant carpenter' means. I'm pretty sure he said his surname is McHugh, so I could probably look him up, if I wanted to.

Wait, why am I thinking about Levi?

I rub my face, trying to push the thoughts away. My mind

is just wandering because things with Mason are so weird and strained at the moment. It probably didn't help that on the night when I told him I got the job, I got a little overexcited and told him that everything would be fine between us because I loved him. And he said nothing. For a long time. Eventually, he kissed me and squeezed me tight.

And said thank you.

He didn't say he loved me back.

That's OK though, because I don't expect him to say it just because I said it. We're not official, so I guess it's a bit out of the usual order of things. Even if *thank you* felt . . . cold?

And I think I love him, I really do. I mean, I've never felt like this about anyone else before and I think what we have is great. Maybe I jumped the gun a bit, but that's OK. At least I didn't accidentally say it while we were having sex.

I haven't said it again just in case it makes him feel weird. Hopefully the next time I say it will be saying it back to him. Maybe once we're official in the future? That would be nice.

I hope he's not feeling too awkward about it. Unlike me. I didn't even tell Pen about it because it was so embarrassing.

I wonder what he's doing right now. I haven't texted him other than a quick *landed safely* which he thumb-up reacted to, but he's at work today so he's probably really busy. It's not like I can expect him to be sitting on one of those plane-tracking websites watching me disappear out of his life. The time difference means he'll be finishing work soon. Maybe I'll try and call him before bed.

Hopefully he'll pick up.

I shake my head to try and knock all the jumbling thoughts loose.

And when I look up, my eyes lock with Tyra's. She jumps with fright, sprints out of the room and slams the door behind her.

Chapter Seven

What the hell? What was she doing in here?

I wash out the conditioner furiously. This was supposed to be my quiet time and safe space and I've somehow already ticked off *roommate sees me totally naked* from my mental list of terrible things that could happen.

I hurriedly dry my hair as best as I can – cochlear implants and dampness really do not mix well – and hurriedly put it up into a bun so the lengths can finish drying. Unless I fiddle about with pinning and hairspraying it down in a slightly weird way, the implant will be on show, but I don't have time to deal with that. I need to have a conversation with Tyra.

Why couldn't I have just had an easy start to this new job?

I get dressed into the outfit I set out, and while I feel like a cute little daisy-print sundress might not be projecting the Serious Conversation about Boundaries vibe I need it to, it'll have to do.

Tyra is in the kitchen with someone else, presumably another housemate of ours. She's a tall Black woman with braids down to her bum, threaded with tiny bits of gold that catch the light. Her softly curved body is poured into a figure-hugging fuchsia wrap skirt and matching cropped bikini top, the colour popping against her dark brown skin. They both look up as I walk in, and Tyra begins spluttering apologies immediately.

I hold up a hand to slow her down, not least because I'm going to get even more of a headache if she keeps talking to me at that speed.

To her credit, Tyra does shut up.

'I'm Sorrel,' the other girl says, holding her hand out for me to shake, though she looks like she'd rather do anything else, probably because I'm trying not to glare daggers at Tyra. 'Yes, that's my real name given to me by my actual parents. They were hippies. Are hippies. But they were gardeners too. It's a whole thing that I'm sure we'll get into after we deal with whatever this is.'

As she says *this* she looks between us.

'Cassie,' I say, taking her hand and giving it a firm shake.

'So . . . what happened exactly? I just got home and this one has been vibrating like an upset chihuahua, and you look like you're about to detonate. No offence.'

'For *some reason*, Tyra walked into my bathroom while I was having a shower,' I say.

Over the top of her comically oversized heart-shaped sunglasses, which Sorrel is inexplicably wearing indoors, she gives Tyra a searching look. 'Girl.'

'I didn't –'

'I would rather you respect my boundaries. I'm not

82

comfortable with people just walking into my room whenever –'

'It wasn't that –'

'You knew I was taking a shower, so how is this –'

'Hold up, hold up,' says Sorrel. 'Let's all take a breath and a step back.'

We do as we're told. Sorrel has some serious intervention skills.

'We just met, but we have to live together for the next however long, so let's take a second to listen to each other,' says Sorrel. As I get used to her speaking, I can kind of tell that she has an accent, a bluntness to how her words end. Her speech is melodic, but slow. If Tyra speaks at a hundred miles an hour, Sorrel is more like two.

'Else, I'm kicking you both out.' She peers over her enormous sunglasses. They'd look like a costume prop on anyone else, but on her they look almost elegant. 'Peachy?'

I nod and turn back to Tyra. 'Explain. Please.'

'OK, first of all, again, really sorry about that,' says Tyra, trying to breathe properly as she speaks much slower than usual. 'You'd been in there a little while, and I knocked on the door to leave you a tea on your side table. You didn't respond so I figured you hadn't heard me over the water. But then it had been like fifteen minutes and I could still hear the water running, so I knocked again, just to check you were OK, and you didn't say anything. Veena and Sorrel hadn't got back yet, and as it was only me here, I just took the risk to check in on you because I was worried you'd had a fall.'

'Well, first of all,' I say, turning the right side of my

head towards her, 'I'm deaf. I wear a cochlear implant, and it's not waterproof so I take it off to shower. That's why I didn't hear you.'

'Ohhh, I'm so stupid,' Tyra says, burying her face in her hands. It admittedly makes me feel a bit better that she's so absolutely mortified.

'Well, that explains that. I'm sorry you had to tell us this way, Cassie.' Sorrel gives me such a gentle smile that I want to reach over and hug her.

Tyra drops her hands and looks up at me. 'Yes, I'm so sorry.'

'It's OK,' I say.

There's something about what she said that keeps niggling at me. *Had a fall.* Most young people wouldn't describe knocking yourself out that way. In fact, it's more like how Pen describes the people they work with at the care home.

And that's when it all clicks. Why she would have been knocking on the door. Why she seemed so familiar.

'You're Sweet Tea & Epilepsy, aren't you?'

'Guilty as charged,' she says, with an awkward smile. 'Though that's a vintage reference. I very rarely get called that these days.'

When I was a teenager, before my first implant broke, I subscribed to a ton of disabled YouTubers' channels. I didn't really know any other disabled people my age, though one of my friends had a cousin who had type 1 diabetes. And so I ended up watching Sweet Tea, a girl based in Texas who had epilepsy, and made a mix of content, about being a teenager with a seizure disorder, but also fun vlogs and *Get Ready With Me*s. She danced too, which is how I found her originally. It made me feel less alone, to know that other people like me were just living lives a bit different from everyone else but getting on with it. To know there were other teenagers out there growing up with a disability.

But when everything fell apart with my implant breaking, I pretty much logged out of that YouTube account and never logged in again. I just couldn't connect with those bits of myself – being different and being OK with it – when things were so difficult, and I had absolutely zero hearing or way of communicating with most people, except Pen and my parents. It wasn't escapism any more. It felt too hard.

I never really forgot about her though. Those videos stuck with me, quietly.

And now, she's here.

In the flesh. And, speaking of, she just got an eyeful of mine.

This is turning out to be a much weirder day than I ever thought it could be.

But at least now I understand that she wasn't trying to sneak a peek.

'I'm really sorry,' she says again. 'I'm not the only one in my family with seizures, so I'm always, like, on the lookout for someone dropping. Plus, heat and travel can be such a trigger for people – I know I'm feeling a bit wonky. First-aid training really kicked in before I could stop it.'

'It's OK,' I say, and I find I really mean it. I get the

hypervigilance she's talking about – I'm always on the lookout for other deaf people, especially people signing. I've helped a few people in shops who were struggling to be understood over the years, and even one girl in hospital while she was waiting for an interpreter to show up. Like, I know the things that I find hard or might not be the safest for me, and must be similar for other people. I guess she's just doing the same thing, really.

'I understand why you didn't want to risk it when we barely know each other and you couldn't be sure I wasn't sick. And to be honest, if I do knock myself out in the shower, I'd rather someone come in and rescue me, even if it means they see my nips.'

'Sounds like she sure did,' teases Sorrel, and we both laugh.

Tyra flushes from head to toe. 'I tried not to!'

'Did you say you made me a tea?' I ask, and before I can finish the sentence, Tyra is in and out of my room with a steaming hot cup. I think of Gemma Collins on *Big Brother* saying making someone a cup of tea is like giving them a grand, because it does feel a bit like that right now. I take a sip and feel more human.

Tyra and Sorrel both watch me a little nervously, as if waiting for me to kick off about something else.

'It's good. Thank you,' I say.

'Sounds like you're on tea duty for the next few weeks to make up for it,' Sorrel says to Tyra who is primed to start up again on her apology cycle.

'I really am –'

'It's OK, honestly. We're even. Plus, it sounds like you're at least as embarrassed as me.'

'Oh, I think definitely more. I would like to go die in a hole right now.'

'Who is dying in a hole?' We're joined finally by the fourth member of our little household, who slams the front door behind her. She's willowy, with earth-brown skin and thick, beautifully curved eyebrows which form a kind of scowl that makes me briefly worry that she's furious at me, specifically.

'Tyra,' says Sorrel. 'She walked in on Cassie showering.'

'I didn't mean –'

The new girl bursts into such raucous laughter that all my nervousness falls away.

'Hi, I'm Cassie who got walked in on,' I say.

'Veena,' she says, and she gives me a curt little nod. She wears all-black athleisure wear, like she's just been for a run, except I get the impression this is how she dresses all the time. Her hair is tucked under a black baseball cap. Holding up the carrier bag in her hand to show us all, she says, 'They didn't have any Fanta Limón left. Like, what am I gonna do if there's no Fanta Limón? That's like a major reason to take the job.'

'The lure of Ibiza and fame wasn't enough?' Tyra says with a laugh.

'No.'

Tyra pats her on the shoulder, clearly confused about what this means. But I get it.

'It tastes of summer holidays,' I agree solemnly. 'Now I'm craving one.'

'See, she gets it,' Veena says to the other two, who seem fairly perplexed.

'Is it that hard to get in the UK?' asks Sorrel. 'It's all over Europe.'

In chorus, Veena and I wearily sigh, 'Brexit.'

'Wow, that was . . . eerie,' says Sorrel. 'And depressing.'

'Well, probably partly that,' adds Veena. 'But also, on that island, we hate anything that might give us pure unadulterated joy. And Fanta Limón tastes like joy. Ergo, no Fanta Limón.'

'What did you get instead?' I ask, looking at the carrier bag in her hand.

'Orangina.'

'Oh, that's all right, then.'

'But it has the bits in.'

I pull a face.

'I feel like you understand me on a deep emotional level,' says Veena, completely deadpan and yet I suspect very genuine. 'Right, then. Are we going to go eat or just stand around talking about Fanta Limón?'

'You're the one who brought it up,' points out Sorrel. 'Like, a lot.'

'Look, I need to find joy where I can. Come on, I found somewhere for dinner.'

We grab bags and shoes, and walk down the road to a little bar that serves tapas. We split a jug of sangria between us, and it's sweet and strong and delicious. For a moment, I imagine I'm just on a girls' trip with three new friends. That feeling is solidified by us all ordering a round of Cosmopolitans and pretty much every tapas dish off the menu.

When we toast our new life and the adventure we're about to embark on, the weight hits me again but it's not like being hit by a fleet of tour buses this time. I might have just met these girls, but between us, maybe we can carry the weight. It's manageable.

Plus, it's easier now that we've gone through something embarrassing and mildly traumatic together.

I take the opportunity to get to know Sorrel and Veena more, not least because I think Tyra is still a bit too embarrassed to talk to me, and I want to give her some space to recover. Plus, weirdly, I already know a lot of details about her life.

Veena, it turns out, is from West London, born and raised in Harrow. She stresses that that's not the same as going to Harrow, the very posh school nearby. 'I teach at a small dance school there on the weekends and in summer holidays. Usually posh kids needing some extracurricular-type stuff for their uni applications,' she says, picking at some patatas bravas with a fork.

'Did you study dance at uni, then?' I ask.

'Nah, I did International Business,' she laughs, miming being sick. 'But I was in a bunch of societies like cheerleading and jazz and stuff. I found out about this job from my boss who runs the dance school. I think honestly she could see the fire dying in me in real time. I don't think the freelance accounting and admin to pay the bills was helping with that.'

'I'm glad you got the job and are here with us instead.'

'Oh, me too.'

'What about you?' I ask Sorrel.

89

'For now, I've got my toes dipped in content creation.' I *love* how casually she says this. 'I've got a nice TikTok following, but it's not dance related. It's mostly mini meditations like *hey, stop scrolling and breathe with me*. I do some stuff about plants that I've learned from my parents – people go nuts for plant stuff so that's a guaranteed way to get on new-for-you pages.'

Veena snorts. 'You've turned up on my feed so that tracks. And I don't even like being outside.'

'Mine too,' says Tyra.

'Are you still creating?' Sorrel asks her, dipping a crispy fried calamari ring into a pot of bright orange dip.

'I was. This job came at the right time. I was having one of those *what am I even doing with my life* moments. It's really tricky to be a mid-tier content creator right now and to rely solely off that.'

'Sounds like you need one of Sorrel's meditations,' adds Veena.

'I definitely need one of those,' I say, making a mental note to follow everyone on socials later. It feels kind of weird to just do it at the table in front of them. Though maybe looking them all up at night when I'm in bed is creepier. I try to distract myself from worrying about being a total weirdo in front of my new friends by shoving a wrinkly little pepper in my mouth, only to realise it's a lot spicier than I was expecting.

'I feel you,' says Sorrel to Tyra, benevolently ignoring my spluttering. 'Anyway, I was working on diversifying my income streams for a bit – editing for other creators, picking up some marketing gigs.'

Veena raises an eyebrow and pushes me a glass of icy water across the table. I try to sip it casually, though my mouth feels a little on fire. Note to self, the cute little peppers are too much for me.

'But I have a dance background. Always on the stage as a kid, and I've been off Broadway a few times as a teenager, but that industry can be just . . . well, super racist, transphobic and fatphobic. It was all skinny white chorus girls or *Hamilton*. Things are changing, but so slowly. Too slowly for me to just stand there and watch and hope I get through the door when I'm battling the odds. Anyway, I had to get out of there and try something new for a bit. Luckily, this job appeared right when I was getting itchy feet.'

She smiles as I spear a little cube of creamy cheese with a toothpick and shove it into my mouth. 'How about you, Cassie?' she asks, once I've swallowed.

My mouth finally feels less on fire, but now that I'm centre of attention it's suddenly dry. 'My housemate applied for the job on my behalf, without me knowing.'

'Oh, wow,' says Veena.

'You didn't want the job?' asks Tyra.

'I . . .'

After today I'm not sure I'm ready to have this conversation because inevitably we'll have to get into my life and my experience with deafness and how that got me dancing in the first place. Everyone has been so vulnerable and open this evening and I'm just not sure I'm there yet.

Clearly sensing my panic, Sorrel leans forward, and pats me on the hand. 'Hon, we don't need to get deep tonight.'

91

I give her a big, relieved smile, and instead cherry-pick a bit of what Pen said to me.

'I just didn't know if I could do it. And they did. You'll meet them soon. Pen. They came with me for an adventure of their own.'

'I like them already.' Sorrel smiles.

Plates keep arriving, and soon we're trying to eat so quickly to make space for the next incoming plates that we fall out of conversation. There's dips and soft flat breads to eat with them. They deliver an enormous pile of olives, stuffed with cheeses and peppers and all sorts of things. I'm too squeamish to try the chunks of octopus, but to my surprise Tyra eats it all up with a satisfied smile on her face. The croquettes are my favourite – truly whoever thought of taking ham and then breadcrumbing and frying it is a genius.

I was about to suggest that next time we order less, but somehow we end up eating everything. We need full bellies before tomorrow, after all.

We walk home before it really even gets dark, determined to get an early night too. When we get back to the apartment, we sit out on the balcony for a while, and soak up the sunset.

I can see so much of the island from here: the mountains in the distance are draped in a thick purple cloud that threatens a thunderstorm, and in the other direction I can see the sea.

'I didn't realise we'd be so close to the beach,' I say.

'Well, honey, we are on an island. There's a lot of beach to be had,' laughs Tyra kindly.

'Maybe we can go investigate on our day off?' adds Sorrel, clearly keen to get exploring already.

'When will that be?' sighs Veena. 'Do we even get weekends?'

'We get weekends.'

'Well, that's a relief. I was worried,' sighs Tyra.

'Why?' I ask.

'Not enough time for drinking European beverages,' Veena answers for her, and we all laugh.

After a moment, Tyra says, 'It's just a lot, isn't it? A lot and not much information about it all. Like, do we even know where the studio we're practising at is?'

Sorrel shakes her head, and I realise she's right. There really wasn't very much in the info pack. 'But they're sending another one of those fancy cars for the four of us in the morning,' she says. 'So come on, girls. Spirit of adventure, and all that.'

'Hmm, we'll see,' says Veena.

As we reach our bedroom doors, we all turn and say goodnight. It's like something out of a movie. But tomorrow, the hard work starts, and our new lives begin.

Chapter Eight

We might not have known where the studio was going to be, but when Bernard picks the four of us up in the morning, I'm pretty sure the last thing any of us expected was to be driven to a huge estate behind ornate gates that look like something out of a fantasy show.

And the thing is that I know that this isn't just any huge estate behind enormous gates.

I've wasted enough time watching *Architectural Digest* video interviews of famous people in their homes to know that this is Rosa Cordova's actual estate. Somewhere on this sprawling piece of land is her *house*. And possibly even her.

In the video, she talked about how her mother was Ibizan, and how she always wanted to come back and live here when she was older. We're inland, where all the rich people live, though probably not on estates as big as this.

I'm not sure the others have clocked it, and so I stay quiet. You never know what kind of nerves people are dealing with, and I don't want to release the idea of us meeting Rosa as being not just possible but possible *today* into the mix without warning.

It is absolutely wild that we are here.

It quickly becomes clear that everything for the next leg of the tour is being prepared here, which I guess makes sense if she wants to rebuild and have complete control over everything – she's probably taking no chances. We don't drive very far in, following the main drive and turning off towards the first collection of buildings. I'm not sure if they've always been here – they certainly weren't in the video – but one building we pass must serve as the workshop for making the stage backdrops, because it's huge. I never thought about how all this stuff is built before. They have to take it from stadium to stadium, so it's not like you can just build it from scratch each time. We pass people carrying construction materials, and rolls of fabric, rushing in and out.

And then next to it, is a more normal building that must be where we're going. Not that there's any indication of that other than the confused-looking people standing outside who all have the hallmark of brand-new backing dancers – workout gear, decent dance shoes, hair tied up, and the unmistakable *what the fuck am I doing here* look in their eyes. We get out of the car to join them in a nervous huddle, but luckily we don't have to stand there awkwardly for very long because through the glass door comes a man with a clipboard. You can always rely on someone with a clipboard to tell you where you're supposed to be going.

'Morning, everyone,' he says, causing us to chorus *morning* back to him. But then he doesn't say anything else, and seems to almost be waiting for us to tell him what happens next.

Then he suddenly seems to remember what he's doing, and leaps to life. 'Follow me.'

We follow him through the building and up some stairs, where we walk into a huge dance studio with a mirror down one end, and barres on the other side. Through the door to a little side room I can see exercise balls and resistance bands and yoga mats stacked up, along with all kinds of weights. This place is seriously kitted out.

'Talk about a control freak,' snaps a girl next to me. Her caramel-brown hair is slicked back into a sleek, high ponytail, the kind that reminds me of Ariana Grande. Her face is thin and long, wearing an unimpressed expression. What kind of person could come here and not be blown away by every single detail?

I'm not quite sure if she said it to me, and I don't really want to be caught talking shit about the boss on the first day either, so I ignore it.

Standing in the middle of it all is the man who's about to whip us into shape. Michael Owusu. He's been Rosa's choreographer for the last few years or so, graduating from being one of her backing dancers. He's the creativity and spark behind the performances I love so much. He has absolutely no social media presence and seems to be intensely private from the few interviews I've read, so I've never been able to find out much about him. I was worried that he'd left in the whole Payton mess.

'Welcome, understudies,' he calls, as we line up. 'I hope you're here to work.'

The response is surprisingly mixed. I nod eagerly because

no one could ever accuse me of not polishing apples for teacher.

Next to me, the girl with the high pony folds her arms defiantly and leans back. I can't tell if she's trying to be cool or not. Perhaps it's easy to be confident if you're not impressed.

'My name is Michael, and yes that is *Michael*, not Mike or Micky or anything else. I am your teacher, your choreographer, your boss. You answer to me, and I answer to Rosa. I am not your friend, but I'll treat you with respect if you show up every day ready to work. Together we're going to create something beautiful.'

He walks around us slowly, eyes forward, but I get the sense that he's taking stock of us all. Watching how we react.

'You have all been selected for this tour not only as dancers, but as ambassadors. You've been plucked by Rosa personally because she liked your applications, your attitudes, your personalities. She saw something in you that spoke to her, and she wanted to bring you onto the team for that reason.' He turns and gives the whole crowd a stern look. 'I'm here to find out if any of you lied on that application.'

My stomach turns. Both at the idea that Rosa knows who I am, and the fact that I didn't even write my application, though I didn't see any lies or exaggerations.

'I'm sure that all of you have seen some things in the press about what might or might not have happened with regards to the original main cast for this tour. All I have to say is, that's not your business. You're here to work. But I do expect dedication, discretion and, this should be obvious, loyalty. I won't tolerate any less.'

I can't imagine what it must have been like for him, losing so many dancers in one go. Knowing he has to train a whole new group. That he has to help redesign the entire show. He must have spent the last couple of weeks rechoreographing half the songs.

'We have the best part of six weeks to get you up to speed before our dress rehearsals on set in Paris where the tour kicks off. I will be training you to cover multiple positions in the choreography, so make sure you're getting enough sleep and coming in sharp so you can retain those steps. We have about twenty full songs for you to learn and be able to execute at the drop of the hat, so this is not going to be easy on you, especially those of you who haven't been dancing in a troupe up until now.'

At this, I hear a snort come from somewhere in the crowd, and my stomach sinks. I had a feeling that not all of us would have come in through the undiscovered route. Of course there's people here who have been dancing longer than me. Hell, Veena and Sorrel have done it for their jobs. I hope it's not just Tyra and me.

Either way, it doesn't feel good. I want to walk out right now, go back to our flat in York. Except it's empty and all our stuff is at my parents' and Pen is somewhere on this island. God, what a mess.

Michael lifts his head and surveys all of us again, his eyes narrowing. He smiles, but it's not a happy one. It's the kind of smile that comes before someone drops a clanger on you.

'I've heard some sassy little noises while I've been talking, and I'm letting you know now that I won't stand for that. There will be no disrespect towards me, end of.' He claps his hands together to signify this, and next to me Tyra nearly jumps out of her skin. 'And,' he continues, once he's sure she's not going to pass out from fright, 'I will not tolerate disrespect for your colleagues in this room. You are a team, and the success of the choreography and this show as a whole relies on you working together and treating each other with respect. There is no hierarchy in this room, except for me. Capiche?'

Suitably scared, everyone nods. Well, the high-pony girl doesn't look scared. She looks the same.

'Good.'

He waves over the guy with the clipboard again, who starts handing him an armful of papers. Michael rolls his eyes, takes the clipboard from him, finds the thing he wants and gives all the rest back. Maybe it's his first day too.

'So, say goodbye to the dance studio because for the first week you're all going to be in the gym.'

This elicits a collective groan from pretty much everyone. But I don't mind this too much, especially if it's all focusing on our own stuff. Plus, I could definitely be fitter cardio-wise, as that run home to yell at Pen taught me. At least I have pretty good arm strength from all the work in the kitchens.

'Yes, yes, but I want to know what I'm working with, and get everyone up to a decent baseline level of fitness before I unleash you on the routines. I've got schedules for you all which my assistant will pass out after we've finished talking. And finally, everyone,' he says, 'just because you got here,

99

doesn't mean you're going to *stay* here. If I don't think you're cut out for this job, if I don't think you display the qualities Rosa and I are looking for in a team, I will be letting you go. You'll notice there's quite a lot of you in this room right now, likely more people than we need because we wanted to be cautious. But that also means I have no qualms about dropping people who don't fit the team.'

My stomach flips. What does that mean? I know they encouraged applications from people with all kinds of experience, but . . . *don't fit the team.* Is this what Mason was talking about? How employers say they want to hire marginalised people but then don't really? Perhaps it was all for good PR, and then if I can't keep up it doesn't matter, because they gave me a chance?

I feel the panic rising in my chest as Michael dismisses us, strolling out of the room like a man with places to be. Clipboard Guy goes up to one of the dancers next to him, and sorts through the mess of papers until he finds the right one. He must have all our schedules.

I feel sick, so I bend over, cradling my head in my arms, and try to breathe deeply into the back of my lungs. Sometimes this helps. I watch everyone's feet leave the room, except for one pair of black Air Force Ones that walk back towards me.

'Babe,' says Veena. I'd recognise her deadpan tone anywhere. She places her hand on the small of my back. 'You all right? You look like you're going to shit yourself.'

I laugh but it's an awkward strangled noise like an upset goose. 'Just having a moment.'

'Moment away. I'm here.'

It's so kind and casual that I really do start to feel better. I mean, I don't forget all the anxiety about how I'm probably going to lose this job before I even start it, but the panic dwindles a little. The breathing comes easier.

After a minute, I straighten up. 'Thank you.'

'No problem. Come on. I got your torture list from that nervous guy.'

'Do you think that's why he's nervous? Maybe they gave him one.'

'I hope, for his sake, that they did not.'

It doesn't seem so bad when I first look it over. There's a . . . really extensive workout plan, plus a meeting with a trainer booked in for me the next day so they can help me with any specific exercises to build up my strength quicker. That all seems fine. I can do that.

It's when I turn the page and realise it's only going to get more intense as the week goes on that my stomach starts to turn.

Veena is similarly grey as she looks over hers. 'Does yours have this many squats?'

'Apparently so.' We seem to have all the same things, but shifted around a bit, presumably so everyone isn't trying to do the same exercises in the same order. It's smart.

'Wow, I guess we're both going to actually shit ourselves, then.'

We make our way down the building towards the gym in the basement, which also turns out to be enormous, taking up the whole floor. There's a fridge with water and rehydration drinks against one wall, and on a table there's boxes of protein bar-type snacks next to rolls of physio tape, brand-new resistance bands still in their packaging and a neat stack of clean towels for us.

There really is no expense spared.

'How the other half live,' says Veena.

Some of the others have already got to work on their programme. A blonde girl is on the stair machine next to high-pony girl's, but she looks almost bored – I've never even been on one but I'm sure they're pretty tough. A couple of people are doing warm-up jogs on the treadmills, and I can see a few others doing planks on yoga mats. There must be people in the weights area at the far end too, because every now and then I hear a loud clang as one of the weights is dropped.

'Did you think it was going to be this intense?' I say to Veena.

'Nope.'

'Do you regret it?'

'Ask me tomorrow.'

I breathe out slowly. 'I guess all we can do is give it a go, right?'

It turns out that Veena might not have been far off with the whole torture thing.

After I've finished the prescribed amount of squats on the first day, I simultaneously can and cannot feel my butt cheeks. My ass exists somewhere on the numb-to-broken spectrum, and my thighs are so exhausted that I'm walking like a cowboy. The only comfort is that my three housemates are equally pathetic. We take turns ferrying drinks and snacks between us once we're back in the flat so that no one has to move from the couches for long.

Thankfully, Tyra logged into her Netflix on the TV last night, so we're able to tune our brains out to the calming tones of an American sitcom I've never seen and am really not taking in now. I almost think about asking for subtitles so I can take out my cochlear implant, but I'm too tired to explain, so I just close my eyes and lie back.

It's weirdly nice. Other than Pen and Mason, I've never really spent so much near-silent time with anyone else. After only twenty-four hours, we're finding a rhythm around each other in our shared spaces. It feels like home already.

Clearly Michael and the team must have anticipated this level of exhaustion, because they drop off deliveries of fresh pasta in a rich sauce, with bright green salads packed with veggies. Hopefully things will become easier as we get used to the routine of working out every day, and just being here in general. It's a lot of change in one go.

Clutching our deliveries, we manage to crawl outside to eat on the balcony and watch the sun set, though after a while we get lost in our phones. I guess we're all a bit homesick.

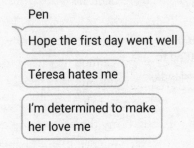

Pen

Hope the first day went well

Téresa hates me

I'm determined to make her love me

103

> But I think she can tell
> I'm a dog person

This makes me snort with laughter.

Cassie

> Just feed her as many
> treats as possible

> First day went OK, I'm so
> tired I could die x

> Please refrain from dying

> Else I'll be left with my only
> friend in the world

> Téresa the heinous cat

As we type, a message comes in from Mason, and my heart flips. I'm too exhausted to worry about what he's said, so I open it immediately.

Mason

> Hey, how was your first day?

> Sorry I didn't text yesterday,
> I thought you would be getting to
> know your new home and friends.

> Do you have time to call
> before bed?

After a beat another message comes through.

Miss you. x

I video call him when I get into my pyjamas. It's so nice to see his face.

'Hey,' I croak, as I clamber into bed. 'I'm not sure how long I'm going to manage to stay awake. I'm so beat. How are you?'

The pillow is so soft. This bed is a cloud. I want to live in here forever.

He tells me about his busy week, and scoring some new clients. He sounds so happy, and it makes me happy, even if I miss him.

I want to stay awake and listen to him talk, but a yawn bursts out of me. 'Sorry about that, I'm so tired.'

'I didn't realise I was boring you,' he says and I'm pretty sure he's joking.

'You never bore me.'

'I know. You must be dealing with a lot, so I'll let you sleep.'

I fall asleep so quickly that the next morning I don't even remember if we said goodbye.

Chapter Nine

Turns out my hopes about things getting easier were wrong.

So wrong.

And whoever said you get endorphins from exercising had clearly never been pushed through one of Michael's workout programmes.

By the time I meet the personal trainer on day two, I'm as weak as a kitten, but manage to at least show her a very passable plank ... for a few seconds. That's better than nothing, though not enough to impress her. She sends me away with a Lucozade and a list of extra exercises to strengthen my core. This came after I did a barre session and pilates, so my core was practically non-existent.

On day three, I burst into silent tears of relief when Michael announces that we've got a half-day off.

On day four, there's a tray of fresh pastries for post-workout treats from Michael, who evidently feels a bit guilty about how hard he's having to work us.

The thing is, I don't resent him. Neither do my flatmates. We know what we signed up for – well, I found out afterwards – and all want the job enough to know that we just have to keep our best professional faces on.

Sorrel is great for keeping us motivated. She's always got something that sounds kind of deep to say to spur us on, but by day four she's so tired that she can only offer us the line 'getcha head in the game' which I'm ninety-nine per cent sure is from one of the *High School Musical* films.

I still haven't spoken to many of the other understudies, or underlings as Michael keeps calling us. None of us are really on the same schedule in the daytime, always moving past each other like ships in the night. It feels kind of weird to barely know anyone else when we're all constantly working out alongside each other. Not that I've been trying to, like, *talk* to people. I did hand a really nice Korean guy called Seojin a bottle of water once. We're in the weights room at the same time a lot. I mean, we've not *spoken* much, but he always wipes down his weights and checks to see if I want to swap. That's a pretty good start for me. Plus, Sorrel says he's nice. Or maybe she just said he looked nice? I'm so tired that I can't keep hold of what thoughts are mine any more, especially when I get bits and pieces about the others from Sorrel, Tyra and Veena.

But it sounds like everyone is pretty nice, if just as exhausted as us four are. It'll be nice when we can all just get to know each other properly . . . though the anxiety in the back of my head thinks differently about that. Perhaps I'm just so desperate to do anything but exercise that I've solved my social anxiety.

A few more texts from Mason have come through this week, which is such a relief. I guess that call and him watching me snore (yes, really, he told me) broke the tension between us. The problem is I don't know what to tell him other than *I worked out again for a whole day and can barely feel my face*. I don't want to leave him on read though, so I drop a few emoji reacts and send *good mornings* and *goodnights*.

But this week would have been way easier if I could read his texts without missing him. And, if I'm honest, I am still a little hurt that he didn't show up to my party, even if I haven't told him that. Maybe that's cowardly of me. Either way, I don't have time to feel emotions! I have more core crunches to do.

Maybe that can be Sorrel's next mini meditation aphorism – zero emotions, only crunch.

It's a Friday and day five, when I'm hoping that maybe Michael is going to give us a bit of an easier time after the guilt pastries, that things all fall apart.

When we get to the gym, Clipboard Guy rounds us all up and directs us upstairs to the studio. There we find Michael in front of the sound system in the corner, and I realise that five days in, when I am so tired I plan to sleep for the whole weekend, Michael is going to finally teach us some choreography.

'Underlings,' he announces. 'We're going to learn some steps and have a run-through.'

Nervous murmurs sound all around me, and I feel Tyra step slightly closer to me.

'I know you're all tired, but I want to see your baseline retention for choreography. I do not expect all of you to be excellent at this, but I do expect you all to give it a go. Now, go line up in front of the mirror.'

We all get into rough rows facing the mirror, with the most confident dancers naturally gravitating to the front. The blonde girl, whose name I think is Giselle, goes front and centre, next to Seojin. I think she's the one who Veena said is French, or went to school there. She seems like a very focused person, not a hint of nervousness on her face.

Michael seems to accept the way we've arranged ourselves and stands at the front facing the mirror.

'Today we're going to learn the first minute of "Diamonds Under My Eyes", from the first verse through the chorus, and then we'll see how we go. I know you're all tired, so I won't be brutal, but I'm not going to go easy, OK?'

We respond with a few exhausted nods, and I swear I hear someone say, 'Yes, chef.'

But secretly, I'm so pleased. This is one of my favourite Rosa tracks – a kind of seventies disco-beat-inspired pop banger. The choreography in her music video was pretty limited, more like a short film than anything. But I've seen her perform this with her dancers on tour and it's always a high-energy crowd pleaser. Well, from what I can tell from TikTok.

Michael's guidance is sharp, to the point – *walk, walk, arms, four* is a complete sentence I'm pretty sure I just heard him say. We run through each set of eight or twelve beats only once, before adding the next one. Sequence after sequence after sequence.

But to my surprise, I can keep up. I'm a bit off beat, especially on one particular move where I'm not keeping my weight evenly distributed, so when I step onto the other foot, it's always too slow. I can work on that later – right now I need to concentrate on keeping up. So far, so good. I guess all that time where I just had half an hour to learn and film a TikTok dance has paid off.

At the chorus, Michael introduces some arm swings, one going a bit too close to my cochlear implant if I keep my arm as straight as I need to. But it's the last move where things start to go seriously rocky. He shows us a half-body drop that turns into a floor roll, ending with chest up and head thrown back. It's the exact sort of move I try to avoid when picking a routine to do.

I follow along just like everyone else, but in the body drop I have to hold onto my implant, as I feel the force threatening to loosen it. I do the same when I fling my head back, using the hand on the far side of Michael in the hope that he can't see.

Though I suspect he did, because we make eye contact in the mirror, just briefly, before he says, 'OK, everyone. Take ten minutes to hydrate, stretch, and then you're going to perform in small groups so that I can track you all.'

Clipboard Guy has brought up ice-cold bottles of water from the fridge downstairs, and I chug one in extremely unladylike fashion, as though I've not drunk in years.

'That was sick,' pants Tyra, who is practically bouncing on her heels in between sips.

'You're going to give yourself hiccups if you keep that up,' says Veena, retying her hair up into a bun. She winces. 'I think I did that last head flip a bit too enthusiastically.'

'I want to go again.'

'Hold your horses.'

'Hey,' Sorrel says, threading her arm through my elbow. 'You OK?'

Her eyes go from my face to my implant and back, and I know that she saw, but I'm grateful she's asked me on the lowkey.

I do a small nod. 'I'll be fine.'

'That's my girl.'

Hydrated, and eager to get the worst part over, we all line up at the side of the room. There's sixteen of us, so that's four groups of four.

Clearly, Michael has spent the week clocking who is friendly with who, and makes sure to split up all the housemates, because no one ends up dancing with their usual friends. That's fine, but when we're still getting to know each other, it's undoubtedly an extra level of nerves. I'm put with Seojin, the high-pony girl who was kind of snippy on the first day, whose name is apparently Fenella, and a sweet dark-skinned guy who Sorrel said she knows from Broadway. He introduces himself as Demi, and I try not to stare at his defined upper arm muscles when he waves at me.

The music is on, and we watch in awe as the other groups perform. Sorrel is astounding. You can tell that she's been dancing professionally for years. She was across the room from me when we started learning the choreography so I didn't get a great look at her, but she's so fast, and sharp with all her movements. There's a couple where she doesn't quite get the body positioning right, but it doesn't look wrong because she throws her whole self into it. I guess that's what comes with the confidence of dancing for a long time – knowing how to fake it.

Standing on my non-cochlear implant side, Fenella says something that I don't catch, but Seojin and Demi nod. I hope that she just assumes I'm concentrating on what the dancers are doing. But then I realise she's looking at me.

'Sorry?' I say.

Her bright green eyes roll in a way that makes them seem much uglier. I hate it when people take me not hearing them as a personal insult.

'I *said* –' but it's lost to the beat of the music again, and I'm straining to hear her so hard that I can feel the headache that was already there really brewing now.

'I didn't catch that,' I say, glancing between her and the dancers because I don't want to see how annoyed she is with me for not hearing a second time.

'Whatever.'

Typically, I hear that.

Our group goes last, so I get to watch the next two groups kill it as my anxiety about performing well enough mashes with my worries about my implant and nerves about whether Fenella is going to tell everyone I'm some kind of snotty stuck-up bitch who doesn't listen, forming a super-headache right behind my eyes.

I try to concentrate on Veena, who doesn't miss a single beat or move, even if she's a bit scrappy at some points. Tyra starts on the wrong foot in a whole sequence just before the chorus and misses a few beats but manages to bring herself back in line for the chorus.

All in all, my roommates do a good job.

And then it's my turn.

We stand in two rows, Seojin and I at the back.

I can do this. I know this dance. Plus, I've had the privilege of watching it three times right before I get to go. I have to nail it.

When Michael hits play, I don't immediately lose myself to the music like I usually do. I know what's happening – I'm too in my head, the nervousness taking over. I try and push it back, because I'm better if I surrender to the music, but it's still there itching away at me. I'm a bit slow into the last move before the chorus, in the same place Tyra got lost, which means I try to speed up in the body drop.

Then the music cuts out. But it's not just the music. It's all the sound around me. Everything is gone.

And I watch as my cochlear implant, which has detached from my head, goes flying across the studio floor.

I freeze as time slows down, but Seojin, Fenella and Demi keep dancing. I've made a fatal mistake – I stopped moving. That's the first rule of dancing. If you fuck up, just style it out and make your way back to the beat. The whole point of group choreography is to move like a single entity, to be part of a bigger organism than yourself. When a part stops moving, it's so obvious to the watcher.

I swear only a few seconds have passed, but I can't pick it back up. I can't hear anything, I can't find the beat. I just have to get out of there.

I scramble to my feet, rushing to reclaim my cochlear implant from the floor, and too terrified and embarrassed

113

to stop and try again or explain or even reattach the implant in front of a room of concerned faces, I race out of the studio.

On the stairs, I sit down and check my implant over. Thankfully nothing seems broken, but I still hold my breath when I reattach it to my ear and the side of my head.

To my relief, there's no beeping or weird noises. I can pick up the end of the song, floating through the silence in the stairwell.

And I definitely hear it when my roommates crowd around me, all speaking at once.

My hands are still shaking from all the adrenaline. I thought my implant had broken, and thankfully it hasn't. But I still fucked up my first assessment of this new job in such a major way that there's probably no coming back from it.

'Guys, shush,' Sorrel says to the others, her hands forming the universal T sign for time out. Everyone goes quiet, and I'm able to take a breath. My headache is still killing me.

'Honey, are you OK?'

She says it so gently that I burst into tears. Huge racking sobs that aren't just about today, but every other time. My cochlear implant doesn't routinely fall off in the middle of a crowded room, but there's still been so many occasions where something happens that means a whole group of people will clock that I'm deaf and different. That the only way I can hear them is through this device attached to my brain.

The three of them wrap their arms around different parts of me. Veena sits on a lower step and puts her arms around my knees because there's not much torso left after Tyra and

Sorrel embrace me. And there's something about her little face perched on my knees in such a way that I can't see the rest of her that makes me laugh enough to stop crying.

Or at least, slow down crying.

'God, that was mortifying,' I wail.

'It's nothing to be embarrassed about,' soothes Tyra.

'Then why do I feel like I want the earth to swallow me?'

'At least you didn't shit yourself,' says Veena's floating head.

'What is your obsession with shitting yourself?' I laugh, wiping a tear from my cheek.

She shrugs. 'Just feel like it's a good low bar for how bad things can get, you know? If that hasn't happened, it's probably still OK.'

'Your logic is fascinating to me,' says Sorrel, shaking her head. 'And, yes, it's nothing to be embarrassed about, but let yourself feel all your feelings. We got you.'

'I'll be OK,' I say.

'Is your hearing aid OK?' asks Veena.

'It's a cochlear implant so a bit different, but yeah. I think so. I have a spare that I borrowed just in case, but still. They're expensive.'

I've only got one backup. And if this keeps happening, I could break both. I really did not need this.

'You know, if you ever want to tell us about this stuff, so we can support you better, we're here to listen,' says Tyra. 'I know we just met but I get it, I know how scary it is to tell people you're vulnerable, but like Sorrel says, we got you.'

'We're a team,' agrees Veena.

'You guys are the best. Thank you,' I say, holding back another wave of tears. 'Maybe later?'

'Babe, I don't want to be rude, but do you think it's time to come back in and give it another go?' asks Sorrel.

I cover my face with my hands. 'I don't think Michael will let me come back.'

'He will.'

'I'll make him,' says Veena, flexing a bicep.

As if on cue, the door to the studio opens and all the other dancers leave, most of them heading towards the stairwell.

'Shit. I blew it.'

'Not if we go back now. Come on.' Sorrel pulls me to my feet and together, we walk back to the studio.

A few people give me sympathetic smiles. Most of them just look right through me. I'm not sure which I prefer.

Seojin stands holding the door open for me, and gives me a thumbs up. 'You can do it.'

I blush furiously and give him a smile of thanks, because there's a huge frog in my throat.

Michael stands, arms folded, waiting for us in front of the mirror where I left him.

'Michael –' begins Sorrel, but he holds a hand up.

'Formation, please,' he barks, and, to my surprise, all four of us line up.

He's . . . giving me another shot? I can't quite believe it, but I have to give it my all. I make the decision then that I'll just hold onto my implant for those moves, rather than worrying about whether it could fall off. I'll work out a solution later, but right now I've got to get through this.

Hopefully, it'll be OK, because he was asking for move retention, not perfection. And I think I can deliver enough of the former and a good enough performance to please him. I hope.

I want this, after all.

In the mirror, I give my roommates, no, my friends, a thank-you smile. They've already done their run-throughs, they don't need to help me, and yet, here they are. Without me even asking.

There's no time to dwell on how nice it feels to be part of a team, because Michael counts down and then the music starts.

Like last time, I throw myself into it. I know I'm dancing to keep my place here, so I give myself to the moves. Not fully, because I'm still so conscious of my implant, and when I go for the flip and roll move, I do hold onto it this time.

When he stops the music and we all look up from our positions, he gives us a nod and says, 'Great. Now go get lunch.'

That was it? Nothing else?

I get to my feet, and Michael, not looking up from his phone, points to me. 'Not you.'

Oh God.

I've fucked it up. He's typing furiously on his phone as I walk over to him. He finishes whatever he's doing before he speaks to me.

'Miss Clyne,' he begins, pocketing his phone. 'I saw what happened earlier. Is everything all right with your implant?'

I nod. 'Yes, I think so.'

For a while, he says nothing, as though he's reading all my thoughts on my face. 'I think the greatest piece of advice I can give you is to toughen up. Things will go wrong, people will be shits, but only you can control how you react in a situation.'

'R-Right,' I stammer, my heart racing. 'Do . . . do I still have my job?'

'For now,' he says with absolutely no reassurance. 'I said at the start of the week that it's my job to decide who can handle it.'

'I can handle it.'

'Then grow a thicker skin.'

He's right. That's the worst part about it. I feel sick and angry and like I want to cry at the same time. But I can't crumble. Especially if I want to keep my job. Otherwise how can he rely on me to be able to go on stage at the drop of a hat?

'You're a hard worker, Cassie. Keep showing me that, harden your heart, and we won't have a problem. Got it?'

I nod. 'And, I'm really sorry about what happened. I won't freeze up again, and I'll find a way to secure it better for when we're dancing so I don't have to worry or hold it.'

'Good. Now, get out of my studio. We've both got weekends to attend to.'

And with that, he leaves.

It's just me in the studio alone.

Well, for about thirty seconds, because the roommates pile back in.

'That went OK, right?' says Sorrel, but it's more of a question than strictly reassuring. 'I think it went OK?'

'He sounded pissed,' says Veena, but because it's her that says it, it doesn't make me feel worse. She's just stating a fact.

'He *always* sounds pissed,' counters Tyra.

'Shall we go home?' suggests Sorrel. 'Cosy clothes and a crappy film?'

'Yes to home,' I say. 'But I think I need to go for a walk. I feel all . . .' I don't know how to describe it in words so I just kind of flail my body. 'You know?'

All at once, they respond with what they think I mean. Sorrel opts for anxious, which is at least a little correct, while Tyra suggests angsty which isn't quite right, and Veena itchy, before both realising that Sorrel got it right.

'Ohh, right, yeah, that makes more sense,' says Veena.

'I mean, I could be all three at once.'

'Sounds minging.'

'Agreed. Urgh, let's go home.'

Chapter Ten

We get back to the flat a little after lunch. I really could get used to being ferried around by taxi for the rest of my life.

I have a quick cold shower but I can't be bothered to wash and dry my hair, so I just put it up in a bun and hope for the best.

I decide to head down to the beach. I can't believe I've been here almost a week and haven't had a chance to go yet. It's not even that far. There are signs everywhere, so I just wander down the roads, and end up walking along a dried-up riverbed that leads to the sea.

When I get there, it takes my breath away. The water is rich blue, bordered by a sandy beach on one side, and a harbour full of sailboats on the other. Alongside the harbour is a boardwalk, dotted with restaurants and string lights ready to be turned on for the evening. I relish the salt breeze that rushes over my cheeks.

It's still early in the holiday season, I guess, which is why the beach is quiet. I settle down on a bench and watch a couple for a while. They must be a little older than my parents, walking along the beach holding hands. Occasionally, one of them will bend down and pick something up to show the other. A shell, perhaps. Maybe a bit of sea-glass. They look happy. I wonder what their lives are like. Do they have children? Have they been together long? Maybe they're both divorced or have lost partners, and found each other later. The only thing I can be sure of is that they're in love, and my heart aches when the woman looks at something in the man's hand, and they both break into laughter.

I feel so lonely. I know I could text Pen and they would drop whatever they were doing and be here, and my roommates are brilliant, but this is the furthest *and* longest I've been apart from Mason. Like, normally even if we couldn't see each other for a week, we'd still be in the same city so it felt like we were close. I could have just walked over to his place. But now I'm an hour ahead and in another country. It feels ridiculously dramatic to say. It's not like I'm in Asia or South America. I'm an easyJet flight away for God's sake. But still.

It'll be easier if I just text him, and can speak to him. Maybe if he knows I'm upset, he'll find the time to call me.

Cassie

Hiya

Had a bit of a hard morning

Are you free to talk on your lunch?

It takes a few minutes for his reply to come through, and my stomach sinks.

Mason

Sorry babe, it's so busy today.

Let's talk tomorrow.

I don't want to act like a demanding girlfriend. I really don't. But I wish he'd give me a bit more. Just . . . something. There's no *you'll be* OK, or *what happened* or anything. It's unfair of me to think this, but part of me feels like he's scheduling me in, like I'm one of his clients.

This is the real cherry on the shit sundae, and combined with the happiness of the couple I'm watching, it breaks me.

Not for the first time today, I sob. There's something kind of freeing about crying on your own on a near-empty beach in a country you're not from. I put my head in my hands and really go for it, like I'm trying to get it out of my system. A tactical cry.

'Hey, are you all right?'

'I'm fine.' I sit bolt upright as a figure suddenly blocks the sun in front of me. 'Minor existential crisis.'

'Ah, I see. You picked a fine view for it at least.'

'Yeah, there truly is nothing like crying in a holiday destination,' I say with a laugh, wiping the tears from my eyes.

And to my confusion and abject horror, I recognise the man standing in front of me.

'Cassie?' he asks, and I want to fling myself into the ocean.

Because not only am I sitting on a beach crying in front of someone I know, but he looks like a glistening topless god who apparently just got out of the sea.

'Levi!' I say. 'Oh my God, hi. Sorry, I must look like a mess.'

I fix my eyes on my feet and try to push the image of his incredibly toned, thick chest and shoulders from my mind, but good God. I am not strong enough. Especially when he sits down next to me on the bench, a beach towel flung over his shoulders.

His sun-kissed, broad shoulders.

Wow, I really am lonely because I'm probably openly gaping at Levi. But also, what is he doing here? No wonder I didn't see him when I arrived, if he was splashing about in the sea. God, how embarrassing is all this? At least he can't hear my inner monologue. I hope.

I brave looking up at his face, and clearly he's as confused as I am.

'I have several questions, but I suppose the first one is, can I help with anything?'

'You're sweet, but I'd feel very rude using your beach towel like a hankie.'

He digs in the bag he drops at his feet. 'How about a tissue?'

'That seems more civilised, yeah.' I take the packet, extracting a fresh one, and try to blow my nose in a way that remotely passes for ladylike, but it ends up somewhere between foghorn and rooster call. I fold it up and hold it in my hand, because obviously this cute little sundress doesn't have a pocket. Normally, I'd just stuff it in my bra or something, but that seems somehow worse than the snotty mess I just made.

'Thank you,' I say. 'That helped.'

'You sound cleared out at least.'

'Oh, don't,' I laugh, swiping the air in his direction but making sure not to touch him with potentially snotty fingers.

'I mean it. I hear it's important for a lady to be clear of mind and sinus.'

'How kind of you to recognise that I'm a lady,' I say, trying to adopt a posh accent, but I'm still too bunged up with tears to pass it off. 'It is very damsel-in-distress coded of me to sit here crying in public, I suppose.'

'Ah, well, you know I'm a sucker for a damsel.'

'I remember.'

'And you know, she wouldn't even take my number.'

'What a tease.'

'I think I'm quite a catch but there we go.' He says this so easily, and I wonder if this is just a guy thing – being able to flirt and exude confidence so naturally, as though it means nothing. I know we're joking, but I don't think I could ever imagine describing myself as a catch. I have a hard enough time working out why Mason is with me, and we've been dating for a year, so I'm pretty sure he likes me.

'So, why are you out here?' I ask, pushing past this spiral in my head in case I start crying again. 'Presumably you've not come all the way to Ibiza to hunt down publicly crying women?'

'Well, not as my primary aim, no.' He leans back, lets his head tip backwards. The sunshine kisses his skin, and now I'm close I can see that his dark brown hair is threaded with golden glimmers, as though the sun is threatening to turn him blond one curl at a time. I can't help but look at his strong

124

nose, and his thick lips. I'm about to tell myself to stop staring at him, when he says, 'I'm working here.'

'Me too.'

'Oh, yeah? Doing what?'

'I'm a dancer. Well, an understudy. But a dancer all the same.'

He gives me a look that I can't interpret. 'A dancer?'

'Yeah.'

Does he not believe me? I guess it's a kind of weird job to be doing out in this end of Ibiza, rather than being a go-go dancer in a club or something.

He looks like he's going to say something.

'Go on. Say what you're thinking, and don't make me regret asking,' I say.

'You're not a dancer on the Rosa Cordova tour, are you?'

'How do you know about that?'

'Who do you think is building her sets?'

'No!' I accidentally yell it, and he laughs a little, but it's good natured. 'Are you on her estate too? In that massive great building?' I remember what he said about being an itinerant carpenter.

'Yep.'

'Wow,' I say. 'Isn't that place wild? Like, imagine that just being your home. I mean, good for her that she's got the space to have us all be there, but also wow. That's her *home*.'

'Honestly, I'm constantly worried a peacock is going to wander in.'

'She has peacocks?'

'I don't even know. But it's the kind of place you'd expect an ornamental bird, isn't it?'

'I wouldn't know. I'm not regularly on fancy estates or in the company of peacocks.'

'Oh, you're missing out. They're truly horrible birds.'

We laugh, and for the first time today, I feel actually good. Though this whole situation is totally wild.

I feel like Pen, and Sorrel for that matter, would insist this was some kind of fate. The universe telling me we should be friends, perhaps? But it's probably just a coincidence. A really weird but kind of good coincidence.

'How have we not seen each other yet? I mean, I've been there a whole five days.'

'Spent much time in the workshops, have you?'

'No. But now I will.' I feel a flush on my cheeks, like I've overstepped or given the wrong impression. 'You know, so I can see your handiwork.'

'I only got here mid-week. When I saw you, I was flying to mainland Spain to organise some supplies, sort some logistics, stuff like that.'

'Wow, look at you. A real man-about-town.'

'More like useful dogsbody, but I'll take the compliment as you're so freely offering it.'

'I can't believe we met at the airport,' I say, shaking my head. 'And now you're here. We're both here. What are the chances?'

'What *are* the chances? No really, I never know what to say when someone says that because, like, is there a way to work it out? Is that someone's job?'

'Probably. There's a niche for everyone. And yours is apparently making enormous sets for an international pop star. Like, how did you even get into that?'

'You say that like being a member of her dancing crew is so normal.'

'I'm just an understudy.'

'Oh, yes, of course, practically a mainstream job. I hear universities are really pushing people into the profession.'

'Almost as much as useful dogsbodies.'

We share a grin, and I feel a bit of today lifting off my shoulders. Maybe the universe *is* telling me we should be friends. After all, I've started to feel much better in the last few minutes of talking to him.

And that's not just because he's half naked. Though that probably helps.

I stand up and stretch my limbs. I'm tight from all the dancing and hardcore exercise this week, but also the tension. I wonder if other people feel that; the way your body stiffens up after you've been worrying. At the moment, I feel like one big plank of wood.

'Can we walk along the beach? I feel like I've seeded pretty bad vibes into this bench, I think I should let it be.'

'That only seems fair to it.'

'Plus, I'm guessing the water is nice?' I say, as he roughly towels his hair, drying the salt-soaked strands into fully sprung curls.

'It really is. Are you up for a swim?'

I touch my cochlear implant. 'Not today. Just a walk.'

'After you,' he says, letting me pick the direction. 'Are you

127

going to let me ask you why you were crying on a bench yet?'

I feel the burn of tears. 'Nope.'

'Fair enough.'

'Why don't you tell me how you ended up here instead,' I say, as we walk down a little concrete slope to the sand.

'Now is that about how I'm an international damsel rescuer, or a carpenter?'

'The latter, I think. For now.'

'My dad's a builder with a big *learn the value of money early* complex, so I started working with him as soon as it was almost legal. Or as soon as I could easily pass as old enough. He taught me a lot at home too, and he's a carpenter on the side which helps. And then I went to uni for structural engineering.'

'La-di-dah,' I say.

'Don't be too impressed, I only did a year and a half. Knew immediately that I was not cut out for being behind a desk, even if it did mean I'd get to occasionally be on site. I wanted to design things *and* be part of the construction, you know?'

'Is it hard?'

'Engineering?'

'Being such a control freak.' It slips out of me and I briefly worry that I've crossed the line from banter to mean, but he throws back his head laughing.

'You crack me up.'

'So how did you go from building-school dropout to this?'

'In freshers' week, I got roped into going to the drama society with one of my flatmates in halls, for moral support.

128

Most of the people there were sound so I kept showing up for socials and that. Acting wasn't my calling, but they needed people to help with the sets, making props, you know, things like that. So I kind of fell into it.'

'But then you decided to quit uni? Or were you kicked out?' I widen my eyes, trying to look scandalised, so he hopefully gets that I'm joking still.

'Somewhere in the middle, let's be honest. But actually I'd picked up some jobs with the theatres in Manchester in the holidays, and then I kept getting recommended for more jobs, so it made more sense to leave.'

'And you somehow ended up here.'

'Eventually, yeah. You do good work for someone, they pass your name on. It's networking, I guess, without me ever having to do the networking myself. Word of mouth.'

'That sounds nice, to know that people like working with you and want to tell other people to do the same.'

'Yeah, it's generous.'

We reach the water's edge, and stand quietly watching the blue rush into white foam, and drag itself back into the deep. Caught among it all is a big piece of green seaweed, being pulled back and forth by the current. I feel a bit like that, I think.

'Do you?' Levi asks, and I realise I said it out loud.

I press my lips together, hoping that nothing else leaps out.

He gently knocks his shoulder against mine. 'Is this part of all the stuff you don't want to talk about?'

Miraculously managing not to cry, I nod.

'All right, then,' he says. And to my surprise, he not only

drops it, but takes out his phone and sets up a timer. 'In that case, I'm going to put sixty seconds on the clock, and we both have to find the best thing we can on the beach and report back to each other. Whoever finds the best thing wins.'

'You're serious?' I say, just as he hits start on the timer, and instead of saying anything else I sprint off along the beach, up to the line where the waves meet pebbles.

From beachcombing with my dad as a kid, I know that the best stuff often gets washed up here, at the edge of the sandy bit. There's some good stones – one with some old barnacles on it – and a few nice intact shells, but I know I can do better.

I risk a glance back and catch Levi scuttling about on all fours in a way that makes me bend over laughing. He looks somehow like both a spider and a Labrador.

'You laugh,' he calls, 'but this is how the experts do it.'

I'm laughing too much to get another word out, but when I wipe the tears from my eyes, I spot something really good. The kind of treasure that Dad said made a beach day. Gleaming in the sand is a piece of sea-glass. It's well worn and rounded from the sea, but a beautiful turquoise, and when I lay it flat in my palm, I notice that there are smaller golden sparkles within it. It feels really special.

'Time's up.' Levi strolls over to me, inspecting a handful of things.

'Anything good?'

'Well, the first thing I picked up was a crab's arm with quite a lot of crab left in it, so that felt like a bad omen. It didn't get much better, but I did find this.'

It's a long thin rectangle in tanned leather, with some curled strings tailing off it.

'A mermaid's purse,' I gasp.

'Is that what you call it?' He holds it up to the sun, and it's totally see-through. 'I was pretty sure it was from a sea creature but then I was briefly concerned it was some kind of ancient, preserved condom.'

'I mean, you're not totally wrong. It's a shark egg case. Probably a ray though, in the Mediterranean? I don't really know what swims in these waters.'

'A real David Attenborough here, aren't you?'

I shrug, because he's not entirely wrong but all that stuff comes from such a squishy time for me.

When I was a little kid and got my first cochlear implant, Dad would take me on special trips, just us. We'd drive out to the beach or the woods or the moors. Quiet places where I could practise hearing without having to sort through a million sounds at once. It's not like rural North Yorkshire is super loud, it's not like Leeds or even York, but being at home with radios on and people talking and doors slamming . . . It would just get a lot and I'd have serious concentration fatigue from processing it all. Now, I can just unhook the processor and have some silent time, but then it was so important for me to train my brain to hear.

We kept up our trips for years, until I got too self-conscious as a tween to hang out with him. I regret that so much, looking back.

But when the same implant broke only ten years later, we

found a new kind of togetherness. I didn't really want to go out that much as it was such a tough time for me. So Dad said he'd bring the outside to me instead. We would curl up on the couch and watch boxsets of Attenborough nature documentaries, which luckily had decent subtitles. So, thanks to my dad, I became kind of a nature nerd, mostly from my living room, for a few months.

My chest suddenly aches with missing him.

'So, what did you get? Can you beat my egg case or whatever you called it?' Levi asks.

I drop the odds and ends of shells back onto the beach and hold out my palm for him to inspect my object.

'Let me guess, a mermaid's glasses? Shouldn't we be returning this poor mermaid's accessories?'

'It's sea-glass,' I laugh. 'Someone must have dropped some glass on the beach, at some point, and then the sea smooths it out to look like this.'

Levi takes it from my palm and holds it up to his eye. 'Almost as good for looking through as the purse.'

'You're silly,' I giggle.

'Most polite people just call me curious,' he says, holding it out between us. 'That's a very good find.'

'So who wins?'

'Oh, that's the trick. I used to play this game with my little brother, and my dad would always say we both won in the end, because it was too hard to choose. So, I think we both win.'

'You mean no one wins.'

'Look at you, Little Miss Competitive.'

'You're the one who made beachcombing into a competition!'

'True that. How about we do something where we're less likely to fight, like grab an ice cream from up there?' He points to a little cafe with outdoor seating under big umbrellas that looks mostly deserted, and we walk up, still picking through the beach for good things.

Even though it's late in the afternoon, it's still warm out, and the watermelon sorbet I pick is instant refreshment. Instead of sitting at the tables, we take our cones back to the beach, and plonk down on the pebbles, eating in comfortable silence.

I think it's because he doesn't push me, that I decide to tell him what happened.

'I had a moment today in the middle of dancing where my cochlear implant fell out,' I say. He doesn't say anything, and I'm so used to people rushing into conversations about deafness with questions or advice, that I wonder if he heard me. As if to confirm he's just giving me the space to talk, he gives me a little encouraging nod.

'And it was just this big moment of, like, *hello, everyone, look how different I am*. I'm sure a lot of them had worked it out before then, though everyone's been pretty polite and not asked what's on my ear or why I talk so weird.'

Levi presses his lips together, and shakes his head, just a tiny bit. Again, he waits for me to keep going.

'Sometimes, I just want to be in charge of how the conversation happens,' I say, realising I've perhaps not said this to anyone but Pen before. 'Or even not have it at all.

I could be, like, here's a QR code, go scan it and find an FAQ about my cochlear implant so you don't have to ask me. Do you think people would go for that?'

'I think it doesn't matter so much what people would go for, Cassie. It's more about what would make you feel comfortable.'

Given that I was expecting a jokey response, this takes me aback. I tell myself that the goosebumps on my arms are from the ice cream, though I'm not sure I believe myself. I'm not used to hearing that how I feel about this matters more than everyone else's opinions.

'Is your implant all right?'

'Yeah. I mean, I think so. It got a real whack so I wouldn't be surprised if the batteries die a little early, but I've got spares on me just in case.'

I take them out of my bag and show him, still in their packet. It's not something I usually show people, but he's a handy guy. I bet he'd get a kick out of some niche batteries. Plus he saw me rush off panicking about them at the airport.

'Oh!' I say, thinking about that first meeting. 'We should take a selfie and send it to Pen.'

'Is Pen on the island too?' he says, and, it's a small thing, but I like that he doesn't guess a pronoun for them. I wish more people did that. They're not even here, but it matters then too, I think.

'Yeah,' I say. 'They're house-sitting for a friend of a friend. Looking after a diva cat. I've not managed to see them all week so hopefully we can catch up this weekend.'

I take my phone out, and we snap a cute selfie, us both

poking out our tongues and winking, like one of those cheeky emojis that no one but your mum uses to try and be cool.

Pen replies almost immediately with a series of exclamation points.

'They seem pleased,' Levi laughs, getting to his feet and dusting the beach off his bum.

My phone starts buzzing, and for a moment I think it's Pen calling to interrogate me, but it's Mason. I hastily decline the call and send him a message that I'll call back as soon as possible.

'I have to go,' I say, getting to my feet. I've got an itchy feeling on my skin, like I shouldn't be here when Mason wants to talk to me.

Levi pauses, watching me, before asking, 'Do you want me to walk you back?'

I shake my head. 'I'm a big girl. I can manage it.'

'All right, then. I'll see you at work?'

I beam. 'At work,' I say, still not quite believing that I'm saying it.

Levi waves as he walks off in the opposite direction down the beach, on his way home. I wonder if he was about to leave when he found me crying. He's a nice guy. I'm glad the universe brought us back together.

It doesn't take me long to walk back, now that I feel a bit lighter about everything. Plus the excitement about finally being able to talk to Mason. I'd have called him while I walked but the traffic picked up along the road, and I didn't want to deal with filtering that sound out and concentrating on a phone call and keeping my body upright all in one go.

The housemates are all in when I get back.

'Hey,' calls Veena. 'I'm going to make carbonara for tea. You down?'

'Oh, yes, please. Just going to do a quick phone call,' I say, waving my phone at them and walking to my bedroom. I lie down on the bed and call him back.

'Hello?' he answers.

'Hiya. It's me. How's your week been?'

'Sorry, babe, I don't really have time to talk right now.'

What?

'But you rang me?'

'Yeah, like twenty minutes ago. I have to get back to work now.'

Oh, of course. We're two hours ahead. I feel stupid for assuming he'd still have time, but it's probably about three on a Friday afternoon over there. Not the busiest time in his week though, I don't think.

'I'm sorry, I rushed home as soon as I could so that I could call you back.'

'From where?'

'I was just on the beach.' He makes a noise I don't quite catch. 'Sorry, I didn't hear that. Can you repeat what you said?'

'I didn't say anything.'

This phone call is so weird. He seems almost pissed off.

'Mason, I'm sorry –'

'I've got to go, Cassie.'

And with that, he hangs up.

What did I do?

Chapter Eleven

The next morning, Pen shows up with a bag full of pastries, instantly making everyone love them.

By the time I make it out to breakfast, Pen is regaling my flatmates with their life story, how we know each other, and how they're staying in a villa up the road. I barely have to add anything as I dig into the flaky, butter-rich croissant.

We've not had much chance to talk this week, though they've sent me a lot of photos of Téresa, an enormously fluffy brown creature with an adorable squishy face and a terrible attitude. When there's a gap in the conversation, I ask, 'How are relations with Téresa the heinous cat?'

'Well, she let me into the living room after two days. Before that, there was a lot of yowling, but I think we're getting there. And we've got to the stage where she's comfortable waking me up for breakfast though I think she was relying on me being so disorientated at 4 a.m. that I wouldn't know what time it was or remember that I already gave her some.'

'This cat is smart,' snorts Veena.

'Has she let you out of the flat?' I ask.

'I think she actively prefers it when I'm not there,'

Pen says. 'I've explored the town a little bit, it's really cute. But yes, we're working on tolerance at the moment. We've established I'm allowed on the balcony, and not many other places, which is why I've got this lovely Rudolph shiner.'

They tap the tip of their pink nose. Pen is very fair and naturally ginger, so they catch the sun the second it hits their skin.

'Plus, I think this is the first week off where someone hasn't suddenly needed me to cover a shift in forever? It's been nice, even if I ended up cleaning the flat from top to bottom the first couple of days because I couldn't settle.'

Sorrel shakes her head. 'That's not healthy. You have to learn to rest.'

'Working on it,' Pen says. 'Though I'm starting to get itchy feet already.'

'Sure you're not just allergic to the cat?' says Veena.

'Hopefully not or this is going to be a painful month.'

'How did you get here?' I ask, in between mouthfuls. Turns out I'm starving, despite the monumental portion of carbonara I ate last night. All the working out and occasional dancing really is making me want to eat everything in sight.

'That's the exciting thing,' they say. 'I rented a car so that we can go out.'

Somehow, Pen has also produced a cafetière of coffee, which I presume they just made without needing to be asked. They pour everyone a cup of the steaming dark liquid.

'Really? Can you afford that?'

Pen shrugs. 'I just got it yesterday for the weekend, so I

can afford that. Plus, it's a bit of space that Téresa and I don't have to negotiate over, so I think it's good for both of us.'

'Do you have big plans?' asks Sorrel.

'Not yet, though I have some ideas.'

'Pen *always* has a spreadsheet of ideas,' I add.

'It's called being organised.'

'And Type-A.'

'Well, I think that sounds neat,' insists Tyra.

'Thank you, Tyra. I'm glad I'm appreciated in this house.'

'Oi! I appreciate you!' I say, waving the last bite of my croissant for emphasis. Subjecting my new friends to Pen's and my ten years of codependency and sibling-like fighting is probably not the easy morning wake-up they were all hoping for.

'I appreciate this coffee,' adds Veena, raising her cup to toast nothing but the air.

The wear of the week is written all over our faces. After stuffing ourselves with Veena's carbonara last night, all four of us nearly fell asleep in front of the TV, before dragging our battered bodies to bed. I'll say one thing about Michael's workouts: I've never slept this well in my life.

'So what were you thinking of doing today?' asks Sorrel.

'Well, there's a really cool cave I found that we could go to, but from the car park it's a two-and-a-half-hour walk –'

A chorus of groans drowns Pen out.

'But we have to book that in advance anyway,' they finish.

'No more moving,' I moan. 'It's my day off. I've done my time!'

'Wow, was it that bad?'

'It was pretty grim.' Veena downs the last of her coffee. 'But I'm hoping that this car you've picked up is going to ferry us somewhere nice?'

'Veena, you can't just ask someone to take you places,' insists Tyra.

'Too late. I think my impropriety filter is broken along with my spirit.'

'I think it's a good thing to voice your needs,' says Sorrel. 'Communication is key.'

'Right? That's what Téresa and I say. Or rather, she just hisses. Anyway, it sounds like you need further refuelling.' Pen may as well have swung another bag of croissants in front of our noses because we all look up eagerly.

'Yes. Yes, we do,' I say.

It turns out that Pen wasn't planning on torturing us with hikes in the sun, but instead had found a famous market that happens every Saturday, even in the off season.

The car Pen rented is like a slightly rougher version of Bernard's car that picks us up in the mornings. It's cool enough today that we wind down the windows, and let the fresh Balearic breeze rush around us. Tyra sits up front with Pen, because sometimes she gets car sick. Every now and then I spy a few giggles or excited gesturing from them both, which is nice. I'm glad they're getting on well. Sorrel and Veena take the back with me, and almost immediately Veena falls asleep in the middle seat, black baseball cap pulled down over her eyes. I can't hear super well with all the wind and chatter and music, so I just decide to give myself a break for a bit and relax into watching the beauty unfold in front of me.

It really is stunning here. The buildings we pass are bright white, with colourful accents, sticking out amid the landscape like beacons.

I feel incredibly grateful to be here. Though it would be really nice if I wasn't quite so stiff.

We drive to a town called Sant Carles de Peralta where we find a huge sprawling market, selling clothes and art and food and shoes and more food. There's something about going to a market that really makes a holiday feel like A Holiday, and we all immediately perk up as we weave between the stalls, which are all covered with white canvas roofs to keep the heat off. As we walk in, a banner overhead proclaims this to be the Hippy Market, and from the occasional wafts of incense blowing our way, it smells like it too.

'It's like going to Glasto,' says Veena, and I have to take her word for that because all I've seen of Glastonbury is the highlights on the BBC.

I walk along with her and Sorrel, who seems so relaxed here, while Tyra and Pen continue to take the lead. We stop just out of the way of everyone so that we can speak.

'This is like my childhood,' says Sorrel.

'Did your hippy parents sell stuff at markets too?' Veena asks.

'Yeah, they were good at bartering. Like, you give me these extremely jazzy trousers and I'll give you a sack of mangoes that'll knock your socks off.'

'Man, I miss mangoes. The UK sucks. I can never get good mangoes without spending my life savings.'

'I'm genuinely sad for you.'

'Thank you for understanding.'

'Anyway, we were mostly at the boujie organic markets that rich white people with fancy tote bags go to.'

'I know the type. London is full of them.'

'What about you, Cassie? Aren't you from Yorkshire? Is that farming country?'

I stifle a laugh. 'Oh no. I mean, I grew up in a village so, yes, there was farmland close by, but we're not farmers. My dad's an electrician and my mum is a teaching assistant at a school, usually working with disabled kids.'

Veena leads us over to the stall next to us which is selling necklaces made of different coloured beads. 'My auntie used to do that until she retired,' she says. 'She loved it.'

'Yeah, Mum does too. She started doing it when I went back to primary school after I got my first implant and was doing really well with my hearing. I think from being with me at home every day practising hearing and speaking, she realised how much extra help some kids need, and probably aren't getting.'

'Does she use sign language? That's the one thing my auntie says she regrets not learning,' Veena says, while she gets out her purse to buy a couple of necklaces. Presumably not for herself as they don't quite vibe with her whole athleisure goth aesthetic.

'A little, yeah. Both my parents are hearing. They learned for me, but they can't sign as much as I can. Me and my sister

142

cottoned on to that pretty quickly and would chat in front of them a lot.' Thinking of her, I giggle and then my chest aches. I don't get to see Vics enough anyway, and now I really miss her. 'I don't think they really have anyone outside our family to practise with unless Mum has a student who signs. Like, now you can learn online and do video lessons if you can afford them, but twenty years ago it was so different.'

'I learned a bit of American Sign Language when I was at college,' Sorrel says, before introducing herself and signing her name in the alphabet one-handed. 'Sorry, I don't know if that was any good.'

'I wouldn't know. We're two-handed in BSL,' I say. I sign *Hello, my name is Cassie* in BSL. Some deaf people have sign names, but I've always finger-spelled mine.

'Oh, wow, I have no idea what I'm talking about, clearly.'

I shrug. 'There's a lot people don't know about Deaf culture, or sign languages. Did you know there's a version of ASL that just the Black Deaf community use? It's a whole dialect.'

'That's so cool. I'm looking it up immediately.' Quickly, Sorrel pulls up a YouTube video of a Black girl with long, brightly coloured nails, signing one-handed in a vlog video. As she signs, her nails clack loudly, taking up space and demanding attention. I love it. 'Oh my God.'

'You should keep it up,' I say, hoping she doesn't feel like I'm pushing her. 'You never know when it will come in handy.'

Veena places the paper packet with the necklaces into her bumbag, and we turn to catch up with Pen and Tyra, who have stopped at a crossroads. They see us coming and Pen signs that we should go eat something.

'Lunchtime?' I ask the others, who agree eagerly.

We follow Pen through the crowd to a little cafe, where we walk past the coffee counter and bar into the back garden. It's a tiny oasis, with plants everywhere and even a water feature. It's so much cooler out here.

We split some bright, shiny padron peppers for the table while we look through the menu. They are covered liberally in salt and charred, and when I take a bite they are richer and nuttier than I expect them to be. Luckily, they're not as hot as the one from the other night.

'OK, can we order like four more of those?' says Veena, reaching for her second.

The table is just about big enough for the amount of dishes we order, though we don't go as overboard as our first night. None of us explicitly say let's order things to share. Instead we order the things that our hearts, and stomachs, desire. Fresh full prawns in a spicy but light tomato sauce. Artichoke flowers with feta and lemon, topped with toasted pine nuts. Grilled octopus in paprika. Bright pink slices of grilled watermelon with nuts and a soft cloud of cheese. Scallops still in their half shell, drenched in butter flecked with red chilli and the bright green of lime zest.

All of our mouths water as Tyra's equivalent of an Ibizan fry-up hits the table: two eggs with bright orange yolks, with chipped potatoes and fried Iberian ham.

'And some more of those,' says Veena.

'Don't watch me like that. I feel exposed.' Tyra laughs

as she dips a crispy potato cube into the egg yolk, causing Veena to lick her lips.

'You'd think you've never been fed,' says Pen, watching us drool over the food.

'I feel like we haven't,' I say, slowly dismantling a huge prawn.

'So, Pen,' says Sorrel. 'What are you going to do with your summer adventure? Are you planning to stay the whole time Cassie is here?'

Pen finishes nibbling on a padron. 'I'm still trying to work it out. That's what Tyra and I were talking about before.'

'Did you decide anything?'

'I'm . . . still working it out.' They laugh awkwardly.

'You're being avoidant,' I sing-song.

'Am not.'

'You are.'

'Following you here is not avoiding the fact that I'm not sure what I want to do with myself right now.'

'It's a handy excuse though, right?' adds Sorrel, before taking a sip of her beer. 'You don't need to examine what you want if you're putting someone else first.'

'Oh no, is this an intervention?' Pen moans. 'We've just met and you're intervening?' They clutch their hands over their heart and lean back, like they've just been shot with an arrow.

'It's good to talk about this stuff. Better out than in,' insists Tyra.

'*Et tu, Brute?*'

Tyra turns to me. 'Are they always this dramatic?'

'Sometimes,' I say with a laugh as Pen mimes choking to death. 'Depends how much they want to not talk about a subject.'

'And speaking of not talking about something,' Pen says, recovering immediately and fixing me with an excited look. 'You've not told me about meeting up with Levi yesterday.'

I roll my eyes, as the others excitedly flutter around me.

The thing is, what do I tell them? I don't really want to tell them I was crying on a bench. They all know I had a shit day, but it might make them feel bad for letting me go off alone, even though that's what I wanted. And I don't want to talk about how we had a deep conversation about stuff, or how I feel like he gets me on some level nobody else does. Part of me wants to keep that just for me.

'Levi is someone we met at the airport, and totally by coincidence I ran into him on the beach yesterday.'

'Not literally, I hope,' says Veena.

'No, not literally. Anyway, long story short, it turns out he's working for Rosa too – he's in the set-production team.'

'And he's jacked,' adds Pen, which starts up another enthusiastic round of cooing.

'Ooh, a handyman,' says Sorrel, with a coy smile. 'A handyman you went for a romantic walk on the beach with?'

'Err, I have a boyfriend,' I say pointedly and then hurry to correct myself. 'Well. We're not boyfriend and girlfriend. But we've been together for a year.'

'Wait, what?' asks Veena.

'Yeah? Mason?'

'You've never mentioned him.'

'I must have.'

'Nope,' chorus Tyra and Sorrel.

'Wait, was that who you were calling last night?'

'Yes, remember, while you were cooking,' I say, relieved that I haven't avoided mentioning him the whole time.

'And then you came out and were really weird.'

This takes me aback. 'Weird? How was I weird?'

'I don't think Veena means *you* were weird,' says Tyra, trying to placate things. 'You just seemed a bit . . .'

Veena clicks her fingers as she finds the words she was looking for. 'Bummed out.'

'The vibe just seemed off for you,' agrees Sorrel.

'I'm fine,' I insist, though I feel a bit embarrassed that I was apparently projecting all that awkward feeling at dinner. 'Sorry.'

'No apologies, please,' says Tyra, patting me on the hand. 'Your feelings are important. Plus, this job is tough. I can't imagine being in a relationship and far away from your person. That must be hard!'

Veena shrugs. 'My husband is chill with it. I'm pretty sure he's been playing *Diablo IV* every night.'

'You're married?' I ask, a little confused. There's no ring on her finger.

'Oh, yeah, like three years? His name's Adam. We're high school sweethearts so, like, we've always been together.'

'What does he do?'

'Teaches primary school.' All of us respond with variations on *aww*. 'Yeah, that's the standard response. He's great.'

'That's so cute,' says Sorrel. 'I was seeing a girl recently,

147

but we decided to cool it off while I'm here, and if the universe decrees it, we'll pick things back up if we're in the same place again.'

'I love that,' Tyra says, before turning her gaze back to me. 'You can talk to us about anything, sugar. We're a team.'

I glance up at Pen who seems to be pointedly not saying anything.

'It's just . . . Well, he's been unsure about me taking this job,' I say, and Tyra nods in encouragement. 'I don't want you to think he's a bad guy.'

'We won't think that unless he's being a bad guy,' says Veena.

'He's just very career-minded. I mean, that's his job, he's in recruitment so he's always thinking about the long term, and he's just a bit worried that I'll get my hopes up and fail and then have nothing to fall back on.'

'You're really good and work hard though,' says Tyra. 'Why would you fail? I bet you'll get a glowing recommendation after our tour.'

I push the hair out of my face and behind my ear. It's nice that she's said that, but I'm not sure I can believe it myself. Especially not after yesterday's chat with Michael.

'And there's always teaching and other stuff to fall back on. It might not always be international tours, but that doesn't mean it's this or nothing.'

'Plus,' says Veena, breaking a piece of bread to dip in some sauce on her plate. 'Even if it is, that's OK. It's about the experience and the memories, and you'll always have those even if the job isn't something you can do forever.'

'That's right,' Sorrel says, nodding enthusiastically.

Tyra turns to Pen, who's been staring intently at their glass of water for the last few minutes. 'What do you think about it? You must have met Mason before?'

'Oh, I don't really know him that well,' Pen says. 'You know, cis straight guys aren't usually my crowd.'

Everyone laughs, and I fake one, but it's a cop-out really. Pen has met Mason plenty of times, but the pair of them are like the two poles of a magnet. They just always seem to repel each other a bit. Like, there'll always be a reason why one of them can't be in the same space as the other for longer than five minutes. If Pen was into straight guys, I'd almost be worried that they had a crush on each other and were overcompensating, but I think it's something worse that I don't really want to think about.

'I think it's more the distance thing,' I say, wanting to stand up for Mason. 'Like, when am I even going to get to see him? We're only one week in and things are so intense that I would only be able to see him at the weekend, which I guess is fine, it's not so different from how we were at home, but it's a lot to ask of someone to fly out to see you just for two days.'

'It's not that far,' says Veena. 'Adam is coming over at the end of the month. We booked a B&B.'

'Oh, that's so cute,' coos Sorrel.

How awkward I'm feeling must be written across my face because Veena adds, a little hurriedly, 'We just got a really good deal on it, you know? Figured we should book it when we saw it.'

I give her a grateful smile. 'Maybe I'll talk to him about it,' I say.

'Yeah, give yourselves something to look forward to, yeah?'

That's a genuinely good idea, though it relies on us actually *talking* which we have barely done all week. I was hoping he would call me back this morning, as I know he gets up early at the weekends to go for a run down the river. But he didn't even send me a *good morning* text today. Mine remains unanswered. Maybe he had a lie-in instead. It sounded like a really busy week, so perhaps he had meetings late last night. I shouldn't always assume the worst of him, or of us. That's not going to help the situation.

Thankfully, I'm saved from this conversation by a realisation from Tyra, who grabs Pen by the shoulder. 'Wait a moment. Why don't we see if we can get you a job too?'

'What, sneak Pen onto the estate?' asks Veena.

'Why not?'

'Security?' suggests Sorrel. 'They probably hired everyone already too. Oh, and does Pen even have the right to work here? Isn't there complicated visa stuff?'

Tyra fixes Sorrel with an annoyed look.

'I'm just saying there's a few logistical considerations, babe. Don't wet yourself.'

Next to me, Veena snorts with laughter right as she drinks her beer, causing a huge coughing fit.

Sorrel raises an eyebrow. 'Plus, isn't this Pen's summer of rest and relaxation? Don't feed the workaholic.'

'I'm not a workaholic. I just am used to . . . working?' Pen winces. 'OK, I heard it.'

'It's not that bad, honestly,' I say in their defence. 'Pen just likes to be busy.'

'And earn money.'

'Well, I'm not letting go of the thought,' Tyra says. 'Pen, you should come with us on Monday. I'm sure it'll help. And if not, you may as well come watch us do a practice session.'

'I think the last thing Pen wants is to watch us sweat our balls off,' says Veena.

'No, I'd like that,' Pen says. 'It'll be nice to have someone to talk to who isn't Téresa or the baker who just sighs whenever I try and speak in Spanish because I'm so desperately bad at it. But seriously, I can meet up with Levi, which would be nice, and I can make sure that he's got honourable intentions.'

'He's got no intentions,' I say with an eye-roll. 'We just had ice cream, that's all.'

'On a beach. At sunset!'

'It was like two hours before sunset. At least.'

'I dunno, I'd put out for good ice cream,' says Veena with a shrug.

'No one is putting *out*.'

'Boring. And what about you lot? You're all single, shouldn't you be having torrid affairs with the other dancers or something?'

'In this dating pool? I think we're surrounded by gay men and heterosexual women.'

'Errr. And me,' says Sorrel, tapping her finger on the table. 'But I take your point, Veena. Someone in our household needs to have a summer romance. The universe demands it.'

Something squirms in my stomach and I'm pretty sure it's not the enormous amount of seafood I've just eaten.

I mean, Mason and I are closed off. We're not dating anyone else . . . I think? I mean, I certainly haven't been. He's always so busy that I don't even know when he would have time to date someone else anyway. The squirming feeling squirms harder as I realise that I don't think we've ever talked about that properly.

Have I just assumed we were closed off? We've been dating for almost a year so I just figured that maybe we were. Have I got it totally wrong?

I don't even know why I'm tying myself in knots about this anyway, because it's not like I'm going to date Levi. We just hung out and got along well and it was really refreshing on a day when I needed someone to be silly with.

That's all.

I'll leave the torrid affairs to the rest of them.

Chapter Twelve

For the first time since I've been here, I don't sleep well. The one good thing I'll say for Michael's back-to-back workout programme is that it gives me no space to think. You can't worry about your relationship when you're counting reps and replaying dance moves in your head to make sure your retention is up to point. The rest of the time you're too tired to think about anything beyond shoving the first bit of food into your face.

And so, as much as I'm glad for a Sunday off which we spend reading, watching films, walking along the beachfront and doing almost nothing else, I'm also not because my brain just will not turn off.

In the end, Mason does ring me back, late that afternoon. Everything seems fine, and it's a normal if kind of stilted conversation. I tell him about the Hippy Market and my new roommates, though I skip over Pen because I worry some of the other stuff might come out too. Like Levi, and the whole conversation about maybe trying to get Pen a job too. And just Levi in general.

Not that there's anything nefarious going on there,

but like, I can imagine how it'd look if the girl you were dating who was working abroad brought up a hot guy who took her for ice cream.

Not that I personally think he's hot. I mean he is, objectively, and friendly, and funny, but that's like a normal thing to say. It doesn't mean I fancy him.

This is why I don't mention it to him: because I can't even say it clearly in my own brain.

I float the idea of him flying out and he says he'll think about it, which is a good start. I guess. Not the most enthusiastic response, especially compared to Adam flying out the first moment he can, but then they've been together forever and are married so it would be weird for Veena and him to be apart. Like Pen and I, I guess. Oh God, perhaps Pen is my spouse substitute. Is this where I've been going wrong the whole time?

In the end, it was nice to speak to Mason, but it's made me miss him so much that I'm not sure I feel better overall. And now I can't sleep because I've been worrying about whether not telling him about Levi counted as lying to him, and when we are even going to get to see each other again.

TikTok ends up being my late-night comfort, as I scroll for hours, bookmarking new dances to learn eventually.

Obviously I must have fallen asleep at some point though, because suddenly it's morning.

I manage to drag myself out of bed, and Pen meets us down in the foyer, bright and early, though notably croissant-less, which is a disappointment to all of us.

'I didn't have time,' they protest, as we clamber into the car.

'That's a mark against you. I'm not sure I can recommend you as an employee if you're not going to come properly equipped,' teases Tyra.

If Bernard has any concerns about gaining a whole extra passenger this morning, he doesn't make it known, and Pen ends up sailing through the gates along with us.

We got an email overnight saying that Michael had some stuff to attend to, so we were supposed to just go over our training programmes as usual, and he'd meet us in the studio later. In my sleep-deprived state, I had half-hoped this meant we could lie in, but apparently he'd anticipated that as he added in bold capital letters that we were to be on site at the usual time.

'Shall we go find Levi?' Pen asks, just as my mind starts to drift that way.

'Yeah, he should be in that building over there if he's in already.'

Like good little employees, Sorrel, Tyra and Veena decide to head straight to the gym, and I feel a very brief pang of guilt before remembering I'm helping Pen. That's a good thing. I'm doing *good*.

If I describe the building as an old barn, it doesn't quite explain the scale of it. It's really tall like it's multi-storey, but when we walk inside it's just one huge, cavernous space, with some smaller rooms around the walls. It smells like sawdust and hot oil.

We find Levi in one of the side rooms, where he has a huge

roll of white paper spread over a workshop bench, which he's mulling over. A pencil is tucked behind his ear. The long sleeves of his shirt are rolled up, exposing his forearms which have already caught the sun.

He looks up from the table just as we get closer, and breaks into a lazy grin.

'Good morning. To what do I owe this pleasure?'

He opens his arms just enough to suggest a hug, the kind of polite move where you could choose to turn it into a handshake, or a high five or something instead. I hesitate. Is it weird to hug him? My brain is still scrambled from the whole *are Mason and I even closed off* thing on Saturday and obviously I haven't asked him because then he'll think I'm running off with someone, rather than just checking on what our relationship terms actually are.

In short, I'm a mess.

Which is probably why I can't stop staring at Levi's arms.

Naturally, Pen walks right into them for a hug. They're a big hugger.

'Nice to see you again,' they say. 'I hear you've been rescuing Cassie from errant benches? I'll have you know that's my job.'

'Maybe we can time-share it? Give us time to explore our other hobbies and passions on the side.'

'Sensible. I'll allow it.'

He leans back against the worktable and for some reason, every time we make eye contact, my palms get kind of itchy, like I can't keep my hands still. It's probably just because last time we spoke, we were so candid, and now

156

Pen is here we've reverted to small talk – what we did at the weekend, what he did, can you get over this weather. I barely pay attention as Pen explains our adventure to the Hippy Market, too aware of my body and its proximity to his.

I feel like I'm losing it.

'Cassie? Are you all right?'

I think Pen asked the question, but it's there in Levi's eyes too.

'Yeah, sorry. Just a bit spacey. I couldn't get to sleep, and I'm supposed to be at work already, so I should probably go get on with that. Get my mind focused.'

I go to turn away and then remember the whole reason we came in here.

'Oh, Levi. Pen's looking for a job.'

'Potentially,' they say slowly.

'Oh, yeah?' he says, his focus on them now.

'I've got very important duties with Téresa still.'

'Is that the terrifying cat?'

'Yes. Exactly. And, yeah, I think I am, though I'm not entirely sure there's any openings here anyway. We just snuck me in to see if I got inspired. But I'm no structural engineer so I'm probably not any use.'

'Well, why don't I show you round and you can hang out with me, and meet up with Cassie later? See how much inspiration we can muster?'

'Great! Thank you!' I bleat, and run out of the door, not stopping until I hit the gym. I end up doing my personal best on the treadmill, because if I run then I don't think.

Literally running away from your problems, a tiny Sorrel in my mind quips.

And then a real-life Sorrel appears by my side, phone in hand.

'Have you seen this?' she hisses.

On screen is an article leaking the set list for Rosa's tour, with detailed information about the costuming, and set design. It's the sort of stuff you want to hold back until closer to the tour, to surprise people.

I slow down and take the phone from her. 'This is bad, right?'

She shrugs. 'I don't think it's good.'

'Who do you think leaked it?'

'I'm sure we'll find out.'

This must have been what Michael was dealing with overnight.

'Oh, before I forget,' Sorrel digs into her bag and pulls out a roll of clear tape.

'Why are you handing me tit tape, Sorrel?' I ask, before instinctively clutching my hands over my boobs. 'I'm not flashing, am I?'

She roars with laughter. 'No, honey. You're good. I just thought it might be good for trying to keep your cochlear implant on when we're dancing? It helps keeps the girls in.' She holds her own boobs.

My heart melts. This is so kind. 'Thank you,' I gasp, before wrapping my arms around her.

'Would you like me to help you, or do you want to have a go yourself first?'

'Let's go try it out together.'

In the changing room, Sorrel cuts the double-sided tape into a few different-length strips while I take my implant off. She hands me a piece of tape and I lay it right in the centre of the battery pack, before reattaching it to my head. It feels like it's on there pretty securely, and I manage not to get too much hair caught up in it the first time. It doesn't feel like quite enough though, so I decide to add some to the processer part, so that the tape attaches to my scalp and the back of my ear too. It's a bit strange for my ear to be stuck down, but it feels OK.

With my cochlear implant taped on securely, I decide to have one more go on the treadmill just to fully test its sticking power. I get another mile in, no problems, before Michael appears in the doorway of the gym, and summons us back up to the studio.

Once we've all made our way up there, Michael gets us in formation and makes us run through 'Diamonds Under My Eyes' almost immediately. I'm extremely thankful that when I couldn't sleep last night, I spent some of that time running back through the routine in my head. I do a pretty decent job considering I'm exhausted from running and hit all the moves, though I could still be more polished. A few of the other dancers miss a move or two, and so as soon as we've finished, Michael resets us and we go again.

And again.

Michael seems pissed off. I'm not surprised, with all the stuff from the tour getting leaked. Even if it's not our fault, he's certainly making it our problem.

159

He doesn't give us much recovery time before he starts teaching us the rest of the dance, which goes by in a blur that's only broken by a mandatory lunch break where we all wolf down some salads that are brought up for us, strangely enough by Pen.

'What are you doing here?' I ask as they hand me a small box packed with grilled chicken, marinated beans, fresh green leaves, some kind of pickled veggies, and a hardboiled egg. It looks delicious.

I watch as Michael storms out of the room, looking like the whole world might collapse at any moment.

'Did you get a job already?' Tyra asks, before stuffing her mouth with leaves. I'm relieved that my flatmates picked up on the whole don't-eat-and-talk thing pretty quickly – it's good manners, but also I can't hear what they're saying or, even worse, end up futilely watching their chewing mouths full of food. Despite the blue hair and e-girl vibes, Tyra has Good Southern Manners (according to her) so it probably didn't even cross her mind to talk while she eats.

'Not quite. Levi was showing me round, and then a delivery arrived at the warehouse door, which I helped him unload. And it turned out it was fabric for the costumers –'

Sorrel interrupts them with something I don't catch apart from 'fittings' and I realise she must mean the fabric is for our tour costumes. That will make all this feel so much more real than dancing in Vics' fancy leggings. We're going to have costumes and need to learn how to change quickly offstage ready for the next songs. It's how dances become a show.

'Anyway,' continues Pen. 'I offered to take the fabric over

160

to them so that they could keep doing whatever they're doing down there. The costumers are lovely by the way. Aoife? That woman has my heart. You be nice to her if you get her making yours.'

'So you were chatting up women, what's new?' I tease.

'Only a little bit of work-appropriate charm, Cass. I don't flirt. Anyway, they needed some stuff from admin, and then admin needed some photocopies of forms, and then I went out in the car with Bernard to pick up this lunch order.'

It seems that Veena does a mental calculation of how many tasks Pen just listed. 'How have you managed all that in barely three hours?'

Smirking, they say, 'I'm incredibly efficient.'

Suddenly, Tyra starts coughing, fork and salad waving in the air. I take both from her, as Veena gives her a big whack on her back. Tyra's eyes go wide, and whatever was stuck in her throat must be dislodged because she says something that I'm pretty sure is not ladylike. She pants and eventually takes her fork and salad back from me.

'Are you OK?' Sorrel asks.

'Peachy keen,' she says, her cheeks flushed with embarrassment as well as the coughing.

I think I've missed something, but I'm too tired and hungry to stress.

'So, you got a job, and no one realises you don't work here yet,' says Sorrel.

'I think so, yeah. It's OK. It was a nice way to spend the morning.'

Before I can suggest to Pen that it might be a good

idea to get paid if they're going to do this much work, Michael storms back into the studio, and waves to us all.

'Attention, please.'

Everyone stops eating and turns towards Michael. The poor guy looks seriously stressed out.

'Now, I'm not sure if you are all aware of the conversations that are happening online with regards to this tour, but I want to reassure you that the member of staff responsible has been removed from the premises.'

I glance at the others, but all the dancers are still here. It must have been Clipboard Guy. I haven't seen him all day, and usually he's trailing behind Michael looking overwhelmed and nervous.

A few people start whispering and Michael barks out, 'Nope, we will not be entertaining gossip in this studio. I need your focus, so zip it.'

Everyone zips it. I sit up a little straighter.

'That means we're short-staffed today and fighting several fires with the press, which is categorically not my job but I'm needed still. So, I am going to set you all a team-building task for the next few days and I expect you to throw yourselves into it.'

A hand shoots up immediately and it's Fenella. 'Will we be allowed to pick our own teams?'

'I do not have time to get into personality politics, so no. You'll be dancing with your flatmates for this one.'

The four of us excitedly buzz next to each other. I'm so happy I get to dance with them again.

'As you might be aware from the leak, Rosa wants to add

a number of her older songs into the rotation. About halfway through the set list, she wants a more artistic performance-led section to some of the songs from her acoustic album *Rose Petals*, and I want you in your teams to come up with a full routine to the song "Damask".'

I can't hold back a grin. 'Damask' is one of my favourites. Spanish guitars duet alongside Rosa's vocals which tell the story of two star-crossed lovers, as the woman realises that loving herself is more important than throwing herself into something that could be bad for her. The song has a deep bass and a beat that I feel in my chest. It's slow, especially compared to her other songs that she performs on tour, so this feels like a real departure from her last international tour which was more of a greatest hits vibe.

Demi raises his hand. 'Do you have any direction for us?'

'I don't want to give you too much, but I want you to pull your inspiration from classical dance. Ballet in particular is what I think Rosa is keen for, but you could even go ballroom or interpretative. Group or two duet pairs. Just try something and work together. Pay attention to each other.' He taps at the Apple Watch on his wrist and sighs. 'I have to go. I want you back here Thursday at 9 a.m. for run-throughs in front of the whole team. If I like what you do enough, we might use it for the show and you will get credit. Now. Go.'

This starts a barely-contained buzz across the room. Our moves could be performed even if we aren't the ones performing them. We could have credits for the tour. For anyone here determined to go into choreography or teaching later, that could be huge.

'Does anyone want to use the studio first?' asks one of the guys who lives with Demi.

'We'll use it,' announces Fenella before anyone can negotiate. I guess she's just a confident person who knows what she wants. We've got two more full days to divvy it up between us at least.

'Shall we go back to the apartment?' suggests Sorrel. 'We can make up a kind of mood board and start thinking of stuff there.'

'Wouldn't the gym be better? We could use the mirrors in the weights room,' suggests Tyra.

My head is starting to ache from all the sound processing, and from all the competing conversations in the room. One of Fenella's pals is playing a song on their phone, probably the video from 'Damask' or something, and all of it is jumbling together to make a dull ache that could easily become a migraine if I'm not careful.

The only people I really talk about this stuff with are Pen and my family, but I live with these three and we're working together for the next few months, so maybe I need to just let them in on some of it. From how they've been so far, I don't think it'll go badly, but still. It can feel scary to ask for help.

I decide to do the brave thing, and speak up. 'Can we go back to the flat? I need a sound break.'

'Sure,' says Tyra, with a big smile. 'Let's get out of here before Fenella starts ordering us about too.'

We grab our bottles of water and bags, and the four of us, trailed by Pen, go to leave the studio, only to be stopped at the door by Michael.

'You!' His bark cuts through the small-talk chatter, and everyone goes silent as he walks right up to Pen. 'Are you the new runner?' How did they hire someone already? Quick now.'

'No, I don't work here. But I've been accidentally helping out,' Pen admits.

'How did you even get in here?'

We shift nervously and Michael works it out for himself. 'If it wasn't obvious, no one should be bringing people to site without express permission, please,' he announces to the dancers still in the room. Michael adds, 'I do not want to contain any more leaks.'

'I'm really sorry,' Pen says.

'I'm sorry, they're with me,' I say.

'Are they your interpreter?'

'No... Erm, just my friend.'

'I'm here for emotional support,' Pen says, and their voice squeaks up at the end so much that it almost sounds like a question.

Michael gives us both an extremely tired look. 'OK, and how did you leap from that to doing jobs for basically every department here? They all told me to come looking for the redhead.'

Pen blushes a little. 'Well . . . People kept asking for help so I've been doing it. Side effect of working for the NHS and in care homes, I think. There's always a job to do.'

Michael looks them up and down. 'You know how to follow instructions accurately? Read and write? Willing to work hard? Know not to speak to the press?'

'Yes. Times four. Or five? I lost count.'

'Luckily mental arithmetic isn't something I need right now. You're hired. Come with me.'

The pair of them disappear down the corridor leaving the rest of us standing in the doorway in bemused silence.

'Well. That was quicker than I expected,' Veena says.

'Nah,' I say with a smile. 'Pen's always found it easy to be helpful. They'll do great here.'

'Let's go home and kick this task's ass,' says Sorrel with a wicked smile. 'It's time to unleash the secret weapon.'

'What's that?' asks Veena.

'Her.' She points to Tyra.

Chapter Thirteen

'When were you going to tell us that you went to ballet school?' I gasp as we get into our car.

Tyra slinks down on the backseat between Sorrel and me, like she wants to disappear into the leather. 'I was only there for a year,' she says. 'It was before the YouTube channel. I was barely out of middle school and I was good at it, but they were just so weird about the epilepsy. No one would cast me as a lead or a bigger part because of, as they kept telling me, "the seizure risk", which sucks and obviously meant I had more seizures because I was so stressed.'

'I'm sorry,' says Sorrel, patting her on the leg.

'It's fine. It was full of girls like Fenella anyway.' Tyra shivers. 'Not my crowd.'

'Anyone else have any secret ballet experience?' Sorrel asks. 'I know I sure don't.'

'Didn't you do it as a kid?'

'Honey, it's hard enough being a Black dancer. Do you think my parents were going to subject me to being a fat Black ballet-dancing kid?' she says it firmly but gently.

'I see. Sorry, that was ignorant of me.'

'Talking about it is how we all learn. I wouldn't know anything about epilepsy or deafness if it wasn't for you two.'

In front of me, Veena turns fully around to face us. 'Me.'

'You what?'

'I have ballet experience. Hang on, Bernard.' She waves a hand at him, so he must have said something to her. Probably, very politely, to get her wiggling bum out of his face. She says his name the British way, and I see him shake his head and laugh at her.

'I worked a couple of summers at a dance therapy camp in Scotland, when I was in university. I was teaching classes, or assisting if it was outside my expertise. But I ended up doing a lot of, like, interpretive, drama, feel-your-feelings type stuff with the kids. One more second, Bernard.'

'OK, so that's good. What about you, Cassie?'

'No specialisms, no,' I admit. 'It was mostly modern, but also, like, years ago. But my mum is really into musicals and ballet and stuff, so I've seen probably every single one that's been on the BBC or made into a movie at some point or other. My sister is named after the ballet-dancing cat in *Cats*.'

'Oh my God!' Veena shrieks, and Bernard must tell her to sit down more sternly this time because she whips back round. Her head pops round the window side of her seat, her cheek squished against the glass. 'I love this. Are you named after one too?'

I sigh. I knew I shouldn't have mentioned this because obviously they'd ask if our names are a pair, and obviously they are. 'Yes.'

'Cassandra is the all-brown one, right? The kind of

168

snooty one?' Sorrel asks, her eyebrows raised.

'Yes.'

The three of them fall into excited cackles.

'At least you didn't get called Grizabella,' says Sorrel. She starts miming some of her moves which gives away that she has also watched the proshot version from the nineties too many times. Or maybe she was even in *Cats*. I want to ask but that will prolong this conversation.

'I'm calling you that from now on,' insists Veena.

'Ladies, I do not know what this *Cats* is but I do know that if you don't chill out, I'm going to park up here and let you walk home.'

'Sorry, Bernard,' we chorus.

Back at the apartment, we start with a Pinterest board, just like Sorrel had suggested. Pictures, costumes, colours, vibes. We listen to 'Damask' over and over, watching the video, chanting the words under our breath. Veena digs out some paper and we make a kind of mind map from the lyrics and movements.

It's an intense creative session that we don't look up from until late that evening when our stomachs start to rumble, by which point we've got a concept to work from.

While Sorrel and I make a rich tomato sauce from scratch to top some fresh pasta, Tyra and Veena start exploring footwork together. There's this feeling like electricity in the air, and yes, that might be a cliché but it's true. I expect my hair to be full of static from it. It's the feeling of connection, of knowing you're on to something cool and the power of working with people you trust.

I'm hooked on it.

So are all the others, though Veena seems a little out of sorts. I watch as she moves a couple of pieces of pasta around her plate.

'Veena?' I ask. 'Are you OK?'

She looks up at me calling her name, and then drops her eyes again. 'Yeah.'

'What's got you worrying?' Sorrel asks.

'Not worries. I just . . .' She shakes her head, and a few errant curls fly loose from under her cap. 'First up, nothing is wrong.'

'So what's got you down? You haven't even mentioned lemon Fanta this evening.'

'Fanta Limón,' Veena corrects.

'That literally just means lemon.'

'But it doesn't *feel* the same, does it?' A bit of the usual Veena flashes across her face. 'I just . . .' She buries her face in her hands, and I'm relieved that Sorrel and Tyra look as nonplussed as I feel. Luckily, she uncovers her face before she carries on talking, though she won't look at any of us. 'I've wanted to be a choreographer for ages, since I was teaching. It's not the same, but you do a tiny little bit of choreo and the kids remember it and perform it, and wow that feels good. But this . . . This is like the biggest of stakes! The biggest version of being an almost-choreographer!'

'And that's bad?' offers Tyra.

'Yes. Because I want it.'

'You're allowed to want it,' Sorrel says.

'I don't like feeling things or wanting things, because if

170

it doesn't happen then I just wasted all that time feeling or wanting for no reason.' She angrily spears a piece of pasta.

'That's being human, honey.'

'I think that sucks, frankly.'

'Me too,' I agree. 'But you're amazing, and you should tell Michael that. Especially if we win this week. Maybe he can point you in the right direction?'

Veena wriggles uncomfortably in her seat. 'I'm not sure about that.'

'What would Adam say?'

Veena takes her phone out of her pocket and as if on cue, it buzzes with a new message. She opens it. 'He says I should stop being a weirdo because I'm talented, and he can be a teacher wherever I am.'

'That's lovely,' Tyra says, her hand over her heart.

'I know. It's gross, isn't it?'

I try to ignore the pang in my chest.

'Well, look. If you want to be a choreographer after this, then let's make a plan,' says Sorrel. 'After all, if we can't help each other get our dream jobs and be happy and fulfilled, then what's the point of all this?'

'I think the point is that we're on an icon's international tour,' suggests Tyra.

'The *cosmic* point,' stresses Sorrel. 'We're in the business of future-making. So why not chase what we want? And help each other get there.'

'What do you want, Sorrel?' I ask.

'This,' she says, with a smile. 'I want to keep dancing on tours. I want to graduate from understudy.'

171

'Me too,' I say quietly, a little nervous of jinxing it. 'Tyra?'

Tyra pats her lips with a paper napkin. 'The usual. To be happy.'

'We all want that, I'm pretty sure,' Sorrel agrees.

'Well, it's more that . . .' She cuts off, her eyes losing focus for just a second. 'The thing about living with seizures is that you have to be adaptable. I feel like making a long-term plan is hard because I've not had the best time with medication controlling my seizures, and you never know when you're going to have one that puts you out of action for a few days or weeks.' She shrugs and smiles. 'It's hard to explain, and I don't want to sound ungrateful! My plan is to enjoy it for as long as I get to do it. And if that isn't very long, well, OK. I'll find something else.'

Veena gets up from the table, walks around to Tyra, and wraps her in a hug. 'You're cool. You're too fucking cool.'

Tyra laughs. 'Get off me, you big lemon. Or should it be limón?'

We all giggle, but I get it. When your body works a little differently, you get used to adapting in ways that people who aren't disabled couldn't even dream of. I feel immensely grateful for the three women around my table. Women who fight, and have hopes and dreams, who push me harder. Sorrel is right, together we could be unstoppable.

Somehow, it's Thursday morning already, but the four of us are ready. I've barely spoken to my family or Mason the last few days, too focused on getting this dance done.

While I'm in the car on the way to work, I text Pen to

see how they are getting on with the cat, and get added to a WhatsApp group chat called Téresa Fan Club. The only people in it are me, Pen and an unknown number. When I click on the profile to see who is in the picture, I realise it's Levi.

Pen sends through a selfie of them sitting on the couch, with Téresa facing away from them, her tail angrily puffed up. It's captioned 'Progress?!'

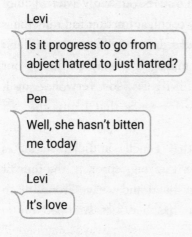

Levi

Is it progress to go from abject hatred to just hatred?

Pen

Well, she hasn't bitten me today

Levi

It's love

I can't think of anything witty to say so I just heart react to the picture.

As an act of mild torture, Michael decides to bypass our 'Damask' performances, and goes straight into teaching us the choreography to 'Dorothy', a boppy song where Rosa teases the person she's singing to that she might disappear, which is met with some grumbles. But I figure he's testing our retention still, and seeing how we perform under the pressure of knowing we have to do something big. It's pretty smart,

173

really. I guess a lot of being an understudy is being ready to go at all times. He's preparing us psychologically for that. It's a fun dance too; there's a bit where we pause while in rows, and all fall back. In the mirror, it looks like a wave.

The amazing thing is that when the time comes for the 'Damask' performances, everyone has interpreted the song in completely different ways.

Demi's group goes first, performing a somewhat interpretive artsy routine that starts out with a lot of floor work. I touch my hand to my cochlear implant as I remember it falling off the last time I did a dramatic floor move. It feels secured with the tape, and managed to stay on during our rehearsals in the flat, but still, I get so lost in wondering if it'll hold up for a proper performance that I miss the rest of the dance.

It doesn't surprise me that Fenella and her flatmates have gone for a classic ballet-inspired approach, the four of them moving in sync as they bend and weave around each other's bodies. Fenella even has her feet strapped up in proper pointe shoes.

It's Seojin and his flatmates who really grab my attention though. Their dance pulls on the Spanish guitar that underlies the music, and instead of dancing in a group, they perform in two pairs in a slow tango. It's romantic and controlled, and intense. The pairs of dancers hold eye contact throughout, and I almost feel like I'm intruding on something, which feels kind of perfect for a song so much about the self. It's my favourite performance, even over ours, though I wouldn't tell the others that.

We land somewhere in the middle of the other three.

At some point, we let Veena loose with her choreography skills. It was a little out there for me to begin with, but the longer I tried, the more I got into it. As we talked through the lyrics together, she encouraged us to react however we wanted to through movement, however the song made us feel. From there, we built and built and built. To sew it all together, Tyra pulled on her ballet experience to create something that looked controlled, thoughtful, and beautiful in slow motion. That's not to say that Sorrel and I sat back, because we didn't. We all pitched in.

In the verses we move as one, with occasional staggered moments out of sync that line back up to give a sense of coming together. For the chorus, we partner up into two duets, never touching but our movements mirrored.

It's nothing like any routine I'd ever have come up with, but I kind of love it.

To my relief, Michael seems pleased. He even looks back to Pen, who now follows him everywhere, and gives them a nod.

'Good work, everyone. You all managed to pull out a decent routine, and there seems to be the same number of you as before, so you didn't murder anyone. Hopefully you all learned a little something about teamwork.'

Across the room, I see some awkward shuffling from Giselle, one of the members of Fenella's group. It's too far for me to lip-read, but Fenella must say something to her, because she stops, stands straight and looks forward, as though there was nothing bothering her at all.

Weird.

I'm even more glad that I got to do this one with my girls. I feel closer to them, and like we understand how each other's brains work a little better. It's really lovely.

On top of all that, my implant barely moved. I breathe a deep sigh of relief. Maybe I can turn that part of my brain off and stop worrying about it every time I'm moving now.

'Thankfully I managed to get back on track with everything so tomorrow we will be returning to your usual routine, though there'll be less solo working out from now on. We have a lot of choreo to learn in the next few weeks, but I'm confident that you'll bring your full selves to that as much as you did to this task.'

A hand shoots up. It's one of the guys, and I know he's going to ask about whose dance we're going to do. I glance over at Veena who is staring straight ahead.

'Yes?' Michael asks, his face a mask.

'You mentioned . . . that perhaps one of the dances would be used . . .' He shuffles awkwardly, and Michael must be prolonging the silence just for effect because even I start to feel uncomfortable.

'I've not made my final decision. I'll let you know tomorrow,' Michael says, a little sternly. Then he softens and adds, 'Tonight, we've organised for you all to go down to one of the beach bars for dinner and drinks.'

Everyone bursts into excited chatter around me.

He holds up his hand to silence them. 'Remember, it is a Thursday and I'll expect you back here tomorrow morning at the usual time for us to start *and finish* learning 'Damask'.

Now, off you go home, and the cars will pick you up in an hour. Have fun.'

I let everyone else leave the room first, including my flatmates, though Pen hangs back with Michael. The echo of chatter on the stairwell is too much for my brain to process, and I'm already pretty tired. The near-enough-to-silence in the room is a temporary relief, and while I should get clean and glam for an evening out, I know I'm probably just going to take my cochlear implant off and lie face down on the bed for at least half an hour. Working full time while processing all that noise and managing the tiredness that comes with it is a lot. I'm still getting used to it.

But I should really be brave and go home. The girls will understand if I unhook in the car.

As I pass Michael, he pats me on the shoulder. 'Good work this week, Cassie.'

For a moment, I think I imagined him saying it because he strikes up a conversation with Pen immediately after, and then they leave the room, presumably on yet another errand. But he did say it, I'm pretty sure.

And that compliment is enough to glide me home.

Chapter Fourteen

I do in fact lie face down on the bed for half an hour, and it is blessed and needed silence. The ache in my head from all the concentrating today starts to lift, but it doesn't completely go and I know it's only going to get worse in a bar where there'll be background music, and people chattering over each other. This is why I don't go out-out super often, but oh well. Perhaps I can convince Bernard to come pick me up after an hour?

I don't want to miss out on celebrating with the others.

Especially when we look this cute. Tyra wears an oversized shirt and matching shorts in bright rainbow fabric, which contrasts intensely with Veena's sheer black mesh dress, though both of them wear big sneakers instead of heels. The only one of us who risks that is Sorrel in an off-shoulder white crochet dress with espadrilles, looking in true holiday mode. I truly have no idea how she is walking in heels but she must have soles of steel.

After a bit of deliberation, I end up wearing a cute sunny-yellow miniskirt with a matching half-jacket over my bikini top. And trainers, obviously. My feet are killing me.

It seems like we're the first group to arrive, but that's fine. We can make our own fun.

The bar is on the beachfront, and while it's mostly open to the air around us, the bar itself is decorated with tiny bits of glass that cover it completely, like a mosaic. As we line up at the bar for drinks, I spot other things pressed into it too – shells, tiny figurines that look a bit sea-bashed, pretty stones, gems. It must have been a huge project by the owners, the sort of thing that's never truly completed.

'Shots? Shots?' asks Veena with a cheeky smile. She orders four tequilas before any of us have a chance to say otherwise, and we all raise the tiny shot glasses in a toast before downing them.

We get cocktails next and then make our way out to one of the tables.

'I swear, Aperol spritzes are bigger in the UK.' Veena peers down at her tiny glass with mild disgust.

'That's because we probably don't know how to make them well. This is the real deal.'

'Aren't they Italian?'

'Then a geographically closer deal?' I say, taking a sip of my chilli margarita. More tequila is probably not the best idea, but I'll just drink it slowly. It's cold and bitter and sour and buzzes at the back of my throat.

'May I just say,' says Tyra, holding up her glass. 'We nailed that today, and I'm really proud of all of us. I feel very honoured to be sharing this adventure with you guys.'

'Aw, Tyra, that's so lovely,' Sorrel says, patting her hand.

179

'Don't get mushy on me. We've got drinking to do,' laughs Veena. 'Cheers!'

We chorus on variations of *to us* and tap our glasses together.

'What are we celebrating?' I look up and see Levi leaning against the table, grinning down at us.

'Oh! Hi!' I say, or possibly shout, enthusiastically.

He's dressed in a light cream shirt that falls open at his collarbones, and it's probably just the angle I'm sitting at, but my eyes are immediately drawn to that patch of sun-kissed skin.

'Hiya.'

'Hi.'

'How did your group dance project go? Good, if we're celebrating?'

I wonder how he knew about that? I mean, Pen, I suppose, or maybe just seeing all us dancers roaming around in packs of four looking stressed.

Still, it's nice that he asked. That he remembered.

'It wasn't a project,' I say with a giggle. I press the back of my hand to my head and pretend to swoon, just so he knows I'm teasing. 'It was the performance of a lifetime, darling.'

'Oh, naturally. With such talent, how could you not wow the crowds? Or Michael and Pen.'

'What do you know about my talent?' I scoff.

'I've seen you dance. You're brilliant.'

He's seen me dance? When? Has he been popping up to the studio without me realising? And he thinks I'm

180

brilliant? I suddenly feel naked, but in a good way, which is weird considering I'm sitting at a table drinking cocktails with my friends.

Thank God for Pen, who appears just as my brain starts thinking about whirring.

'I didn't know you were coming,' I say, trying to sound casual about it but I'm excited to see them both.

'Michael let me out for good behaviour,' says Pen, before jutting a thumb at Levi. 'And I made him take a break.'

'Well, it was hard to resist when you said you were going to the beach,' Levi says, with a lazy smile. 'And I figured the present company would be nice too.'

I can feel myself blushing. 'You say that, but if you're not careful, I'll challenge you to a beach hunt again,' I say. 'And this time, I'll win.'

'I told you, everyone's a winner on a nature hunt.'

'Not this time. Not with my new rules.'

'Oh yeah,' he says, with a laugh. 'And what rules are those?'

I don't know what possesses me to say, 'I guess you'll find out,' in such a coy, smirky way, but those words literally do come out of my mouth. And I swear there's a moment where I almost wink, but think better of it. I cannot be winking at men; they might get the wrong idea.

Clearly, he wasn't expecting it either, and for a minute we just watch each other, and I can feel my heart beat furiously in my chest.

There's a tap on my shoulder, and I spin round to see all three of my roommates watching us both.

'Are you going to introduce us properly to your new friend?' Tyra asks.

'Oh! Yes. Levi, this is Tyra, Sorrel and Veena. We absolutely nailed it today because of Veena and Tyra's direction, and all our ideas pooled together. They're the best.'

They chorus in variations of hello, and Levi gives them all a broad smile and a little head-bob. 'It's lovely to meet you all. Friends of Cassie are friends of mine. Can I get any of you a drink?'

'We're all good, I think,' I say.

'Cassie, don't turn down a free drink from the nice man,' says Sorrel.

'Maybe later, then.'

'Preordering, are we? Youse are going to rinse my wallet at this rate.' Levi laughs, and puts his arm round Pen. 'Come on, let's get a drink.'

The moment they're gone Sorrel, Tyra and Veena turn to stare right at me.

'What? Do I have something on my face?'

'I think you could if you wanted to,' Veena says with a laugh, glancing over to the bar.

'That man looked like he was near ready to eat you up.' Sorrel fans herself. 'The heat! The spice!'

Veena nods her head in agreement. 'Potential spice.'

'What are you talking about?'

'Cassie, honey. He's very obviously into you,' Tyra says.

'No, he's not.'

'Yes, he is,' the three of them chorus like some horrible audience reaction.

'Do you think he has a mandingo?' Veena giggles.

'A what now?' asks Sorrel.

'A big dick.'

'Veena!' I protest, but I'm holding back a laugh.

Tyra frowns. 'What did you call it? A duolingo??'

That gets even me, and we all fall apart laughing. Sorrel can barely catch her breath. 'A duolingo? Did she just say a duolingo?'

'That's what I thought she said!'

Veena wipes the tears from her cheeks.

What the hell was in those shots? I try to bring things back to serious conversation without us talking about the contents of Levi's underwear. 'One, I don't think he's interested in me, and two, it doesn't matter even if he is. I'm with Mason.'

Sorrel looks at me, takes a sip of her drink and says, 'The guy who makes you cry and didn't want you to take this job?'

I'm a little taken aback by that. 'Hey, isn't it Veena's job to be blunt as a rock?' I laugh awkwardly.

'That it is,' Veena says, pointing a finger in the air. 'And I second that this guy made you sad and so I hate him.'

'Hate is a bit strong, Veena,' Tyra admonishes. 'Be nice, girls.'

'All right, not hate. How about I'm predisposed to dislike?'

My cheeks flush and I want to defend Mason, but nothing they're saying is incorrect. It's not like he's been trying to make it up to me since then either, but still, I feel weird about it. He matters to me.

'It was only one time,' I say. 'Or two. I can't remember.'

'You can't remember how many times he's made you cry?'

183

Tyra's eyes are wide, and she takes my hand in hers. It makes me think of my mum, and then I want to cry because I miss her. Apparently it's feelings central for me this evening.

'No, I just mean . . . I'm not interested in Levi and I'm not breaking up with Mason, so that's that.' I look back to the bar and luckily Pen and Levi are still over there.

'Can I ask one tiny thing though?' adds Veena, her forefinger and thumb in front of her face for emphasis.

'Fine.'

'OK, it's not really a question, but he's not your boyfriend, right?'

I feel a lump in my throat. 'We've been dating eleven months.'

'But you're not exclusive? So really there's nothing wrong with you eyeing up another man, not necessarily Levi, but *someone*.'

Why does it feel like Veena is pressing a bruise? 'Guys, can we not talk about this?' I say, taking a sip of my drink.

'Sorry, hon, it's just the shots talking,' says Tyra. 'We're all being a little too much.'

Sorrel leans forward with a wicked grin. 'So, you're saying Levi's single and available, then?'

I splutter. 'Um, well. Yeah, I don't know?' God, what is *wrong* with me? It's like I don't want to share my friend at nursery or something. I flick my hair over one shoulder and say, in the calmest tone I can muster, 'You should ask him out, if you want to.'

Sorrel bursts out laughing. 'Don't worry, babe, I'm just teasing you. Not my type. Too . . .'

'Conventionally attractive?' Tyra fills in.

'Straight coded, I guess?'

'Who is?' asks Pen, as they return with drinks and Levi in tow.

My head is spinning from all the Levi and Mason chat, and all I want is for us to go back to talking about silly stuff. 'How about –'

'Levi,' says Veena.

'Oh yeah. You've got the vibe,' Pen says to him.

He shrugs, but it's the usual relaxed Levi. 'Sure. I'm like . . . a Kinsey 1.'

'Oh, OK,' says Sorrel, raising her eyebrows. 'Consider me corrected, Mr Incidental.'

I realise I have no idea what this means.

'It means he's maybe a bit fruity,' explains Pen, and Levi roars with delighted laughter.

'I'll take it.' He smiles easily. 'I just don't think it's beyond the realm of possibility, you know? You love who you love.'

'In that case, you two are in the minority at this table,' Tyra says to Veena and me.

'I didn't say I'm straight.' Veena shrugs. 'I'm just married to a man.'

'So it's just me?' I say.

'It's OK, honey, we accept you for who you are.' Tyra pats my hand again and we all burst out laughing.

'You're so brave for living your truth,' adds Sorrel.

'I'll be the best ally that ever was,' I promise.

'Oh, that's what I used to say,' says Tyra. 'I kept kissing the shes and theys because I was just so darn supportive.'

At *theys* I notice Pen's eyebrow twitch.

185

The roommates ask Levi about himself. He fills them in on pretty much all the details I know already. He's relaxed and so easy and not trying to impress them. But because he's not trying, he wins them over easily.

Then the conversation is cut short by all the other understudies arriving at once. Seojin starts chanting for shots, and Patrick insists that we play beer pong, but no one has a ping pong ball to hand, so there's a lot of discussion about what would make a suitable alternative. We give up when we realise the only options are ice, rocks or shells, none of which seem particularly safe to be lobbing around drunkenly.

We end up pulling the tables together so that we can all sit in one big group, which is great in theory but I truly cannot hear half of what's going on.

The one thing I am deeply, far too aware of is that Giselle is sitting next to Levi, and seems to have looped her arm inside his. My stomach aches, and while my brain keeps saying that it's probably just the chilli from the margarita I've been nursing, the hum in my body says otherwise. That hum dials up to a furious spark when she leans her head against his shoulder, laughing one of those *haha we are flirting and I am wonderful* laughs that girls who are more comfortable in their own bodies than I am seem to execute easily.

I need to stop thinking about it, and to stop looking over because I am probably less subtle than I hope I am. When I drag my vision back in front of me, Veena catches my eye, and presses her lips together, eyebrows raised. Hopefully, she's just thinking *awkward*, not *it's awkward that the guy you might have a thing for is snuggling some girl.*

186

Except I don't have a thing for him.

Do I?

Determined to stop thinking about any of this, I finish my margarita in the hope that an empty drink might allow me to get away from it all, but Sorrel is already up, getting a round in, so I have to stay where I am, without a drink to fiddle with, and it feels antisocial to get my phone out.

Instead, I try to focus on whatever conversation is happening around me. It's hard, and I can feel the ache in my head start to build up again.

During one long anecdote from Demi's roommate Kev about the last time he was in Ibiza on the club scene, I get totally lost when everyone starts laughing and interjecting, but it's fine, I don't want to bother anyone.

Across the table, Pen catches my eye and signs, 'Do you want me to translate?'

I sign back no, but I'll ask if I need to. I was hoping that no one would say anything about the fact we're using sign at the table, but Yanni, who seems remarkably drunk already, leans towards us.

'What are you two talking about?' He giggles, and then burps.

Pen looks to me, seeing how I want to handle it. 'Pen was just asking if I needed translation,' I say. I push my hair back from where it mostly covers my cochlear implant. 'I'm deaf.'

'That's so cool,' he says, and I genuinely believe him. 'Will you teach me some sign?'

'Maybe,' I say, trying to keep it light. 'But then you'll know all my secrets.'

He finds this far too funny, but it's enough to move the conversation along. Though perhaps not the way I was hoping it would go.

'Speaking of secrets,' says Fenella's roommate Natalie, an American girl I suspect is eye-wateringly rich from the clothes she wears. 'Why don't we play a little game of Never-Have-I-Ever?'

The response blurs into one big groan, and I wince at the noise. That headache is back now that I'm in a circle of drunken yelling, but I don't want to go just yet, even if it does mean that we have to play some silly games.

I try to keep up with the questions but as Natalie starts and they go round the circle, the people furthest away from me are coming up with Nevers first so I can't catch what they say. The only one I do hear is 'Never have I ever cheated on my partner', which obviously I don't need to drink on. I'm a little relieved that no one from my group drinks then either.

My eyes slide over Levi. Giselle's hand is on his knee, and I try desperately to ignore the hot feeling rushing up through me.

It's just the tequila.

Nothing else.

As always happens with this horrible game, the questions get progressively more intimate and I manage to lip-read a few – *never have I ever had a threesome, never have I ever done something illegal, never have I ever got with a friend's ex.*

Veena offers *never have I ever faked an orgasm.* I take a sip, and when I look back up, I catch Levi's eye. He smirks,

188

and I feel a rush of goosebumps over my skin.

Eventually, Demi announces, 'Never have I ever lied to get a job.'

There's a sonic boom when a load of people at the far end of the table drink and then everyone else yells or cheers, and it's hard to tell how the group feels about this. Everyone is so loud that I can't pull out any individual sounds from the blur.

To my surprise, Veena drinks too. She sets her drink down and faces me when she speaks. 'Not for this. When I was a teenager I lied that I had experience to get a gig tutoring this incredibly rich kid in Maths. He was a little shit, but that kept me in decent trainers for years.'

Now, that I approve of, I think.

The game breaks up – thank God – as people go to the bar to refill their drinks, buy shots, or dance on the tiny bit of space in front of the ornamental jukebox that I think is supposed to be a dancefloor, but is basically just a bit of bare ground.

Giselle says something to Levi, tries to pull him up, but he shakes his head. He says something I can't catch over all this noise, or read because his face is turned up towards her, away from me. Whatever it was, I think it had something to do with me, because she looks straight at me, eyes burning with fury. I don't know what I did, but she storms off.

I'm so confused that I don't really notice him actually coming over to speak to me.

'You all right?' he asks, and it takes me a second to clock, but I realise he just used the BSL signs along with verbally asking.

'Where did you learn that?' I ask with a smile, pointing at his hands.

He gives me one of his signature smiles. The kind that I want to know more about. 'I know things,' he says, though I read it from his lips instead of hearing it as someone has fired up the music.

It's an intimate thing to look at someone's lips to read what they're saying. And being this close to Levi and doing that makes me feel . . . I don't know. It's intense. Right now, standing in this bar looking at him, I feel exposed, but in a good way which I think is new to me.

It's probably just because I'm worried that other people will think I'm looking at his lips because I want to kiss him. Everyone thinks that's universal body language and don't think to take into account the fact that lots of us are just trying to communicate.

Probably.

I get goosebumps along my arms, which I rub at, trying to warm myself up. 'I'm sure Pen had nothing to do with it.'

'Nothing at all. Anyway, you didn't answer my question.'

'I'm OK. It's just –'

As if to demonstrate the point I was about to make, Fenella and her roommates all scream with laughter at once.

'Loud,' I say, when their screeching dies down.

'Just say if you want to go. I can always drive you home.'

'Not if you're drinking.'

He gently flicks his glass. 'It's just Coke. They jazzed it up for me. Didn't want me to go without a funky straw.'

I squint, feigning suspicion, and take a sip from his neon green curvy straw. He's right. It's just Coke.

'All right, I believe you. Do you not drink?'

'I do,' he says. 'But I have work early and I figured there should be at least one sober person here tonight just in case.'

'You're always looking out for people, aren't you?' I say.

'I try to.'

I lick my lips, tasting the sweet sugar of the Coke.

That must be what he tastes like.

I curse my traitorous brain as my face flushes with heat.

What is wrong with me?

I turn away and take a slow, long sip of my margarita in the hope that the remains of the ice cool me down enough to banish any blushing. It doesn't help. I just feel hot *and* buzzed.

'I'm just going to go to the loo,' I say, nipping out from the bench quickly.

I don't actually need to wee, so I just splash my wrists under the cold tap. In the spotted and warped mirror, the blushing has subsided, and just looks like I'm a bit sunburned. I'll take it.

When I walk back, I go round the edge of the tables, which is my first mistake. The other group of girls have taken to sitting along the pebbles at the top of the beach, and as I pass, I hear Fenella loudly say, 'Well, not everyone here is a diversity hire because they're supposedly disabled, are they?'

I freeze.

'We didn't need to pretend we were disabled just to get a job,' she continues, though I can't be sure it's still her because

191

my brain is frozen. I'm not imagining this, and I'm nowhere near drunk enough to have misunderstood what they said.

It's very, very clear.

'We're talented enough to get it without ticking a *pick me* box,' adds someone else.

They laugh nastily, and I want to fall through the earth.

When I turn to face them, they're all side-eyeing me. So they knew. They knew I was standing here, and they said it anyway.

If I was braver, I would say something but instead, my insides feel like they're melting and on fire, all at once. In my chest, my heart beats wildly, and I can feel the edges of a panic attack coming along. I can't move.

Suddenly, Pen is there, storming across the sand right to them.

And in front of me stands Levi. 'Cassie?'

I shake my head softly, the only tiny movement I can command my body to do.

'You should have picked the box that identified you as ignorant fucking arseholes,' spits Pen.

The laughter not only cuts out but feels like it was just sucked down a drain. I can't look at them. I can't move.

'We're just joking,' says one of them in a tone that suggests they think Pen is taking this too far. I can't tell who is saying what; I just wish I didn't have to hear any of it. I wish I could move. I wish it wasn't happening.

'You were being ableist.'

'Pricks, more like,' Levi barks. He stands in front of me, facing me, and looks me in the eyes. 'Cassie?'

I could fall into that grey. It's the only thing keeping me steady.

'You don't need to resort to name-calling,' snaps Giselle, I think.

'Never mind name-calling, Cassie should take this to HR,' Pen barks.

That changes the atmosphere. I feel it, like all the eyes have turned to me, and my hands start to shake. I look down, and Levi holds his hands out, not touching me, but they are palm up, right underneath my own, as if waiting for permission to hold them. I grant it by putting my hands in his. It's a moment of stability in the chaotic, television-static feeling rushing through my body.

On the beach, Pen is still tearing into the girls, now joined by my flatmates, and while I'm grateful, I just want to get out of here.

'Are you going to repeat what you said to my face?' asks Tyra.

'I think they're too cowardly for that.'

Their voices swim around my head.

'Come on, babes, tell us. Tell us how we got this job by ticking a box,' snarls Veena.

I want to sink right through the world, and go back to being unperceived, forgotten about, ignored. This is so much worse.

Levi takes me by the arm. 'Come on, let's go.' It's soft, a promise, and I feel safe with him.

We walk slowly to his car and I get into the passenger seat wordlessly. I can't imagine speaking, or even signing, right now.

I zone out the whole way home, and when Levi takes me up to the flat, he gives me a look that suggests he would rather do anything than leave me here.

'Are you sure you're going to be OK? I should probably go get Pen and the others, but I can be back here –'

'I just want to be alone,' I manage to say.

'All right. We won't be long.'

There's so much I want to say to him, but I'm overwhelmed by so many terrible feelings that all I can do is give him a weak smile as I close the door behind me.

Chapter Fifteen

I don't really sleep at all. Or at least, it takes me so long to fall asleep that I wake up feeling like I haven't.

When all the roommates came home, they texted me, correctly anticipating that I had taken my implant off and lain down. I couldn't find the words to reply, so I just heart-emoji responded to their messages so they wouldn't worry.

I didn't even text Mason when I got in. What would I say, after all? The thing that I worried would happen, happened.

Some time in the early hours, I change my mind and text him that I've had a bad day, but I don't get a response. He puts his phone on airplane mode overnight so he doesn't get bothered. I always hoped he'd put me on the exception list, just in case, but apparently not.

To make it worse, the one person who did text me from home was Mum, telling me she hoped I was having a good week and that she knew I would be doing my best always. Way to twist the knife, mother. A dose of parent pride-guilt without even knowing she was delivering it.

I don't want to face today.

This all feels too hard, even if it is my dream job.

Too unfair that I've showed up, worked hard to keep up, and this still happens. It's still all presumed special treatment. It's horrible, and makes me feel so small.

There's no escaping Fenella, Giselle and the others. They'll be in the studio no matter what happens, because it's easier for them in so many ways.

The light brightens and I know that I should get up, have a drink of water, attach my implant, and try to be a normal person.

But I can't.

It feels like . . . like everything terrible is happening again. Like going to a hearing high school when my implant had malfunctioned and I couldn't hear anything. I was too good a lip-reader to not know that people were talking about me while standing right next to me. It made me feel like I wasn't a person. Like I wasn't real. Frankly, it totally sucked.

I sit up in bed and reattach my cochlear implant, clicking the magnet back into place, and hear my phone vibrate on the table. As if on cue, the one person who made that whole time in high school bearable texts me.

Pen

Are you getting up?

Cassie

No.

I'm not leaving this bed.

The bed and I will become one.

196

I am become bed.

Destroyer of worlds?

What?

Never mind

I've been around too many
men in the workshop

They're getting inside my head
with their opinions on Nolan movies

And while I absolutely very much
respect your super valid choice
and decision to become a bed
goblin, I also think that you
should go to work

Shan't!!!

Do you want me to come
pick you up?

no.

I'm not going.

Cass.

no.

fine.

but you better bring treats.

Open your door then x

Of course they'd already be here.

I drag myself out of bed, and open the bedroom door, to find Pen, Tyra, Sorrel and Veena waiting there for me.

'Hug?' Pen asks.

I nod, and am enveloped by all four of them, squeezing me tightly. Holding me together. Supporting me through one of my worst days.

I feel the rumble of someone speaking, but everything is so muffled I have to push us all apart so I can hear.

'What did you say?'

Tyra speaks. 'I'm so sorry that those horrible little twerps were so ignorant to you.'

'Thank you,' I say, before realising that I've been a little bit self-involved about this. It was about Tyra as much as me. And given how white people like to talk shit about people of colour in the workplace, it would have hurt Veena and Sorrel too. I should have fought back, for all of them. But I couldn't. I just froze. And for that I feel so incredibly ashamed.

'Are you all OK? I'm so sorry I didn't check in last night. I just . . . wasn't in my body,' I say.

'The most important thing was getting you out of there,' says Veena. 'You did not look OK.'

'I wasn't,' I admit. 'I just . . . I can't believe they said it, you know.'

'With their full chests.'

198

'Are you OK?' I ask Tyra, who just shrugs.

'I'm not sure they've realised that I've got epilepsy. I don't want to pretend it wasn't technically about me, but . . .' She waves her hand over her body.

I get what she means. Passing as not disabled comes with its upsides and downsides – you might escape people being randomly ableist to you, but also people don't see all that you're doing just to keep up with them, or the cost of it.

'They said I was faking it,' I say, shaking my head. 'Like, what the actual fuck? Why would I have a magnet on my head if I was faking it?'

'They're just ignorant.'

'Luckily, we were all there to protect each other,' adds Veena.

'I think Pen did a good job of that for us too,' says Sorrel.

'Yeah, where did that come from? You're so cute and charming and little and then you turned into some kind of fury beast.'

'Protector mode was engaged,' says Pen, folding their arms like a bodyguard.

'Terrifying.'

'Speaking of,' Pen begins and I know exactly what they're going to suggest.

'No. I don't want to dob them in,' I say before they can finish.

'Are you sure?' they ask again, but I know they understand why I'm not going to take this to Michael or someone else. At the end of the day, they'll get away with it because they were drunk and all I'll have done is made things really awkward.

They won't lose their jobs over it, and it could end up turning into a lengthy investigation that will just make things worse for me. It won't change. It never does.

And I know Pen gets that because of the amount of transphobic microaggressions they've had to deal with.

It really sucks that this is the way, that people can get away with being horrible bigots to our faces and not face any consequences.

'I think you embarrassed them enough,' I say, and Pen nods. They won't bring it up again.

'You sure did. After you left, pretty much everyone got involved and made them go home. Seojin was kicking off.'

'Everyone was, really,' agrees Veena. 'When Levi came back with the car, he talked to them in this, like, serious teacher mode. Everyone else had been like yelling at them, but I think they thought we were all overreacting, or pretending to, until Levi sat them down and gave them a talking-to.'

Sorrel snorts. 'Given Giselle had been all over him last night, she looked like she wanted to be sucked into the void. I think she thought he was coming over to flirt.'

Something twists in my stomach. 'He went back to talk to them?'

'To confront them, honey,' Tyra insists. 'They weren't having a picnic.'

'He schooled them,' says Veena with a nod.

I can't decide how to feel about this. I mean, people have stood up for me. *Levi* stood up for me. I guess it means that people care about me, but I wish I hadn't found out this way. And I wish that it hadn't happened in the first place.

I'll still have to see those girls at work, after all.

If this was any other job, I'd give myself the OK to go lie in bed and get in my feelings about it. I think I deserve that, but at the same time, I feel motivated after talking to my friends. I will not let them beat me. I will not let them define what I can or can't do.

I deserve to be here. That's the only thing I'm certain of.

'Come on. We should all get to work,' I say, ignoring the ache in my head and the swirl in my stomach.

I feel so much better that I decide to text Mason about what happened. I never want people to worry, if I can help it, so I try not to tell my family and Mason about anything bad that's happened to me until I feel in a better place to share it. I just don't want to upset them with my feelings.

The others are already ready, so I dress quickly. I don't want us to be late.

Bernard is waiting downstairs and greets us happily. I'm actually feeling ready to face the day, and then, as we pull into Rosa's lot, I make the crucial mistake of checking my phone.

Mason

> People are going to have questions about how a deaf girl can dance. I'm sure they didn't mean it the way you took it.

I'm so flabbergasted that I just shove my phone away and bite down on my lip so that I don't cry. Of all people, I had hoped he would have my back.

He just doesn't get it.

The atmosphere in the studio doesn't exactly make me feel better. The other girls stand in one corner, icily projecting fury at us. I don't look at them, or I try not to.

To their credit, pretty much all of the guys come over to say hi and to ask if I'm OK, and I know it's because they care but I kind of wish we could move on so I could stop thinking about it for just a little bit.

Saying that, I don't mind when Seojin wraps me into a hug and lifts me off my feet. That man gives good hugs.

For once, I'm actually relieved that Michael works us hard. When I dance, I can get out of my own thoughts and focus on the movement of my body. I can become part of the music.

We work on 'Damask' and I feel very smug that we end up using a whole section from our choreography, blended in with the boys' tango-influenced duets. Michael pairs us up boy-girl, and Seojin and I commit to having a lot of fun with it, making it the horniest, hottest dance we can. We perhaps go a bit far, because Michael asks us to take a cold shower afterwards.

At lunch, Pen pops their head in and the mean girls scatter like a flock of pigeons, eager to get out of the way.

'How's it going?' they ask airily, as though nothing happened last night, as though they're not checking up on me. I love them for that.

I want to tell them about the message from Mason. My phone is in my bag in the locker room, but now that I'm still, all I can think about is what he said. How he took the other girls' side without even asking me how I felt. But I know that

202

if I talk to Pen about it they'll go into protector mode again, and I don't need that right now. I'll just have to work it out myself.

I try to put on a peppy, all-is-OK vibe but I obviously fail, because Pen gives me a kiss on the cheek when they leave.

We start marking out the steps for a new dance in the afternoon. It's for 'Bye Bye', a song that reminds me of Pen and I dancing in my bedroom as teenagers. It helps lift my mood, a little.

Once he's satisfied that we won't immediately forget everything, Michael sends all the girls to the costumers to get fitted for the tour. Thankfully it's the last thing we need to do for the day, and then we're allowed to leave a little early.

I didn't think it could be more awkward than in the studio, but the costumers have us wait in a queue, stripped down to our pants and workout bras before they call us up to take our measurements which they silently record in a spreadsheet. No one really speaks, which I'd normally be fine with but the tension in the air is thick. Fenella stands next to Veena and is probably afraid she will literally bite her head off from the looks she keeps sending her way.

Luckily, the team are incredibly efficient, and we're all done in about ten minutes for initial measurements. I pull my leggings back on, and step out of the door, and almost walk directly into Levi.

'Creeping around the women's changing rooms, are we? You'll get a bad name for yourself, Levi McHugh.'

'I don't think it counts as creeping if I'm standing in a well-lit corridor clearly waiting for you.'

I feel a catch in my chest, like I've missed a step when walking downstairs. 'Waiting for me?'

'I thought you might need cheering up.'

I groan. 'I don't want to think about what happened last night.'

'Exactly. So, you and I are going on an adventure.'

After today, I would kill to get away from everything, and he's offering me a way out. 'All right.'

'Perfect.'

I see Tyra hesitating in the corridor ahead, her head tilted in question. 'I'll be back at the flat later,' I tell her. 'I think Levi is kidnapping me.'

'Just a light one,' he insists.

'I don't think there's a spectrum for kidnapping. It is or it isn't fully kidnapping. That's it.'

'I guess you'll have to take that risk.'

Tyra watches my face a second, and says, 'All right, then. You have fun, and text me when you're on the way back.' She gives me a squeeze before she goes.

Levi smirks at me. 'Coming?' he asks, sauntering off.

For just a second, I wonder if I should be going off to hang out with him alone. I mean, the day at the beach was an accident really. He found me. This is a choice to go. It's not a date but a guy and a girl hanging out alone . . . I mean, men and women can be friends, obviously. But there's chemistry between us, I think. The roommates spotted it last night. Even if I'm not actively pursuing anything with him, is saying yes to this kind of the same thing?

My head feels scrambled.

All I can think of is the difference between how they reacted to what happened to me last night. How Levi scooped me up versus how Mason essentially told me I wasn't being considerate enough of someone else's feelings.

And so, I barely wait three seconds before running after him. We walk downstairs and he leads me towards his car. 'You haven't told me where we're going.'

'That's part of the surprise.' He opens the door for me. 'I promise, I'll be careful with you.'

The feeling of my heart flipping over itself in my chest is so intense that I just get in the car so that I'm not standing so close to him, so that I'm no longer at risk of falling into his shining eyes.

Chapter Sixteen

When we pull out of the car park, I look out of the back window and see Pen waving furiously through the open workshop door.

'Checking out my reversing?' Levi asks.

'No, just noticing our fans. Did they put you up to this?'

'Of course not, it was all my own idea,' he says, his hand on his chest as though I've offended him.

'Your own idea which you still won't explain to me.'

'Where's the fun in that?' That twinkle of mischief in his eye again. 'Though, if you want to know, I can actually tell you. I don't want you being anxious that I'm taking you to a gladiator match or something.'

'As long as it's not a gladiator match with loud music and people yelling at me, we'd probably be OK.'

'OK, note taken. Silent death matches are permissible.'

We both giggle.

'But really –'

'No, it's fine, you can surprise me.'

We drive along a different route to the one Bernard brings

us on every day, heading north on the island as far as I can tell. 'Oh no, you're not taking me to that cave I have to hike to that Pen was going on about, are you?'

'No hiking either. A few steps maybe.'

'Hmm, all right, then.'

'To their credit, I should say that Pen was worried about you today. They care a lot about you.'

'I care a lot about Pen too.'

'It's nice to see youse together, so easy with each other. I haven't had a pal like that since . . . well, maybe primary school really.'

'More of a lone wolf kinda guy?'

'Well, more that I was always part of a group of people who hung out for reasons. Like, school or rugby –'

That explains the shoulders.

I flip down the sun visor and pretend I'm checking my hair in the mirror. No blushing. *Get it together, Cassie, you have Mason.*

'Or all the jobs I've done. We'd go out and stuff, have a nice time, but my life is just a bit transitory. Hard to hold onto people when you're moving around so much.'

'What about your flatmate who took you to the drama club?'

'Mercedes? Oh yeah, I dunno. I think she's settled down back home, engaged to her high school sweetheart, baby on the way.' He rubs his hand through his hair. 'Look, I'm worried I'm now giving you the impression that I'm terrible at keeping friends.'

I burst out laughing. 'A little, I'm not going to lie.'

'I was trying to say that you're lucky, the pair of you. To have that.'

'We are,' I agree.

Everywhere is so green here. Not quite the same green you get in Britain: it's both richer and sandier at the same time. We pass occasional huge trees at the side of the road that tower over everything, and drive under a grove that grows over it, forming a little tunnel of cool air. I open the window to smell the rich, warm, baked ground and the sappy scent of the spindly pines.

'Smell good?'

'Like holidays,' I sigh.

My phone vibrates in my bag with a text.

Pen

Have funnnn x

Cassie

Why didn't you come too?

I thought you two could hang out just the two of you

You know

As friends. No biggie.

This is not helping the whole getting over this summer crush thing

Oopsie x

You're a nightmare

No, I just love you and I think he's nice and good for you

I'm with Mason

And that's fine, Cass

Levi can just be your pal

But he's a nice person and you don't get to hang out so much so here we go

It's a little friendship date

What is it about that sentence that makes me feel a bit weird?

I'll talk to you later

bye bye x

We turn off the main road we've been driving along, and start to wind through small towns with big white churches in the centres. The road rises through some hills where the pine forest gets thicker until we're completely off road.

'Are we allowed to go down here?' I ask, grabbing hold of the inside door handle to steady myself.

'We are, I promise. It's just a bit of a secret.'

'How did you find out about this secret place?'

'Martin, one of the other guys in the workshop. He's a Swede who used to come here on holiday a lot, so is full of good tips.'

The car lurches dramatically in and out of a pothole, and Levi laughs with wild abandon.

'I promise the destination is good, even if the road is not.'

'I'm holding you to that, Levi.'

The glove box in front of me suddenly pops open with the all the lurching, and a notebook falls into my lap. It's a really nice one, with tanned leather on the outside, and kept together with a band of fabric.

'What's this?' I say.

'Oh no, don't look at that.' Levi tries to reach for it, but the road is too pothole-riddled for him to take both hands off the wheel.

'Is it your secret diary?' I tease, waving it at him.

'Worse.' He laughs, and a blush runs over his cheeks. 'It's my songs.'

'Your *songs*?'

'Yeah.'

We pull over then and I offer the notebook to him.

'You can have it back. I won't look.'

He rubs the back of his neck as his whole face flushes. And I mean it, he goes entirely strawberry pink. It's kind of adorable. 'I mean, you could look, but I wouldn't want to know about it. You might hate them. And I think sometimes song lyrics can look so weird on their own. It can be a bit corny.'

'Yeah, but that's part of the fun of them. I can't always

hear the lyrics when a song is playing, so I go read them later online so I can learn them. I'm used to it.'

He nods, clearly still nervous about it.

'Have you been writing songs for a long time?'

'Yeah. Since I was a kid. Terrible yarns about not wanting to do my homework and how adults sucked. That was my early *Busted* era.'

I laugh, imagining a tiny version of him jumping around singing 'What I Go to School For'.

'What came next? A little Bieber?'

'I wish I could say you were mistaken.'

I start to croon 'Baby' at him and the awkwardness gives way to laughter.

'Yeah, yeah. I know. I was a real heartthrob.'

'I bet.' I put the notebook back in the glove box. 'Come on, I believe you have other secrets to show me.'

He gives me a relieved smile and then we get out. From the boot, Levi pulls out a cooler box and dons a beefy-looking backpack.

'Ominous,' I say.

'The cooler?'

'Is that where you hide the bodies? Or perhaps bits of them.'

He closes the boot, and leads me towards a path that runs through the trees. 'Guess you'll find out soon. If you're brave enough.'

And once again I find myself chasing after him.

I'm glad that I wore decent trainers to work today because the path gets a little rockier and steeper, but we take it slow. The floor is strewn with pine needles from the trees above us, and that rich sap smell fills the air. It reminds me of the Hippy Market a little – like the incense and oils they sold.

There's no rush, it seems. And we've got quite a few hours until sunset, thanks to Michael letting us out early. It's a nice change of pace, and the air is so cool here under the canopy.

I think back to the notebook in the glove box.

'So you're an artist?' I say, as we pause to take in the view.

'I wouldn't say that.'

'Why? You make art. Therefore you're an artist.'

He squirms. 'Maybe.'

It's strange. He's normally so relaxed and easy, and yet bringing this up has changed everything about him. 'I can drop it, if you don't want to talk about it?'

'No, it's OK. It's just . . . how do I put it? There's nothing more embarrassing than being earnest about something.'

'What do you mean? Because you care about it?'

'Maybe, but I guess it's more than that. It's all very soul-baring, isn't it?'

'Have you ever played for anyone?'

'Girlfriends when I was younger, sure. I wrote some real bops. Rhymed Lisa with *I want to please her*.'

'Ooh, smooth. How did Lisa take it?'

'Not well, because she was called Sarah.'

I burst out laughing so hard that we have to stop walking so I can catch my breath.

'Please tell me you're joking.'

'If I was it would have saved me a lot of hassle. That's what this scar is,' he says, pointing to the little nick in his eyebrow.

'She threw the guitar at you?'

'Luckily only the can of Diet Coke she was drinking. What girls did you grow up around if they were throwing guitars at people?'

'Oh no, they were all quite normal. I was thinking about what I'd do.'

'I will keep my guitar very far away from you in that case.'

'Just don't write a song about me, and we'll be OK.'

He gives me a little smile as we start walking again, and I feel a squirm in my stomach.

'I kind of get it though. How hard it is to share that vulnerable part of you.'

'Oh yeah?'

'Did Pen not tell you how I got the job?'

He shakes his head, so I fill him in on all of it. 'Until then, I was just dancing on my own in my bedroom. It was all mine.'

'And now you have to share it.'

'Yeah, but that part wasn't too bad in the end. It's just the . . . you know, other people.'

'The other people indeed.'

We let it hang in the air between us, and I'm glad he doesn't push it. We keep walking on. Just as I'm thinking about stopping him to ask more about his songs, the path crests over a hill, the trees falling away to reveal we're standing on a ragged, rocky coast, looking out over a rich azure sea. Sailboats dot the water, but otherwise we're alone.

'Wow,' I gasp.

'It's a bit of a good view, isn't it?'

I nod. It's breathtaking.

'We're going down there if you're OK to walk?' He points

below us to a sandy cove, bordered by the cliffs. There's no one on the beach. It'll just be us. 'We'll go slow.'

'This is amazing,' I say, walking alongside him down the path cut into the rock.

Halfway down, I slip a little in the loose scree on the path and grab onto his backpack to steady myself.

'You all right?'

'Yeah. I think so.'

'Just hold onto me. We're almost there.'

It feels too much to reach over and hold onto his shoulders or arms or any part of his bare skin, so I stay attached to the backpack, which appears to be straining at its seams. 'What do you have in there? Did you bring the guitar?'

'I don't think they've invented fold-up guitars yet.'

'I'm sure someone has. One of those guys who loves to travel because he's super rich, and then goes into tech. Tesla will be making one any minute, I bet.'

'You've thought a lot about this.'

'It just seems like something someone really rich and annoying would do.'

Levi bursts out laughing. 'If it helps, I promise I'm not the kind of guy who whips it out at a party or on a train.'

'Hopefully you mean the guitar.'

We almost fall off the cliff from giggling, but we do make it down without either of us injuring ourselves. Levi leads me to a natural rock formation that makes a kind of bridge over the water, and we settle down on it. The rock is still warm from the summer sun, even though the strongest heat of the day is long gone.

Luckily the cooler isn't for dismembered human parts, but is instead packed with food, and his enormous rucksack turns out to have a picnic set built into it.

'Where did you get all this?'

'Martin.'

'He really pulled through for us today.'

Levi hands me a plate, and starts filling it for me with fancy olives from a can, a few crisps (Paprika flavour, the quintessential holiday crisp) and freshly made sandwiches filled with thick slices of fresh mozzarella, bright green pesto and basil leaves, all nestled inside crusty ciabatta rolls.

'Did Martin also make us dinner?'

'No, that was me. I snuck home this afternoon and filled everything up.'

'This is really nice of you, Levi.'

'Seemed like you needed something nice after yesterday. And to be clear, we don't have to talk about it. We can just sit and eat the sandwiches and you can make fun of me for being a wannabe Hozier.'

'Hozier?' I say, raising an eyebrow. 'I was expecting more of a Lewis Capaldi crooning vibe.'

'I can be versatile, though I'm definitely not a good enough singer to match either of them.'

'So, you want to write but not perform?'

'Basically. I could be that lady who wrote "Toxic" and "Can't Get You Out of My Head" about that vet from the telly. The Supervet? That guy Noel with the border terriers.'

'I have no idea what you're talking about, but I support you if you want to write love songs for a television veterinarian.'

We laugh and he hands me an ice-cold Fanta, which I run across my collarbones. It's heavenly. I don't know if I'm imagining it when Levi's eyes follow the path of the cool can.

'How do you sell the songs you write?'

'Great question. I wish I knew.'

'You've not looked into it?'

'Not yet. They're still mine, for now. Maybe one day.'

I take my shoes off and let my feet dangle into the salt spray that splashes up the rock face to us. It's bliss for my aching feet, though I hope Levi doesn't look at them too closely. Dancing hardcore for a few weeks has done a real number on them. I'm becoming more blister plaster than human.

We eat our sandwiches in comfortable silence, watching the waves splash below us.

'Did you always want to be a dancer?'

'Yes and no. I found dance because my audiologist suggested to my parents that it would help me practise hearing, but instead it brought me a kind of freedom that I didn't have anywhere else. I didn't think I could do it for a job. It didn't seem like that was possible.'

'You know, I admire you a lot for chasing your dream.'

'Technically, Pen chased my dream for me.'

'But you came. You stuck it out. That takes courage.'

'Especially when I have to deal with people who know nothing about deafness.'

'Does it make it harder for you?'

'What? Being deaf?'

'No, the misconceptions. The way those girls treated you is obviously shit, but I imagine it's more than that.'

I'm a little taken aback by his question.

'No one's ever asked me that before. But, yeah, to put it simply, I always think about how I might be the first deaf person they've met, or that they know they've met, and so it kind of puts pressure on me to give the right first impression.'

'An instinct to teach them?'

'Yeah.'

'Must be tiring to always be educating.'

'It is. Sometimes I wish I could just *be* but I'm not just a dancer. I'm a dancer with different needs from everyone else. The disabled dancer. The deaf dancer.'

'I can imagine mixing that with the need to be the best version of yourself out there makes a real cocktail.'

I shake my head in disbelief. 'You get it. That's exactly it. Have you been reading my secret diary?'

'Not yet, but now I know there is one, maybe I'll catch up in the bath later. Is it a good one?'

'A messy one.'

'I look forward to it.'

I nibble on a crisp as I think about whether I want to be honest with him. There's stuff I'll tell the roommates, but I still sanitise much of it.

'I know a lot of it is from me trying to be the best, but the pressure of being the only visibly disabled person in the room can be hard. Like, I don't pass. Most people clock my voice, or the CI, so I'm always managing reactions to some extent.'

'Would you rather people didn't comment at all?'

'Somewhere in the middle. I want them to recognise that I might need something hearing people don't, and to ask if I need anything, but to leave it at that. Those videos on YouTube of people getting their implants turned on and suddenly being able to hear make people think they can ask me really personal stuff about the experience.'

'I think I know which ones you mean.'

'They're weird, because I remember when my new one turned on when I was a teenager all I could hear was . . . I don't know, too much? Everyone's voices sounded all robotic and distorted. It was too loud, and my brain couldn't keep up. And that was after me using one for ten years so I knew what to expect, but I was starting over in a lot of ways. Sometimes I try to think back to when I was a little kid, and it was the first time I'd ever heard anything at all, so it must have been really scary for me.'

'You don't remember?'

'Not really. I was only six. Do you remember much about being six?'

'Only obsessively watching *Cars* over and over.'

'What a film to pick.'

'Look, there's a lot of existential questions in that film. Like, have you ever thought about how that town works? Where is the line between machine and animated car?'

'You were a very advanced six-year-old.'

'Plus,' he says, fixing me with a serious look, 'life . . . really is a highway.' I burst out laughing at the way he delivers it like a priest giving a sermon.

'You're so unserious.'

'Good. Who wants to be serious all the time?'

'You don't think it's the same as being ambitious?'

'No, I don't. I can care about my job and trying to develop my art, which is the wankiest sentence I've said for a while, and still enjoy my life. I don't want to change who I am as a person for that.'

'I'm glad,' I say. 'Also, I know I said I didn't want people asking about how it worked, but I meant like people I don't know. Friends can ask.'

'Have I officially achieved friend level?'

'I think cheering me up on two separate occasions definitely gives you a fair shot.'

'I'd better not screw it up,' he says. 'And thanks. I wanted to ask about it if you were comfortable, only in case something went wrong and you needed me to help. But there's no pressure. I'm sure there's plenty of information online that I could look up?'

'Hush,' I say. 'You asked for the life story, so now you're getting it.'

'Yes, ma'am.' He sits up straight, and I know he's not joking around. The look on his face is keen, but he's patient. I trust him with this.

'So, I was born deaf in both ears, but my parents didn't find out until I was, like, one, I think? They're both hearing so it was kind of a surprise to them. The doctors tried me out on hearing aids first but they just amplify the sounds, so rely on what amount of hearing you already have. And obviously we found out later that I have none at all.'

'So it wasn't doing anything for you?'

'Nothing. The damage to my hearing is inside and out so they were just decorative, I guess.'

'I imagine a lot of people don't really understand the difference between the two?'

'No, which can make things tricky. Anyway, so when I was six I had surgery to put in my implant.'

I turn my head to the side so that the implant is facing him.

'Under here, under my skin, is an internal part which has a receiver and there's also been electrodes put in my cochlea, which is like this spiral-shaped cavity deep in your ear. Anyway, it basically bypasses any damage in my ears because those electrodes send signals straight to the auditory nerve, which go to my brain as sound.'

'That's kind of incredible.'

'It is. Also be impressed with how much of that I remembered off the top of my head.' I grin and he smiles.

'I'm always impressed by you.'

I'm too scared to hold his gaze, because there's so many feelings trying to burst through my skin. All I can do is go straight back into science mode.

'I'm going to detach the outside bit, so my voice will change a little because I won't be able to hear myself speaking, but then you can see it properly.'

He nods. 'Only if you're sure.'

'I'm sure,' I say.

I pull my hair back, and tap the top of the part attached to my ear. 'So the microphone is here, on the tip of it.'

I unhook my cochlear implant from my ear, and pull the coil gently from the side of my head, so the whole processor comes away.

The silence is peaceful. So very peaceful.

'Underneath where the coil was is a magnet,' I say slowly, focusing on my words. 'Which sticks them together and activates it, so the implant in my head works.'

I slide the battery pack off the cochlear implant to show him. 'This is why I had to leave at the airport. The batteries died on me. Normally they last two or three days.'

I press the button to activate the implant, and the tiny light flashes green to say it's working, so I reconnect it and the sound of the world floods back in.

'When the batteries start running out, I can hear a beeping in my head from the implant and it always wigs me out a bit, even though I have spare batteries basically everywhere.' I pat the little bag I have slung across my body, knowing there's at least four batteries in there, even though I only ever need two. You never know when you'll need a backup.

'There's a few different types of implant, so they can function a little differently. It's all what works best for the person, I guess. And it's supposed to last for life, but my first one broke, so this one is only four years old. I think that's pretty much everything.' I laugh awkwardly. 'Here ends the lecture.'

'That was really interesting. Thanks for trusting me with all that.'

My cheeks burn a little, and for once I don't rush to hide it. 'Thank you for understanding that it takes trust for me to share all that.'

He holds my gaze and it feels like looking into the sun.

'Well, you're my friend. I want to keep hanging out with you, and knowing you, and that means knowing all of you.'

I feel a traitorous heat rush up my body at *knowing all of you*. This crush is getting embarrassing.

'You know when you said people always get them mixed up with hearing aids?' he begins, and I nod. 'I guess that means people get a lot of stuff wrong about them. Like those videos you were talking about.'

'Yeah,' I say. 'Like, it wasn't an instant fix once the implant was in, and I'm not not-deaf now I have one – that always confuses people. Plus, I had to work so, so hard on training my hearing when I got it both times, and there's still stuff I can't pick up. It's an aid, not a fix.'

'Can I ask something else?'

'Go for it.'

'If someone asks me about it, what do you want me to say? Like do you want me to explain or just encourage them to google it?'

'Whichever you feel comfortable with. It's nice of you to ask permission.'

'It's your life. And I think that my being part of it should be contingent on me respecting you and your boundaries.'

I feel like my breath has been stolen right from my chest. I'm not sure anyone but Pen or my family have ever spoken to me like this before. I want to hug him but I'm frightened of what I might do, or might think about doing. What I'm already thinking about doing.

Instead I ask him to take a few photos of me on the land bridge to send to my parents, which he does. When I send them to the family group chat, the first person who replies is my sister.

Vics

You look happy x

Mum

LOOK AT MY BEAUTIFUL
GIRL XOXO

Dad just sends a heart emoji, but I know he'll be crying because he cries any time I send him a photo. Something about being a parent changes your brain chemistry in truly fascinating ways, I suppose.

'Come on,' he says. 'We should do a selfie too. The golden hour light is too good.'

I squeeze up against him, and feel my skin prickle at the touch. I smell *boy* – that deep oud-and-pepper smell that you always find in men's shampoos, that I also love in my candles. Plus a hint of sawdust. Maybe a hint of liquorice. I have to concentrate on smiling when his arm wraps around me. It's hard to not look at him in the phone screen opposite, and I try to just look up into the camera, but my eyes keep getting dragged to him.

It's as I sit here in his arms that I realise that this is more than just chemistry. This whole date, the last few weeks of knowing him, I've felt things that I've never felt before. Knowing I could be vulnerable with him, and not being afraid of taking up that space. Not feeling like I have to shrink myself.

But it's not just about how he makes me feel about myself.

The hair standing up on the back of my neck as he breathes is proof of that.

'OK, smile?' he says.

We're still touching as we look through the photos we took. I don't kid myself that it looks like just a friendly date.

'Ah, that's a nice one,' he says, and I feel his words rumble against my body.

What if I kissed him? What would that be like? Would he even want that? I could just turn my body slightly, tilt my head up, and his lips are there.

I scramble to my feet, and stretch out my legs. 'Cramp,' I say, with a laugh.

'Come on, I should get you home before curfew.' Levi holds his hand out. 'Hand or backpack?'

'Backpack,' I say a little too quickly. 'So you can keep your eyes forward.'

I'm not sure if that's disappointment on his face or not, but whatever it is he quickly covers it up. 'Backpack it is.'

We start making our way up slowly.

'Did Pen set one?' I ask.

'What?'

'A curfew?'

'Oh, they absolutely did. Insisted you had to be home before sundown.'

'They're such a dork.'

'You're like siblings.'

'Pretty much. Pen comes on all the family trips and dinners. They were at my leaving dinner.'

I drop the rest of that sentence, because then I'd have to

say the truth. That Mason didn't come. That I even have a Mason. That in my mind, Mason isn't matching up with the man who took me out today, just because he knew I was sad. Who asked me how I felt and thought about things, without making any decisions about them. And it's not that I only like Levi because he's maybe better at those things than Mason is. I think I just *like* Levi in a way that's kind of terrifying to me.

I could just stop us when we get to the top of the hill, spin him round, and tell him how I feel. Would he say he felt the same?

'Does Pen get on well with your fella? What's his name? Mason?' he suddenly asks, as if he can read my mind.

So he already knows about Mason. I wonder how he figured it out. Pen probably told him, I suppose. I haven't been purposefully hiding it from him, it just never came up. Plus, things with Mason aren't exactly super fun right now with all our miscommunications so it's not like I've been talking much about him with anyone – last time I did, Veena said she hated him.

God, I'm such a dickhead.

A heavy feeling runs through my torso, like someone dropped a weight into water. Have I been acting like a fool this whole time? Clearly he's saying this to flag to me that he knows the boundaries of our little friendship. There was me going off in my head imagining stuff, and he must have been feeling awkward that maybe I was getting the wrong idea.

Obviously my roommates were wrong and he doesn't fancy me, because he knows I have Mason. I really hope he hasn't picked up on my silly little crush. This is kind of embarrassing.

'They haven't really spent that much time together. He's always busy, and Pen used to work shift hours at home. Ships in the night, you know.'

'Hopefully, when he comes to visit you, you all can hang out. I look forward to meeting him.' He keeps his eyes on the ground.

I feel mortified.

'Are you all right?' he asks me, and I realise we've made it back into the forest already but I've been too busy yelling inside my own brain.

'Just tired,' I say, which is true but only half of it. 'I get a headache at the end of the day from all the sound processing.'

'Do you want to turn off when we're in the car?'

'Turn off?' I laugh. 'I'm not a robot, Levi!'

Now it's his turn to look mortified. 'Sorry, that's not what I meant! I just meant . . . I don't want to say the wrong thing.' He shuffles about as he puts the things in the boot. 'I mean, how would you say it. Unhook?'

'I'm teasing you,' I say, helping him close the boot, though he needs no assistance from me. 'Tune out, I guess.'

'Yes. That.'

'Thanks, I'll keep my implant on. But is it OK if we don't talk? Let's just put on some terrible music.'

'Now *that* I can do,' he says with way too much excitement.

As we drive away from the cove, I shouldn't be surprised when the first song he plays is 'Life is a Highway'.

Chapter Seventeen

I half expect Pen to be waiting for me at my flat when I get home, but they're not here.

In the living room Veena and Sorrel are watching old episodes of *Love is Blind*. My stomach turns at the thought of sitting down and watching people profess their true love for each other, and to my relief Sorrel hits pause as I walk in.

'Hey, how did your date go?' asks Veena, and Sorrel lobs a pillow at her.

Can they tell how I feel? That I nearly kissed him? Or at least, I thought about it way too much.

Sorrel gives me a reassuring look. 'Your *day out* she means.'

Perhaps it's OK. I flop down between them. 'It was really nice. He's . . . he's just a really good guy.'

Veena gives me a wolfish smile.

'Stop thinking about his mandingo,' I tell her, and she barks with laughter.

'You're the one who said it, not me.'

'Anyway, he cheered me up a lot, and we had this really in-depth conversation about creativity and bravery. There was a whole picnic and stuff. No Fanta Limón though.'

Veena winces. 'Ooft, marks deducted there.'

'I'm glad he looked after you all right,' says Sorrel.

'Where's Tyra?' I ask, thinking it feels a bit quiet in here.

'Went out for a walk about half an hour ago,' says Veena.

I take my phone out of my pocket and see that there's a few notifications, almost all of them from Mason. I can't bring myself to open them though, not right now.

First things first, I have to work out what's going on with me. With Levi. Not that there's anything going on, he's made that clear, but the way I keep imagining stuff can't be good.

My phone buzzes, and it's Vics. Perhaps the one person I can talk to about this, as she's always a good neutral sounding board. After all, my flatmates have gotten a bad impression of Mason and seem to have staked themselves as Team Levi, and I get the feeling that Pen would be happy if I dumped Mason . . . It's a feeling I've tried to ignore for a long time, a kind of itch at the back of my head. They've never said outright they don't like him, and they've respected our relationship. But we're too close. I just know, as much as I want to ignore that.

So, that means time to talk about it with Vics.

Vics

How's my lil sis

Cassie

Having a crisis

Oh no, lay it on me

Terrible day, mean girls, etc, etc

Who am I killing

That's not even the main crisis

Uh-oh

Nice boy took me out to cheer me up

Listened to me talk about my CI

Has just been really kind

UH-OH

Now you get it

I'm joking, pet, you can have a crush even when you're dating someone else

You are a human with feelings

It happens!

I still feel bad about it

In what way

Just the daydreaming about it

It's probably because he was so nice, asked a lot of good not intrusive questions about being deaf

I pause as I realise something, and I'm a little afraid to say it to someone else.

I just wish Mason would do that more

He doesn't ask about it?

I think he just ignores it

Err you're deaf, he can't just ignore that

I'm really sorry that he's being an arsehole about this whole job

How did you know??
Did Pen tell you??

Sisterly intuition

Plus the whole not showing up for the party was a red flag

You seemed so sad about it

Oh God, did the parents notice

Don't worry about them, they'll be fine

I think they'd like Mason a lot

If they ever met him

Ummmmm

What does that mean

I think they would be happier to see you with someone who saw all of you, including your deafness

I would too

Plus it doesn't matter if I like him, it matters if you like him and if he treats you nicely

Does he treat you nicely?

I know he's not your boyfriend or whatever parameters you've set

> But seems like he's kind
> of having his cake here,
> if he can have that
> freedom but you can't

> Let yourself have some
> fun with this nice boy

God the irony of me not knowing what the parameters are.

> We've been together
> a year though

> Look, just take this new
> boy out of the question
> for a minute, and think
> about your relationship
> with Mason

> Is it a good relationship
> for you?

What a question. And it's telling that I'm not leaping to defend him for once. This whole time I've been trying to convince people over and over what a nice guy he is and . . . is he? Is he *actually* a nice person? Is he kind to me?

I think back to when we were first dating and he'd take me out to clubs with his work friends, and I'd have to leave early because the migraines always sucked. He used to get so huffy with me, so I told him to just go without me.

And no matter how many times I ask him to face me when I speak to him, or uncover his mouth, he doesn't do it. He gets irritated when I ask him to repeat things.

He never learned sign either, even though he knows it was my first language and that it's important to me.

Even Levi learned some sign, and I've only known him two weeks.

Though Vics is right. I need to stop comparing the two of them and work out if my relationship with Mason is enough for me.

The worst bit is I think that's the first time I've ever thought about that. That I've ever asked myself if I was happy in the relationship, rather than just focusing on him. He was worried this job would change me, and I think it has. But for the better, because I'm starting to realise that it's not just Pen and my family who love and respect me for who I am.

And yes, there are still people who are terrible, but I have Veena and Sorrel and Tyra and Levi, and Seojin and Demi too. Maybe even Michael. We're not friends but I think he respects me and cares about how I'm doing.

This whole time I thought that Mason was too good for me. That I was punching up, and that I should be grateful that someone would put up with me when I'm such a burden to them.

But maybe . . . maybe I'm not actually the burden I've spent my whole life thinking I was. Maybe it's OK that I have different needs to other people, and that doesn't make me unlovable or difficult or too much effort. If these people

I've just brought into my life can meet me where I'm at and love me for it . . . then why can't Mason?

I feel a hand on my wrist, and Sorrel is there. Her touch is so gentle, like she's worried I could shatter at any moment.

'Sweetheart?' she says. 'Talk to me. Are you OK?'

It turns out that I'm crying. I don't even know when I started, but now the dam has burst.

'Oh. No, I don't think I am,' I sob.

'Hug?' Veena asks, also appearing, and I nod. The pair of them envelop me in a cuddle and I feel safe and loved and also desperately aware of what I need to do.

'I think I need to break up with Mason.'

They don't say anything, don't ask why or when or how. They just hold me and let me cry my heart out. Sensing that a dating show might not be quite right, Sorrel puts on one of the reality TV shows about baking terrible cakes, and I only notice that time passes because eventually someone wins. I take my cue to sit up and get a hold of myself.

I can be sad about it, but I need to do this.

It isn't technically a break-up if we're not boyfriend and girlfriend, but it feels like one. Maybe because I was kidding myself the whole time I said I didn't care about us being together properly.

'Thank you,' I say to my friends. 'This is going to suck.'

'What do you need from us?' asks Sorrel.

'Just sit with me? I haven't opened his messages all day. I think, subconsciously, I've kind of felt it was coming.'

'We're here,' says Veena, snuggling against me.

The smell of their perfumes and beauty products blend

234

together, forming a comforting cloud of cocoa butter, vanilla, roses, and the occasional hint of Fanta Limón.

'There's nothing like the first true heartbreak,' says Sorrel, pushing my hair away from my wet face. 'Even if it's you doing the breaking.'

I nod. 'I knew break-ups hurt but this *really* hurts and I haven't even done it yet.'

'Deep breaths.'

Sorrel shows me some breathing patterns and we breathe together, slowly in and out. Veena even joins in.

'OK. I'm going to read his messages now.'

We crowd together as I open my message thread with him and there's a lot, sent over the course of the day.

Mason

> Hey, I've not heard from you. How are you doing? x

> I saw you got tagged in some photos on Instagram so I guess you're having a good time without me.

I frown, and Veena whips out her phone. It's just some selfies with the roommates, plus one of Seojin and Demi doing shots with me in the background, Levi sitting right next to me.

> It would just be nice if you could maybe message me once in a while.

I guess you're just off having fun with your new friends.

I'm not going to ask why so many of them are men, but think about the optics, Cassie.

It's embarrassing.

Most people wouldn't behave like that with their colleagues.

Not that this is a proper job anyway.

I suppose you're just going to ignore me now?

You know, I've spent all day worrying about how you're getting on. Distracting me from my work. You could at least treat me with some respect.

Especially when I do so much for you. Not everyone would go out with someone disabled.

Sorrel takes a sharp intake of breath, and Veena tenses next to me. There are more messages, but I've seen enough. More than enough.

How dare he weaponise my deafness, like there's something shameful about being with me?

My body feels hot with fury. I've never felt so angry before. Not even when those girls were horrible to me at the work drinks.

This is the man I've wasted months trying to please, and this is how he thinks of me? Like I'm some kind of burden.

Fuck this guy.

'If you weren't about to break up with that man, I would be about to tell you to break up with that man,' growls Sorrel.

'What a nasty little shit,' snaps Veena.

'It's bad, isn't it?' I say.

Veena spins round and takes my hands in hers. 'Has he said something like that to you before?'

'Which part?'

'Implying that he's some kind of saint for being with you?'

I don't say anything because I don't need to. The truth is written across my face.

Veena presses her lips together, walks to the balcony and shouts, 'I'M GONNA MURDER HIM!'

'Sit down, will you? You'll scare the neighbours,' says Sorrel sternly.

She stomps back over and wraps me up in a fierce hug. 'I will though. If you want me to.'

'I'll help,' agrees Sorrel.

'Thanks. I'd rather say what I need to first though.'

It takes me a long time to write what I want to say. Part of me wants to write a long essay, really chew him out. But in the end, I just send him the most important bit.

> Mason, the way you've spoken to me is absolutely disgusting. I hope you never, ever date a disabled person again. We are over. Do not contact me.

And for good measure, I block him.

The adrenaline comes out in my shaking hands and more tears, but I'm not afraid. For the first time in a long while, I stood up for myself. I *chose* myself.

I fill Vics in by text. She offers to go pick up my things from his, and as I'm about to make a list I realise there's nothing important there. After a year together. How depressing. She sends a row of heart emojis.

I suspect she might have messaged Pen to let them know what happened, because about ten minutes later both Pen and Tyra burst into the flat, adding themselves to the cuddle pile. The one time someone moves is to order pizzas, and then collect them from the front door, only for us to go right back to our nest on the couch. For maybe the first time in my life, I feel invincible thanks to the love of my friends.

Chapter Eighteen

In my post break-up funk, I had been hoping that I could throw myself into my work. But when we arrive at the studio on Monday morning, it quickly becomes apparent that something is up.

I don't know what happened before we got here, but the rest of the dancers look pretty anxious, and we're only met with a few smiles that don't meet eyes. Michael isn't here. Nor are Fenella and Giselle and the other two girls they live with.

After a little while, Pen walks in, clipboard in hand. 'Hey, guys, we'll be getting started a little later this morning. Michael's asked for you all to run warm-up together, and if he's not back by then, start some rehearsals together. You can do group critique. Thanks!'

The rest of the dancers burst into a sea of confused noise, and so I follow Pen out into the hallway, catching them by the elbow.

'What's going on?' I ask.

They look from the studio door to me, and sigh. 'I think you're going to be called in so I may as well tell you now. Michael got wind of what happened at the bar.'

My stomach sinks. They're in trouble? Everyone is going to blame me for this. This is going to totally fuck up the camaraderie of the underlings. Well, not that I necessarily had any with those girls in the first place, but this is definitely going to make that worse.

'This is all my –'

'Nope, it's not. Do you want to go talk to him?'

I shrug. 'Maybe.'

How did he find out? I asked Pen, Levi and my roommates not to tell Michael about it. God, this sucks.

Before I can decide, Michael walks up the stairs, with Giselle and the other two girls from their group in tow. The three of them walk right past me into the studio, eyes averted. Fenella is not with them.

'Michael, I –' I splutter.

He holds up his hands. 'I said from the beginning that anyone who didn't have what it takes would get cut.'

I feel like my stomach is going to fall out of my body. Does he mean me? But he walks past me and gets everyone started in the studio, so I don't have time to ask. I can't let this get in my head. After all, being an understudy is about showing up to work even when things feel rocky.

And boy, does this week feel rocky. As if the break-up wasn't enough to deal with.

But all I can do is throw myself into the work, and show Michael that I am cut out for this. Over the course of the week, it feels like something really starts to click. Yes, I've been working hard this whole time, but I feel like I've finally found my rhythm, excuse the pun.

And that's not because Fenella is gone, or because I'm not with Mason any more. I think it would be unfair to place all the blame for my low self-confidence on them, though Pen is particularly eager to – turns out my gut instinct was right there. Though saying that, working without worrying about how Fenella is going to behave or speak to me is a definite boost.

It's more that without that distraction of wondering when Mason was going to text me or what our relationship actually was, I've been able to recognise how *good* I am at this job. I can't believe he took up so much space in my head.

Michael takes us through four new songs in a week, the most new steps he's thrown at us at once, and gets us to practise 'Damask', 'Bye Bye' and 'Diamonds Under My Eyes' in between, really testing how well we've retained steps. With my intense post-break-up focus, I nail it all.

I struggle a bit with the quiet opening of 'Autumn', one of Rosa's ballads, but Michael gives me a visual cue for the start of the track, where there's quiet sparkly sounds that my cochlear implant doesn't pick up. On stage, this will be signalled by the lighting cue at the start of the song that will happen whether I'm on stage or not, which we'll practise in dress rehearsals, all arranged by Michael and the lighting team. I think if this difficulty had happened in the first week, I'd have been devastated, but three weeks in I don't feel like I'm causing a problem. It's just an access need. It helps me do my job, and doesn't interrupt anything for anyone else. I'm grateful for Michael doing the heavy lifting on the problem-solving for me, rather than just cutting me out or something. I feel like part of the team, even if the other group of girls have been ignoring me since then.

There's no more rogue bond-building tasks for now, and I think we all take a deep breath at the joy of being able to feel like we're doing it. We're *really* going to be understudies.

I do try to process everything I've been through with Mason too, but I think that will take time. We didn't have an *awful* relationship, but the more I talk it through with Pen and the others, I realise that there was a lot I needed from him that he wasn't willing, or capable, of giving. Pen keeps insisting that none of those things were big asks, and they should know given that they've been around me for basically forever. The girls agree. Logically, I get it. But it's not sunk in for me yet. That's the part that is going to need the most time, I think. It takes a lot to trust a partner at the best of times, but I think it'll take a little longer for me to rebuild that possibility for trust in someone else.

Which is why I've been avoiding Levi at work. Quite literally. I've taken to walking different routes so I don't have to go past the workshop, and avoiding him if I spot him. The other day, he was right outside the main building talking to someone, so I crawled around the side of one of the cars, hoping he wouldn't spot me. I know that Pen filled him in on what happened, so I don't know if he's giving me space on purpose. I don't hear from him immediately, which I'm glad of in a way, but he does send me a text partway through the week.

242

Let me know when you
need a new adventure x

He must have gotten my number from the Téresa Fan Club group, even though I don't tend to reply much there.

Everything I feel for him is so big and confusing that I'm scared to look at it, especially when I'm in this vulnerable, heart-battered state. A small part of me longs to run to him, bury myself in the scent of him, but even if he wanted that too, I don't want him to feel like he's a rebound. Considering I wasn't exactly upfront about Mason to start with, I suspect he wouldn't feel particularly *chosen*. And I don't want him to feel that way, if I do decide to pursue things with him.

Not that I know what *he* wants, beyond what my friends keep telling me he must be feeling. I kind of want to ask Pen about it, given they're practically best buds at this point, but I'm not ready to think about it, or know the answer. He's not told me, and that's OK. Like, now would be the worst timing for him to drop feelings, or worse, to say that he doesn't have them at all. But it does leave me in some kind of limbo there.

I probably ruined my chances with him anyway. Any time I think of him asking about Mason, about how I fantasised about kissing him just before, I cringe. What a weirdo.

It turns out that my hope that we were out of the woods for weird bonding activities was premature, and as we wrap up our session on Thursday evening Michael makes an announcement.

'Good work today, underlings. I come bearing good news. Tomorrow, you've got a day off.'

It's not just me who is unsure how to take this news. God, who else is getting fired?

'Stop looking at me like that. It's *good* news.'

We all relax, a collective breath let out.

'As things have been a little tense round here this week, Rosa insisted that you all take some time to get to know each other outside of the studio. And without quite so much alcohol,' he says pointedly. 'So, tomorrow after you've done your workouts here –'

A few groans escape.

'Hey, it's still most of a day off! After that, you'll go to a beach club for lunch.'

Pen clears their throat, and Michael gives them a look, before sighing heavily. '*We* will all be going to a beach club for lunch to get to know each other.'

'Bring your swimmers, factor 50 and a hat,' adds Pen, and I beam at them for always being the sensible one.

'Yes, yes. See you tomorrow.'

Michael leaves as we burst into excited noises. God, chilling by the pool is *exactly* what I need after working my butt, and the rest of me, off all week.

And I'm not disappointed when Bernard drops us off at the club the next day. We seem to be the first people there, because the place is empty. Just waiting for us to come and relax.

A couple of very handsome waiters stand behind a bar making cocktails under a big shaded area, dotted with barstools. Everything is wood and white canvas – I think this place might be *fancy*. No wonder Michael wanted us on our best behaviour.

There's a bright blue pool with a clear edge, infinity style, that looks out onto the beach. Loungers are dotted around in rows under umbrella shades made of palm leaves. On the sand on the other side of the bar is a volleyball pitch.

'I could get used to this,' says Veena, who is unsurprisingly in all-black – a cute sporty bikini and her signature baseball cap.

'Being waited on by hot bartenders? Or the prospect of free-flowing Fanta Limón?' asks Sorrel, peering over her giant sunglasses. She looks radiant in a plunging bikini in bright pastels, and I catch one of the bartenders checking her out.

'Baby, it's both.'

The four of us set up on a few loungers, and are immediately greeted by one of the hot waiters taking our drinks order. It's almost lunchtime, so I figure it's OK if I have a little cocktail, as I'm here. It's only right.

The raspberry daiquiri he returns with is an enormous mountain of slushy, and when I make the mistake of using a straw to suck it up I get the worst brain freeze.

'Put your tongue against the roof of your mouth, honey,' Tyra says, applying another layer of factor 50 onto her skin, even though she's wearing board shorts and a rash guard top. She looks ready to surf rather than sit by the pool.

I do so, groaning with the ache. 'Why's this always happen to me?' I moan.

It's not the most mortifying thing ever, but honestly I could have done without Levi appearing right then. 'Everything all right?'

I knew that I would most likely see him today and might have to admit that I've been kind of avoiding him and have broken up with Mason and am trying to deal with my definite unrequited crush on him.

It absolutely doesn't help that he's standing in front of me in a short-sleeved shirt, entirely unbuttoned, so I've got an eyeful of his toned stomach, and the defined lines around his hips, the hint of a V-shape that leads down under his purple shorts.

Lord save me. There is something wrong with me.

'She's got brain freeze,' Sorrel helpfully offers for me.

I nod sadly, one eye squinted shut from the ache.

'Well, I'll catch up with you when you've recovered,' he says. With a soft smile, he turns away and heads over to the bar.

'Girl, what is up with you?' asks Tyra.

I point to my forehead. 'Brain freeze.'

'I think you've got brain freeze of the more general kind.' Veena snorts.

I whip round and stick my tongue out at her, but this makes my head hurt more, so I dramatically flop back onto the lounger.

When I manage to speak, I say, 'We just haven't had a chance to properly talk.'

'So . . . talk to him now?' Sorrel suggests.

I make a noise that's somewhere between *no* and *urgh*. At least I look good – I chose a heather-coloured bikini in this cute, recycled, ribbed Lycra fabric with a high rise over the hips that makes my long legs look even longer. Weirdly, Levi and I are almost matching. Even if I'm not going to get into the water and risk nuking my implant, I can look good in swimwear. And work on my tan. And avoid looking at Levi.

Luckily, I'm saved from the girls' attempt at making me talk about my feelings by the arrival of the rest of the dancers and crew. There's a few people I recognise from Levi's workshop, and the costumiers.

I was expecting everyone to dive into the pool the minute they saw it, especially given how hot it is, but the minute the boys spot the volleyball pitch, all talk turns to making teams.

'Are you guys going to play?' I ask.

'Absolutely not, babe', 'I hate sports', and 'I'm busy relaxing' are the responses I get from Veena, Tyra and Sorrel in turn.

I've never played volleyball properly, but I'm not sure how much longer I can manage sitting in my thoughts trying to avoid looking at Levi, so I make the decision to walk over.

'Cassie, are you joining us?' Seojin asks excitedly.

'Patrick and I are captains,' Demi tells me, bouncing on his heels.

'You can't just pick who is captain,' says one of the girls who lived with Fenella, and this is the exact moment that I realise I have no idea what her name is.

'Err, I think we already did, Tori,' says Patrick.

Tori. That's it.

'How many people do we need?' I ask.

'Six per team?' Tori says to me. 'I think?'

'Room for two more?' asks Pen, as they and Levi join the crowd.

I give Levi a nervous smile and regret ever thinking I should get up and engage in some kind of bonding activity, but there we go. Too late now. It takes a little while to divvy out, but we end up with two teams: Patrick picks Seojin and his roommates Kam and Raphael, plus Pen and Levi. Tori and I go with Demi, and his other two flatmates, Whyley and Jan. We're one short, so Tori goes off to the loungers to find someone to join, and to my horror she comes back with Giselle. She doesn't even look at me.

At least we're on the same team so she can't lob a ball right at my face. Not that I particularly want to play on the same team as someone who was possibly awful about me either. I still haven't really found out what happened that night, mostly because everyone's known I just didn't want to talk about it. But it does make me wonder why Fenella is gone, and the other three are still here.

It quickly becomes apparent that none of us really know how to play beyond not letting the ball touch the floor, so we go along with that as enough rules. I take position up front near the net, and typically I find myself face to face with Levi.

'Are you ready for this, Clyne?' he says to me, and my heart does such a huge flutter that all I can do is laugh very loudly and awkwardly.

Smooth work, Cassie.

To start with, everyone is quite tentative with their

hits and throws. Like we're playing a game of catch rather than volleyball.

And then, when the ball sails high over the net to Giselle, she leaps into the air, spikes it and it lands hard in the sand on the other side.

'Woahhh,' gasps Raphael, looking down at his feet. 'She came to play.'

Giselle wipes her hands. 'I did.'

Things really kick off then. All the frustrations and exhaustion of the last few weeks burst out of us in fury for that little ball, and determination to beat the other team. Their team scores, then us twice, then Levi manages to tap it just over the net and I miss it, instead faceplanting into the sand. He's a gentleman and steps under the net to help me up, which is even worse. I get one back and screech so loudly in excitement that half the people on the loungers look over.

At nine points all, things really get intense. The boys on both teams at the back just keep lobbing it as hard as they can at each other, the ball sailing right over our heads. It goes on for so long that I start to zone out, and end up watching Levi, even though I don't mean to. I wonder what he's thinking? I wonder if he's upset that I've not really talked to him? I hope he doesn't think I'm icing him out.

Lost in my thoughts, I don't hear what someone shouts at me, and it's only when I look up that I see the ball sailing right towards my face. I don't have time to duck out of the way, and to my relief, someone jumps in front of me and spikes it away.

It's Tori. 'Are you OK? I didn't want it to hit your . . .' She searches for the words but comes up short.

I blink hard, still not quite with it. I think the last few weeks are catching up on me today. 'Yeah, I think so? Thank you.'

'Guys, let's call it a draw. It's too hot,' sighs Kam, wiping sweat from his forehead. Everyone agrees, and heads off towards the bar, but Tori stops me.

'Hey,' she says, 'I just wanted to apologise for what happened last week at the bar.'

Her other roommate, Natalie, joins us and nods. 'Same. It was unacceptable.'

'We should have stopped Fenella from saying what she did, and by staying silent we were condoning it.'

'Well, my memory is pretty fuzzy from that night,' I say, crossing my arms. 'But I remember a lot of laughter too, and that wasn't Fenella.'

'No, it was us,' admits Natalie, and Tori cringes. 'I laugh when I'm nervous. It's a horrible habit.'

'We tried to get Fenella to apologise to you, and she wouldn't, so we went to Michael about it on Monday.'

Well, that solves that mystery, I think.

'Anyway, you don't have to talk to us or anything. We get that we blew it. But we are going to try harder to show up for you, as part of our team.'

'And you don't need to accept our apology either. That's our fuck-up.'

They're both nervous, and clearly feel bad about it, but I'd rather know the truth. 'Do you agree with what she was saying?'

'Not at all,' blurts Tori. 'I came in the same way as you. I laughed along because . . .'

'You were scared of being her target, right?' I finish.

'Yeah. It's cowardly, we know.'

'It is,' I say. 'But thanks for the apologies, I appreciate it.'

And with that, I walk off. I'm not ready to forgive them, and I don't want to talk about it any more, but I feel a bit better now that they've at least tried to make amends.

I spy Veena and Sorrel in the pool, along with most of the volleyball teams and some of the crew. Tyra and Pen are both chatting in the shade, too pale to be out in the sun for very long. It's then that I spot Michael sitting at the end of the bar, drink in hand.

'Cassie, come sit,' he says, patting the stool next to him.

I sit down, and automatically the bartender asks if I want another daiquiri. 'Oh no,' I bleat, keen to avoid another brain freeze. 'I'll have whatever he's having.'

'A Moscow mule,' Michael answers.

'What is that?'

'Vodka and ginger beer.'

Blergh. I'm not sure that's better, but oh well. Too late now. 'Great.'

'I saw Tori and Natalie went to speak to you. Everything all right? They were apologising, I hope?' His face is a stern mask, not unusual for Michael, but his words seem soft for once.

'Yeah. They said they told you what happened.'

'They did. As did pretty much every other dancer on staff.'

My heart flips in my chest. 'What?'

Michael nods his head towards the pool. 'You've got a lot of people who want to stand up for and *with* you here.'

'I didn't realise,' I say as the bartender plops down my drink.

'Cassie, when I said anyone who didn't have what it takes would get cut, that includes anyone who can't work as part of a team. Fenella was not a team player, nor was she willing to accept that what she said was wrong, and I do not want that kind of person working for me or representing Rosa. Giselle is on thin ice. According to all three of them she didn't say anything near Fenella's opinions, but I want to reassure you, a single toe out of line and she's gone.'

My mouth is dry, and so I take a sip of my drink for courage. I slightly regret it, as it's extremely fizzy.

'Thank you,' I say quietly.

'You don't need to thank me, Cassie. Looking after you all is part of my job. I'm sorry that you had to hear that.'

'It's not the first time someone has been ignorant about my deafness.'

'And it might not be the last,' he says a little sadly, and I can't imagine the things he must have had said to him as a Black, gay dancer who came up in the ballroom scene in New York. 'But know that this team has your back.'

I nod, my heart swelling as I think about these people, who I've only known a month, who have stood up for me.

'Now, with all due respect, I'm off the clock.' And with that, he drops his sunglasses over his eyes, and walks off to a sun lounger as far away from the pool and the dancers as possible.

I don't really know what to do with myself. Pen is still over in the corner with Tyra, so I could go sit with them, but they seem to be having a really in-depth conversation, and I don't want to intrude. It's nice to see Pen making friends.

252

I know what I should do is go talk to Levi, especially now I don't have brain freeze. He's out of the pool, on a sun lounger drying himself off. Now is the time to talk to him, and hopefully his being partially wrapped in a towel will stop me from horning all over him so much.

'Hey,' I say as I approach him. 'Can I sit here?' I gesture to the lounger next to him.

'Please.'

'Did you have a nice swim?'

'Yeah, though a few people started playing chicken and it got a bit intense. I decided to get out of there.'

'Good idea.' I perch at the edge of the lounger next to him, too uncomfortable to lie back. I was about to move closer so I can lip-read, but he sits up and leans toward me so quickly that I feel a flutter of something in my chest. 'Hey, erm, I'm sorry I haven't replied to your text yet. I am looking forward to some more adventures. I'm just . . .'

'In the mourning period?' he offers.

'You heard, then?'

'Yeah. I'm sorry.'

'It's OK. The mourning period does suck, but was my choice, after all.'

At this, I swear he sits up a little straighter. 'Oh yeah?'

'Yeah. It just wasn't a good relationship for me. Or whatever it was. We were never exclusive, so who knows. I'm still unpacking it all.'

He nods slowly. 'You deserve more than uncertainties.'

'Yeah, I'm starting to realise that.' I smile but it's a little sad. 'Erm, and on that note. I think I need to apologise.'

'What for?'

'Just. You know.' I gesture between us. 'I think I got the wrong idea about what was happening here, and I'm sorry you had to bring up Mason to, like, remind me of normal friendship boundaries. And that's why I've been avoiding you. Sorry, it's true, I have. I was just a bit embarrassed.'

He watches me with a bemused look, and I feel even more confused.

'What?' I ask.

'Cassie,' he says, wiping his hand over his face. 'I asked you about Mason because he was in your life, and I care about you and your life.'

He hesitates, mulling over his words. I feel a prickle of heat in my stomach. Did I get this all wrong? It feels dangerous to hope.

'I like having you in my life,' he says finally. 'And I want to support you through this change, so you can talk to me, you know? It sounds like you have a lot to unpack, and you owe it to yourself to take that time.'

I nod, but my whole body feels stiff.

So that's it, then. We are just friends. We're only ever going to be just friends. And even though I knew that was the case from our hangout, hearing it confirmed again only makes it all the worse.

I'm worried about how much of that disappointment is showing on my face so I say, 'Yeah, thanks. I appreciate it. You're good to talk to.'

'And you.'

'So we're in agreement that we're good conversationalists?'

I laugh but it's so forced, and I think he can tell.

It must be so uncomfortable for him to have to brush me off, let's be real, for a second time. I'm so embarrassed, I can't believe I put him in this position again.

'Well, then,' he says, looking away from me. His eyes seem dull, for once, the shine gone. 'I'm going to get a drink. You want anything?'

I shake my head, and half-heartedly raise my glass to show I'm good, and perhaps because I don't follow him when he goes to the bar, he doesn't come back either.

Chapter Nineteen

The next Monday finds us in the studio dressed and ready to dance as normal. Only this time, when Michael and Pen come in, they're flanked by a petite blond woman in high-waisted wide-leg trousers and a blazer, carrying the biggest mobile I've ever seen. Pen has a huge, excited smile on their face, but is trying to hide it.

'Good morning, underlings,' Michael begins, and we chorus a reply of *Good morning, Michael.*

'Dancers, this is Hannah Tewksbury who does the PR for the wellness brand Hart. This week, we've got something a little different lined up for you. Over to you, Hannah.'

'Thanks, Michael,' she says, effortlessly practised at holding a room's attention. 'At Hart we are huge fans of Rosa Cordova, and you might be aware that we've worked with her for several campaigns for our products over the years. It's a long-running and fruitful relationship. When Rosa put out the open call for dancers for this tour, we were immediately interested in working on something new. And that's where you come in.'

Tyra does an excited shuffle up against me.

'We're launching a new campaign called *The Hart Inside* which will showcase all our products across a wide variety of body types and genders, highlighting that wellness and self-care truly are for everyone.' Hannah is absolutely giving us the corporate pitch, and yet there's something in her delivery that makes it feel like she just came up with this, straight from the heart. She's really good. 'Over the next few days, we're going to film a series of adverts with you guys as the stars of the campaign.'

A buzz of excited noise sounds around me, and Tyra squeezes my arm. She's worked with a lot of brands as an influencer, but never Hart. They're a huge relationship to land, with only the top models, artists and influencers working with them. This could be massive for her channel's future, and for the rest of us.

'It'll be shared across socials, and, of course, some key television spots. We can't guarantee that everyone will be featured or get particular focus, but we're keen for you all to come along and be involved.'

'You will be compensated for your time by Hart on top of your regular wage, and if anyone isn't comfortable with being in this campaign, it's not a mandatory assignment and you can let me know in private,' Michael adds, though when I glance around I can't see anyone who doesn't look extremely excited for this.

They lay out the plans for the rest of the day which involves us running through the choreo, followed by meeting the production team who are set to arrive later this afternoon. Filming will take place in one of the other buildings on site tomorrow, when we'll also meet the director.

'Oh my gosh,' gasps Tyra. 'This is a *dream*.'

'Nice of them to be upfront about all kinds of body types,' adds Sorrel.

In the back of my head, Mason's voice pipes up, questioning whether they really want that, and I chase it away by imagining I'm snarling at the horrible thought.

'Cassie, did you just growl?' asks Veena.

'Sorry,' I laugh. 'I was scaring away bad thoughts.'

'Whatever works.'

Hart have brought in their own choreographer, an American girl I recognise from Instagram called Katie Woo, who does a lot of work on dance-themed episodes of television shows. Clearly, she and Michael go way back as they greet each other with huge hugs, before getting down to work.

The choreography draws on K-pop, blended with some street, and is refreshingly different from what we've been doing for Rosa, even though with Michael I think we've touched on pretty much every dance discipline by now. The music we dance to has apparently been composed for the campaign, and the dance clocks in at only about a minute long. It's fairly simple, but has some intricate hand work, and when it's all sixteen of us dancing in sync, it looks powerful. I can just imagine how it's going to translate to screen.

Katie is clearly familiar with Seojin though I get the sense they just met. On her encouragement, he performs a solo moment, a break-dance that ends with an extremely controlled backflip. The way he moves is so *cool* that all of us are rapt, and the Hart team insist that he performs that when we start filming proper.

When he rejoins us, I give him a high-five.

We practise the choreography until Katie and Michael are happy. We've worked so hard and been so high on adrenaline all day that we all crash once we're home, which is lucky because we've got a really early start tomorrow morning.

The next day, we're dropped off on the other side of Rosa's estate at another old farmhouse building, though this one has been less extensively renovated than the ones we've been working in. The inside still has the vibes of the old barn, but a set-design team have been in and added lighting, some different backdrops, and a multi camera set-up is here, with wires taped down running across the floor. On one side of the room are rails of clothing all ready for us to wear.

We're walking onto a real set.

The thing with being an understudy is that you can never guarantee you'll be on stage in the limelight. But in here, in front of cameras, it feels like even more of a chance to be seen.

'My hair is enormous,' gasps Veena, whose sleek black hair has been put up into an Ariana Grande-style hairline-challenging high pony.

'Me too,' I agree. I'm also sporting the high pony but given I didn't have a huge amount of hair to begin with, they added a lot of extensions to make mine even near the length of hers.

The slicked-back style shows off my cochlear implant in a way that I never thought I'd be comfortable with. Well, I'm not *comfortable* necessarily, but I'm not panicking about it being on show. Especially because Hannah said there's no guarantee that we'll even be seen in the campaign. I'm happy being a background dancer, after all. That's my job.

'I cannot tell you the relief of seeing some melanin in that hair-and-makeup room,' adds Sorrel, whose natural hair has been beautifully styled in a gorgeous halo around her face. 'They actually had shades to match me.'

'Same,' says Veena. 'My face matches the rest of me for once, instead of being five shades too light.'

We're all in black bodysuits with sequins sewn into them, that catch the light as we move. It's going to look amazing on camera, though it doesn't half make me think of Mum and her obsession with *Cats*.

Once we're all dressed and buffed, we return to the backstage of the set.

The first person I spot is Levi. I'm still reeling from our conversation at the bar, and I haven't replied to his invitation to adventures text either.

He and Pen hung out at the weekend – all I've heard from Pen was a couple of pictures of Téresa and, as much as this makes me feel like a weirdo, I recognised Levi's hands in one of the photos.

I got so in my head about it all, thinking he might possibly like me, even though he very clearly does not. God, after all Mason's confusing behaviour no wonder I'm all mixed up.

I know I should have talked to my roommates about it, but Adam was over this weekend, so Veena was out the house, and Tyra was doing her own thing, and Sorrel had some freelance work come in, so I spent most of it resting. Or, let's be real, moping. But when else can you mope, if not after a break-up and repeatedly embarrassing yourself in front of the man you like?

All I can do to resolve this situation is to stop acting so weird, so I walk over to say hi.

'Hey,' he says, and I see him quickly assessing my outfit. 'Wow, you look . . . Wow.'

Heat rushes into my cheeks. 'Thanks. It's good, isn't it?'

'Yeah,' he says, and then suddenly stands straighter, looking a little past me. 'Yeah, you're all going to look really good on screen.'

The compliment is nice, but I try and push it to the back of my mind. Better to stick to the safe topic of conversation: work. 'What are you doing here?'

'Ah, I'm helping with the sets. And lifting things, you know, the usual stuff.'

If we hadn't had that awkward conversation, I'd have said 'ah, yes, you're good at that I bet.' But I can't face it now. The easy, friendly, not-quite-flirting banter we had feels impossible now. I spend too long in my head over it, until Levi eventually says. 'I think you're about to get started.' He nods behind me, where the dancers are gathering around Katie Woo.

'See you later,' I say, trotting over to join the others.

Behind one of the cameras is a woman in a wheelchair, adjusting the camera for her view. When she turns to face us, the first thing I notice is her amazing Barbie-pink silk blouse, and then I realise who she is. And I'm starstruck.

'Everyone, I'd like to introduce you to your director. The esteemed Keah Thomas,' announces Katie Woo.

261

Katie gives Keah's credits, but she needn't have bothered for me. She's an established filmmaker – started out acting on a few shows for the BBC, before moving behind the camera. The reason I discovered her was because she presented and directed a brilliant documentary for Channel 4 about the importance of Deaf culture and schools for Deaf children, as part of a long-running series about things affecting disabled people's culture and lives. After I watched that, I went through and watched all the other episodes, which touched on things like online abuse, the purposefully inaccessible benefits system, and the way disabled people are failed in healthcare. She was saying all the things I knew were true but barely heard anyone talking about, putting fact and people's stories alongside it.

Basically, she's kind of a hero to me, which is why my mouth goes completely dry.

'And she just wrapped on Rosa's next music video which we'll be dropping when you're on tour,' adds Michael.

'Making her the perfect person to handle this project,' adds Hannah, who is somehow typing on her phone without looking at it.

'It's lovely to meet you all. Let's make some good television,' Keah says, with a sharp smile.

Typically, just as one of my heroes is talking about what her vision for this campaign film is, my implant starts beeping. I know I have some batteries over in the changing room, but I can't just leave in the middle of her speaking so I try to concentrate on what she's saying. But the beeping is just too distracting.

There's a break in speaking where we seem to be briefly

dismissed, so I take the opportunity to rush off to the changing room to find my little crossbag. At first, I don't see it hanging on the hook, and it's not tucked inside my change bag either.

It's on the floor.

When I pick it up, I know something is immediately wrong. The bag is soaking wet.

'No, no, no, no,' I moan, as I reach inside and find the cardboard packaging completely soaked through. The batteries are swimming in water.

Thank God I put my phone in my bag, but still. This is bad. I can't risk putting these batteries into my cochlear implant and breaking it, even if I do have the borrowed backup processor at home.

On the bench above where it was is Giselle's enormous water bottle, which has tipped over, and leaked all over the floor. I know it's an accident, but it feels personal, after everything else that's happened.

'Cass?' I recognise Pen calling me from the door, and I rush to them, soaked battery pack in my hands. 'Ah, shit.'

'Yeah. They're running out. I didn't think to change them this morning as I was too caught up in –'

'Let me see if Levi can drive me back to yours. Hang on.'

'No, Pen –' but they're rushing across the room before I can stop them.

To my surprise, when Pen reaches Levi, he doesn't rush off to the car or tell anyone that he's got to nip out. He just reaches into the satchel slung across his side, digs through it for a second, and hands Pen something.

It's not the keys though. Totally the wrong shape. And I only realise what it is when Pen scurries back.

It's a full packet of batteries. The brand of batteries I use. I'm speechless. Why does he have these?

I look up at Pen, and they give me a shrug. 'He's just that kind of guy.'

With shaking hands, I change out the batteries and thankfully they work perfectly. I hang up my little bag in the hope that it might dry, and make a mental note to toss out my old batteries along with these wet ones when I get home.

I put the rest of the new packet inside my kit bag safely, and rush back to the group.

'You OK?' asks Tyra. 'You look flushed.'

'I'm fine,' I lie.

There's no time to think about Levi right now. I have work to do.

Standing with my colleagues in front of a real camera kind of feels like a full-circle moment. Barely two months ago, it was just me in my room with my phone camera.

Now I'm on set.

I'm being filmed for real.

I think I might have gotten a little used to being able to see myself in the screen when I'm dancing or being able to watch it back, because as we stand there and the camera gets sorted, I feel like my stomach is going to fall out of my bum.

'It's really happening,' sighs Tyra next to me. I want to squeeze her hand, tell her that we've reached an amazing new step in our career, but the crew is almost ready.

When we begin, it feels just like dancing in the studio really, though deep in my brain I'm aware that usually I'm in my hand-me-down Lululemons and not a figure-hugging bodysuit. The rest of me is as immersed in the performance as always.

The camera shoots us at all kinds of angles, and pans across us in close-ups – our faces, bodies, even our feet as we work on the intricate steps.

While we dance in the background, Seojin aces his solo. We reshoot it a couple of times just to make sure they get all the angles, and even though I've seen him work on these steps several times today, I really have to concentrate on not watching him.

Which is why I don't notice the first couple of times Katie Woo apparently tries to call me over after the last take.

'Cassie,' hisses Tyra, tapping me on the arm and tilting her head towards Katie. 'Go.'

'Me?' I say, pointing at myself while looking at Katie, who enthusiastically nods. I walk over, a little nervously. 'Hello. It's really lovely to meet you.'

'And you, Cassie. The director and I were just talking, and we'd like to do some close-up shots of just yourself.'

'Oh!' I say with genuine surprise. 'What do you want me to do?'

'We're thinking a . . . in fact, let me show you.'

Katie strides to the centre of the room, and catwalks back towards me. Despite the baseball cap and baggy joggers, she looks like she's wearing couture, strutting in non-existent heels.

'And then when you get to here,' she scuffs an X into the floor, 'turn.'

She turns just enough so that her hair flicks, and I realise it means my cochlear implant will be facing the camera.

My heart starts to race. Is this really what they want? To show off my implant?

This is a bit of a step up from being an understudy on stage because only the people in the closest seats would see it for definite . . . and then everyone on TikTok, I suppose. But still, this would be face-on. This would be . . . a statement.

'Does that sound all right?' asks Katie.

'Umm –' What do I say? I'm still processing the question, never mind the implications of it all.

In the middle of my quiet spiral, Keah comes over to me. She takes one look at me and beckons me to follow. 'Come.'

She takes us over to one side, just out of Katie's earshot, and tells me to sit down on the chair next to her.

'You're nervous?'

I nod. 'Yes. Sorry, I –'

'And I take it it's the implant being visible?'

I nod again. I feel so ignorant saying this to her, but it's the truth of how I feel.

'Now, listen,' she says kindly, taking one of my fidgeting hands in her small, thin ones. Her skin is so soft, and I can smell the lavender hand cream she must use. 'I'm about as visible as it gets, and I don't get a choice about that. And I struggled with that too, the visibility that goes with being on camera. Throughout my whole career, really. So I understand. If you want to do this, we can take it slowly.'

'Sorry,' I say, feeling the catch in my throat as I breathe out.

'My rule is no more sorries on set.'

I laugh, and instead reply, 'OK. I just . . . it's kind of you to offer more time but I don't want to be a trouble to anyone.'

'Remind me of your name?'

'Cassie. Cassie Clyne.'

'Now, Cassie. I am offering you space *to be* without any expectations. If you want to do this solo cut, then we will do it. If you change your mind, that's also fine. What I want is for you to stop trying to shrink yourself for our presumed comfort.'

I feel a blush rise on my cheeks. She's right. I spent the whole of my relationship with Mason shrinking myself, and maybe I'm doing that here too. Perhaps I got too used to being out of the way, when really I'm allowed to take up space.

I take a deep breath.

'Could you talk me through what you're thinking? With the shot, I mean,' I say.

She gives me a bright smile. 'We were thinking a dramatic zoom close-up, right at the end, to highlight the occurrence of beauty and power and disability all at the same time,' insists Keah. 'It won't be long, just an effective couple of seconds cut away. How does that sound?'

I try to picture it in my mind, and I can feel the nerves trying to creep in, anxiety whispering that my implant will fall out again, and embarrass me in front of all these new people. It's taped up as usual, but still. I worry.

I swallow, and Keah squeezes my hand.

'It's important to me in these projects to never take a pity angle, so I promise you I won't do that. What I want from this campaign is "we are hot and cool and disabled and different".' As she says this, she snaps her fingers in the air.

We share a giggle, and something lifts a little.

When I glance around the room, I see Veena giving me a covert thumbs up. Tyra beams and Sorrel shimmies a little. I can't help but look for Levi in the crowd. He's already looking at me. My heart aches at the sight of him, and I get a little thrill when he gives me a bright Levi smile.

Pen appears and hands Keah a bottle of water with a straw poking out of the top. 'Do you need anything else, Ms Thomas?'

'I'm all good, darling,' she says.

As they turn away, Pen gives me a shoulder squeeze. My friends are here, and they've got my back. I'm not alone, and in fact, I'm sitting opposite one of the greatest disabled creators of our time. I'm never going to have an opportunity like this again in my life. I can't let nerves ruin this. And Keah is the best placed to position me and my deafness. I have to do this.

Time to shimmer.

Time to show them who I am.

'Yes,' I say, snakes squirming in my stomach. 'Yes, let's do it.'

Swallowing down the burst of *ohmygodiloveyou* I want to yell at Keah, I follow Katie's directions, making sure I know my mark. When I stop and spin, I feel my enormous ponytail swish behind me, but it doesn't go so far as to cover the implant.

'Perfection, darling,' calls Keah. 'Let's commit that to film.'

We take it a few times and then Keah calls it a day.

'Thank you,' I say to her. 'It means a lot. From you, especially.'

She gives me a sweet, knowing smile which saves me from gushing everything I want to say. 'We have to carve our own futures, and break the barriers. Society will always be surprised by what we can do, so why not surprise them on our own terms?'

With one final wink, Keah sends me back to the understudies. I hear her call Sorrel from the line-up to do a short choreo segment, similar to Seojin's – though no backflips. Sorrel is such a pro that she gets it in a couple of takes.

The whole thing is done in one admittedly long day, and I'm a little sad to part with my bodysuit at the end of it. I feel like we went through something together. Plus, Levi really seemed to like it.

'I'm going to miss you,' whines Veena as she hangs the bodysuit back up on the rail. 'What are they going to do with these afterwards anyway?'

'We're taking them with us,' says Pen, putting a protective cover over the rack ready for it to be wheeled away. 'Backup costumes for just in case.'

Veena blows out her cheeks. 'Well, that's annoyingly sensible.'

'Why don't we go get some dinner? Y'all can mourn your bodysuits and we can celebrate?' Tyra suggests.

'What are we celebrating?' I ask.

Tyra shrugs. 'It's Sorrel's birthday, isn't it?'

Veena and I shriek, while Sorrel rolls her eyes. 'Yes, it's my birthday.'

'Do you not like birthdays?' I ask.

'I'm not totally ambivalent. I kind of celebrate it over the turning of the year. Celebrating me with every step.'

'You're such a hippy,' says Veena, slinging her arm around Sorrel.

'I'm just magical, actually.'

'Precisely why we should go out to celebrate,' Tyra insists, kissing her on the cheek.

With a snap of the brakes, Pen starts wheeling the outfits away.

'Are you coming too?' I shout.

They reply with just a thumbs up.

'I'll text you,' I add.

I'm almost positive there was a red flush across their face. I wonder what that was about . . .

Chapter Twenty

Once we've showered and changed into cute outfits for dinner, we walk down to the beach, to a seafood restaurant that Pen had sent us a location to.

The sun is heavy and low in the sky.

'This is so romantic,' swoons Veena, grabbing my hand. She gets down on one knee and a passing couple stop to stare at us, the lady resting her hand on her chest in delight at seeing an in-the-wild proposal. 'Cassie Clyne! Love of my life!'

'Stop that,' I laugh, yanking her up to her feet.

The woman looks genuinely disappointed so I give her an apology wave, while Veena skips along snickering.

'You're a menace.'

'Pretend public proposals are my favourite thing to do.'

'Oh, I know,' says Sorrel. 'She got me three times at the supermarket last week. Once when I was trying to pay. The checkout girl looked so confused.'

'It's the best game in the world.'

'Did Adam propose to you in public?' Tyra asks, but at this Veena snorts.

'No, thank God. Can you imagine? I would have thought it was a bit much.'

We arrive at the restaurant – a small, family-owned place right on the seafront, so we can listen to the sound of the waves as we eat. The waitress leads us to the outdoor seating and gives us today's menu with a few different options fresh off the boats.

'Those moules frites have my name on them,' confirms Veena, putting the menu down.

I wave over Pen, who walks inside the restaurant looking for us. 'Hello, campers,' they say, sitting down between Veena and Sorrel. 'What did I miss?'

'Veena tried to propose to Cassie,' says Tyra.

'Veena?!' They dramatically clutch at their chest over their heart. 'Love of my life, why would you do this to me?'

'You turned me down,' she huffs. 'Twice.'

'Wow, you really got everyone,' I laugh.

'Not me,' says Tyra with a little bit of annoyance. Naturally, Veena takes this cue to get out of her chair, and Tyra fixes her with a glare. 'Don't even *think* about it.'

'You're right. I'll wait until the restaurant is full.'

'Menace!'

We order drinks and our food at once, and we're all grateful when the waitress immediately brings us fresh bread with oil and vinegar to dip. All of us bar Pen descend on the breadbasket almost as soon as she's put it down, like we've not eaten for weeks.

'I think we could take another of those,' Pen says to the waitress, who looks a bit nervous about our devouring, like she might need to warn the chefs we're going to eat everything they have.

'Come on, tell us how Adam actually asked you?' I say.

The cutest thing about Veena is the way she goes all coy when she talks about Adam. The rest of the time she's so blunt, or the epitome of the smiling devil-face emoji, that I'm never sure how she really feels about things. But it's clear how much she loves Adam.

'He did it the traditional way, I suppose. We went out for dinner in central London, got a bit drunk, walked down the Thames in the middle of the night and when we sat down on a bench for a breather, he just asked me. There was no one else around. Just us and the stars hidden behind the Zone 1 pollution.'

'Awww. That's so cutesy,' says Tyra.

'Tyra loves pollution and hates the Earth, confirmed!' The old Veena doesn't take much encouragement to return.

'I take it all back. You are a menace.'

'So still semi-public?' I say.

'No, no, the rules of a public proposal are that it has to be in, like, an area full of people who can watch, plus maybe with a flash mob.'

'Gosh, remember flash mobs? I used to think that was the height of romance,' sighs Pen.

'Is that why you're always hanging around dancers?' giggles Veena.

Just for a second, Tyra stiffens next to me.

'Are you OK?' I ask.

'Yeah, honey,' she says. 'Why?'

'Oh, nothing. I just wanted to check. It's been a busy few days.'

She gives me a soft smile. 'Don't worry. Brain is OK. Just a bit chilly.'

I reach across to take her jacket from the back of her chair and drape it over her shoulders.

'Thanks, sweetheart.'

'Now, talking about romance,' says Sorrel. 'Cassie?'

'What?' I laugh awkwardly. 'I'm still just-dumped.'

'No, no, you're the dumper. It doesn't count,' insists Veena, digging into the second basket of bread.

'It does count.'

'Isn't Adam your first boyfriend turned husband?' asks Sorrel.

'Yes.'

'So you're intimately familiar with the rules of dating.'

'I watch a lot of dating shows. It's basically the same.'

The others clearly do not agree, but don't challenge it.

She swings her gaze round to me and I feel, very seriously, like I might have a spotlight on me. 'We should talk about Levi though.'

I groan. 'There's nothing to say!'

They all fix me with a look that says *bullshit*. Well, Tyra would probably find a politer way to say it, but still. That vibe is being very clearly communicated from all angles.

'Urgh, well. I may have gotten confused about the whole situation.'

'How so?' asks Tyra.

'When we went on that hangout, he asked me about Mason,

right? And I realised he was doing this whole *I'm drawing a line and reminding you we are just friends* thing, because I think the silly banter we had was like crossing a line. At the beach club last week, I apologised to him for like . . . getting the wrong idea about that.'

'So you apologised for liking him?' asks Sorrel, clearly baffled that someone would do this.

'Well, yeah, because I made it weird. He doesn't like me that way.'

'Well, obviously he does,' says Pen, and everyone turns to look at them, waiting for more.

'No, he doesn't, Pen,' I sigh. 'If he did, he would have told me then.'

They shake their head as they sip their beer. 'No, he wouldn't.'

'Why's that?' asks Tyra.

'Because she's in the mourning period,' Pen says, eerily echoing the words I used in that exact conversation with Levi.

'Oh, bless his heart. He's a gentleman.'

'He said that to you?' I ask, not quite believing what they're saying.

'Well, over the time I've known him he's asked about all the things you like and what your favourite foods are, so either he's into you or about to throw you a surprise birthday party.'

'Pen.'

'Yes?'

'Did he tell you he liked me?'

They let out a groan.

'I'm pulling bestie privileges here,' I insist.

'Yes. He obviously is not going to have a conversation with you about it just after you broke up with Mason because he's a good guy, but yeah. I'm certain that he likes you, Cass.'

'Oh,' I gasp.

He didn't want to pressure me. What was it he said? I deserved the time to unpack it. He was giving me space. Oh no, I am a total idiot.

'When is your birthday?' Sorrel asks casually, as though we're not having a life-changing conversation right now.

'February twenty-fourth,' I answer automatically.

'Hmm, Pisces. Makes sense,' she says. 'You're in your own head a lot.'

'What's that got to do with anything?'

'You're overthinking.' Tyra taps the centre of my forehead. 'We can see it all whirring in there.'

My cheeks flush. 'Sorry.'

'You don't need to apologise. We just know your tells now.'

'Are you *sure* he likes me?' I ask Pen.

They roll their eyes. 'When have I ever been wrong?'

'Well, you did let her go out with Mason,' says Tyra.

'Oops,' says Sorrel, as the air goes kind of frosty.

Pen breaks up a piece of bread into very small pieces. 'I'm not in charge of Cassie's life. She can do what she wants.'

'Besides, I kind of knew Pen didn't love Mason,' I jump in. 'But at the beginning I just thought that was us both being codependent and disliking change.'

'Rude but fair,' Pen agrees.

'Wait, so Levi was fishing for info about Mason on your date-not-date?' Tyra asks.

'I mean you barely brought him up with us,' says Veena. 'But somehow, you thought that was him telling you to back off, instead of saying, "Please come kiss me instead, I'm very tall and pretty."'

I can feel my face burning, and I'm briefly saved by the waiters bringing our meals. I'm thankful that I can fiddle with the fresh clam pasta dish and not look them in the eyes when I say, 'Well, I didn't tell him to start with.'

'Uh-oh.'

'And the reason I thought that was because when he asked me about Mason . . . Well, it was right as I was thinking about maybe kissing him.'

'UH-OH,' repeats Veena, much louder, and we have to shush her because the other restaurant patrons all turn to look.

'Is Levi psychic now?' asks Sorrel, raising her eyebrow.

'Well. No.'

'OK, so you weren't upfront about the man who kept insisting he wasn't your boyfriend.' Tyra shrugs, and her putting it like that makes my stomach squirm. 'He'll understand that.'

'You've already explained most of that to him,' Pen says. 'You're overthinking it again.'

Tyra nods eagerly in agreement.

'What does he not know at this point?' laughs Veena.

'That Cassie likes him, which is the whole problem!' says Pen. 'Obviously I didn't tell him that.'

I slump in my seat.

'What's going on in there?' Sorrel asks, gently poking me on the forehead. 'You're whirring again.'

'I'm just . . . there's so much that's happened, that I feel like I'm running to catch up. I keep misunderstanding things, and I'm constantly having to rewrite the truth. I feel like I can't trust my own judgement! I'm glad I have you guys to unpack it with, but it's just a lot.'

'Is one of the things you're worrying about him being awful with the disability stuff?' asks Tyra. 'After Mason's texts, it would be understandable.'

At the mention of his name, Veena growls.

I sigh. 'Yes, but I think it's my own irrational hang-ups. He's been so great on all that. I mean, guys, he had batteries for my implant just in his bag.'

'I sense a *but*?' Sorrel says.

I nod, shrug, move in a non-committal way so I don't have to say yes out loud.

'I get it, hon. I really do,' Tyra says. 'It's hard to trust someone is always going to be good about stuff, right?'

That's exactly it. 'I'm sorry that you know how it feels.'

She shrugs, but I can sense war wounds under there. 'But let's consider the evidence. He's been pretty great so far and you even told him all about how your implant works, right? Do you think that maybe you're carrying over some of the hurt that Mason left you with, and applying it to him unfairly?'

My stomach sinks. 'Yes. It's ridiculous, I know it is. I'm just a bit . . . scared. What if I'm wrong *again*?'

Tyra reaches over and strokes my forearm. 'I don't think you are, hon. He looks at you like you're the last slice of pie.'

'What else is wrong with him?' Veena asks. 'Does he have bad breath? Does he play golf? Is he a very bad DJ?'

'Nothing,' I say, trying to hold back the smile threatening to burst across my face. 'He's kind of perfect really.'

No one says anything and when I look up they're giving me the kind of look that you might give a puppy.

'Don't you think it's too soon?' I ask.

'Only you can answer that,' says Sorrel. 'Does it feel too soon?'

'No.' I blurt it out before I can hold it back.

The truth is, I can't stop thinking about him.

I tried to keep this all down and bury it deep inside my chest so that I could get on with getting over Mason. But I think in some ways, I already was over him, and I'm not sure that really had anything to do with Levi. I think, in my heart, I knew what we had was over when I got the job and he didn't want to celebrate with me. He didn't like the idea of me changing. I just felt I needed to get over the hurt, the damage he wrought at the end, and before, so I swept myself away into a neat box. Like he'd do to me.

And my friends are right. I have been overthinking this, all of this. Overthinking how much time Mason deserved in my head. What is a mourning period if you have nothing left to mourn?

And Levi . . . Levi has been so good. So, so good. And he makes me feel good. That's what made me realise I was falling for him in the first place. The kind of guy who keeps spare batteries, who picks you up for adventures, who respects your feelings first. He feels rare. Special. I don't want to let him get away from me, and I don't want to squash down all my feelings any more.

I want to tell Levi how I feel.

When I look up from my plate, Pen meets my eyes across the table. They mouth 'go' and I get up.

And I run. I just start running down the beachfront in the direction of Levi's place, thankful that I wore trainers to dinner. Though I realise I have no idea what building he actually lives in.

To my relief, my phone buzzes and it's Pen dropping me a location pin to Levi's place with his address. He's not far away, especially not at the pace I'm running.

It's silly and dramatic to run to him, but the buzzing in my limbs tells me I have to. I have to tell him how I feel right now. It's like that moment from *When Harry Met Sally* – when you know you're in love with someone and you want the rest of your life with them to start right away. That's how it feels.

I want this new part of my life to start right now. The part where I tell Levi that I want him. And I ask if he wants me and hopefully, he says yes.

Perhaps I'm just setting myself up for more heartbreak, but I know now what I've been trying to figure out this whole time – that it's worth the risk that this could work out. We could be something real. Something true. The passion, the spark between us demands to be felt. I'm choosing it.

I get to the building not too out of breath, and make a note to thank Michael for all his insistence on hard work on my cardio in the early weeks of us being out here. There's sweat on my upper lip and my top is probably damp too, but I just don't care. My mind is so focused on getting to Levi that my heart beats his name.

I race up the stairs to his apartment, and after a deep breath, I knock on the door. Time slows as I wait, but there's no answer.

I knock again, and once more.

But there's still no movement from inside. No one comes to the door.

He's not here.

I feel so deflated. I was ready! I geared myself up to tell him that I like him, and he's not here!

'Fuck,' I groan.

If I was Sorrel I'd probably consult the stars or blame mercury in lemonade or something. As it's me, all I can do is leave.

Except, when I turn, he's there, standing in the hallway holding a bag of groceries. That beautiful broad man with intense sparkling eyes. He's here.

'Hi?' There's a flicker of a smile at the corner of his mouth that sends my heart racing.

He's here.

'Hi,' I say.

'What are you –'

'Do you like me?' I blurt out, taking a step towards him.

'Yes.' He looks a bit confused but like he'll go along with it.

'Not just like a friend.' It comes out too quiet, like I'm afraid to say it. But I have to be bold. I ran here, for fuck's

281

sake. I take a deep breath and steady myself to ask him once and for all. 'Do you like me as more than a friend? Forget the mourning period. I just need to know. Do you?'

The corner of his mouth twitches, and he walks closer to me. I can smell him now, that ever-present scent of sawdust, and oud and liquorice. My heart thunders in my chest.

The smile grows. 'Cassie, are you asking if I *like-you* like you?'

He's so close to me now that I could just reach across the tiny gap between us, and kiss him. My eyes keep darting to his lips, his beautiful full lips, that I desperately want to touch.

Can he hear how hard my heart is beating?

'Don't tease me. Please. Just tell me.'

His dark eyes lock on mine, and when he speaks, it's a growl that I feel through my body. 'I didn't realise I was teasing you.'

'I think you do,' I gasp.

My heart is hoping, so desperately hoping that he's going to tell me how he feels. I need that clarity.

His eyes sparkle and he licks his teeth, as if weighing up what to do. 'Cassie, I didn't think I needed to spell out to you that I've thought about you non-stop since I saw you at the airport.'

'Spell it,' I whisper.

'All right,' he says, stepping closer. He brushes a strand of hair from my clammy forehead, runs his hand down the side of my jaw and tilts my chin up, just a little bit. 'Cassie, I adore you.'

When our lips meet, I melt. I'm not sure who moves first,

or if we move together, but we kiss. He opens his mouth and I kiss him deeper, relishing the sweet, delicious taste of him. I run my fingers through his hair, up the back of his neck, and he lets out a groan when I press my body up against him. At some point I realise he's lost the grocery bag because his hands are all over me.

I've wanted this for so long. Longer than I could ever admit to myself. And I don't care that I'm standing in a corridor of an apartment building with groceries all over the floor, because I'm kissing Levi.

We break apart, just for a second to catch our breath.

'Wow,' I say.

'I take it the *like*-you-like-you is reciprocated, then?'

'Oh yes, very much so.'

'I'm glad we got that cleared up.' He leans forward to kiss me some more but I, very reluctantly, put a finger to his lips. 'Cassie, are you shushing me?' He tilts his head and moves back ever so slightly so we can look at each other. It aches to be separated from him when I could still be kissing him, but I need to think with my head not my . . . other parts.

'No, I just . . . I want us to have a date. A proper date. I know most people would consider hanging out in a cove together, alone, for like nine hours was probably a date but –'

'It wasn't a date. It just had date vibes.'

'The aesthetic of a date.'

'Sure. That wasn't intentional by the way. I really was just trying to be a good friend.'

'I know. I believe you. Which is why I want us to knowingly go on a date together. Have everything clear and in the open this time.'

He nods. 'That sounds great to me. When?'

'Tomorrow night?'

I feel a rumble in his chest. 'I was hoping you'd say now so I didn't have to wait to kiss you more.'

Goosebumps run over my body and I desperately want to press him up against his front door and kiss the sense out of him.

'Friday,' I say. 'After work. Let's go to dinner. Though I'll need time to change. You don't want to take me out in my dance clothes.'

'I think I'd love you in whatever you wore.'

My heart skips a beat when he doesn't hesitate over that word.

'I know a place. I'll call and book,' he says.

'Another recommendation from Martin?'

'The man has good taste.'

'OK, Friday. At Martin's mysterious recommendation.'

'Friday.'

I sigh. 'I'm going to go home now.'

'I was worried you'd say that.' His hands find my waist again, gently, softly holding me in place. 'Don't go.'

'I should.'

'I know.'

'Absence makes the heart grow fonder.'

I stay long enough to help him put all the spilled groceries back into his carrier bag, but make sure to run before he can get his key in the door. If I hesitated there's no saying what I'd do.

There's so much I want to do with him.

But I want this first. One date, one evening where we're both on the same page, and then maybe I'll let myself give in.

I can still taste him on my lips when I get through my front door, and at seeing my flushed cheeks and kiss-bitten mouth, everyone cheers.

Chapter Twenty-one

That Friday night, I open the door to our apartment expecting Levi come to pick me up for our date. Except it's Pen who stands there, waiting.

'Hello?'

'Hiya. I've come to swap.'

'Swap?'

'One Cassie Clyne for one Pen Jones for the evening.'

'Oh, good,' says Tyra, dragging Pen into the flat. 'I thought you were going to be late for dinner. Veena is cooking.'

'Glad to see you all getting on so well without me,' I shout as they disappear into the kitchen.

I start to close the door, but a hand reaches out to stop it. Levi sidesteps into view, dressed in a linen shirt rolled up at the elbows, and a pair of chinos. He looks good. Really good.

'Were you hiding?' I ask.

'Only a little bit. I was worried what might happen if your flatmates caught wind of me being here.'

'You tease. What if I shut the door and thought you'd bailed?'

'I'd never bail. Plus, in that situation, I figure I'd just

knock on the door like most people do.'

'Good point.'

He takes my hand and raises it above my head, so that I spin to show off my outfit. The periwinkle blue dress I picked out is fitted around the body and then flows out in sheer waves, with a big split up one side, showing off my tanned legs. I wore my hair down, but curled and pinned back at the side with a moon-shaped clip Veena lent me. At first, I almost put it on the side where I don't have my implant, but instead I pinned my hair back around the implant, putting it on full show. *Disability and beauty coexisting*, just like Keah said.

'You look beautiful.'

I really *feel* beautiful. I know I look good in this dress. But then there's the way Levi looks at me, like I'm a glass of water in the desert.

'Ready to go?'

'Yes. Bye, everyone!'

There's a chorus of *bye*s as we shut the door. I'm nervous about tripping down the stairs in my dress, so we take the lift and I'm so desperately conscious of how we're in a tiny box together. He's so close.

Neither of us look at each other, and it somehow feels like the most excruciating trip downstairs of my life, especially as just before the lift doors spring open I swear his pinkie finger touches mine.

It's hard to breathe.

His car is parked right out front, and like a true gentleman, he goes to open the door for me. As I try to sit down as elegantly as possible, I catch Levi awkwardly laughing.

'What?' I ask. 'I think I did that pretty gracefully.'

'Not you. You're perfect.'

I kind of hate the thrill that sends through my body.

He gets into the driver's seat, and points above us. 'I'm pretty sure one of your gang just shouted down something about the importance of birth control.'

As we drive away, I risk a glance in the wing mirror up to the balcony of our flat, and see the four of them waving us off like we've just got married. They're so ridiculous.

'It's like having my parents here,' I say.

'Are they also intense and overly invested in your personal life?'

'A little. They're just very supportive of me, and Pen too, given they're practically family. What about yours?'

'Eh, I speak to my dad a bit. We don't have a lot in common but he loves rugby so I try and keep up with it, you know? Something to talk about. He's closer with my little brother, Ezra. They still work together.'

I notice he doesn't mention his mum, and has never mentioned her. I take a leaf from his book and leave the space, just in case he wants to fill it himself.

Eventually, he does.

'My mam died a few months after I was born. Ovarian cancer. I think they might have known while she was pregnant. Just bad luck.'

'What was her name?'

'Rachel. She's who I get the thick hair from. Sometimes I'll be doing something, and Dad'll say *ah, that's your mother there*, so I know I take after her a bit too. It's strange knowing you have traits of someone you don't remember, but I like it too. Keeps her alive in me.'

'That's so nice. I'm sorry you didn't get to know her.'

'Ah, me too. She used to take in all the waifs and strays – not just pets, people too. My dad kept that up a bit as I was growing up, where he could. But it's only really been the three of us. No stepmum either, though he dated a little when we were younger. He's just a very self-contained man, I think. Happy with his life as it is.'

'That's the aim, isn't it? Being that happy in your own life no matter how it looks.'

'Yeah, I think so. He goes on enough holidays with his friends, and he's got Ez with him a lot, so I know he's not lonely. He's just living his own path, and that doesn't have to mean re-marrying for the sake of it.'

'Do you think he'll fly out and see you?'

'I think when we get to Paris for the first show of the tour he'll come down on the train from Manchester, yeah, I offered to get him a hotel room, but he said no when he found out the company was already paying for one for me, because why pay for two? Insisted that if it's just one double we top and tail like we did when I was a kid. Heart of gold, but unless the money is going to someone who needs help, he could peel an orange in his pocket. Never knowingly paid for anything unnecessary.'

I laugh hard. 'I look forward to meeting him. Do you look like him?'

'Hey, now, don't you be making moves on my dad before we've even had our first date.'

'Got to keep my options open. He sounds canny with his finances, at least.' I wink at him and he smirks.

'What else could a woman want?'

As we pull into a car park alongside a marina, my heart whispers *you*.

Typically, when we park up, Levi nips round the side of the car to help me out. As I do, I glance at his glove box wondering if his lyrics notebook is still in there.

He drops my hand as I stand, and I fight the urge to take it back. For just a moment, he rests his hand in the small of my back as we walk on, and my body sings.

'Been writing anything new?' I ask, trying to maintain my composure.

He smiles over at me. 'Aye, I've had a bit of inspiration, you know? Lots of feelings.'

'I can imagine trying to have a conversation with me when I had brain freeze from drinking a daiquiri too fast was a major spark for you.'

'It was but you wouldn't believe how few words rhyme with daiquiri.'

Bone-white sailing boats bob in the water, and as we walk down the boardwalk that runs along the little marina, I relish how wonderfully quiet it is. There's hardly anyone here, but somehow that makes it even more special. It's like the world opened up a space just for us to exist together.

The restaurant sits over the water on wooden decking. The waiter leads us to a table in a corner strung with rows of golden lights. We're right over the sea, and on the table the furthest away from the kitchens. Levi holds my chair out for me to sit, before sitting himself.

'Is this OK? I wanted to make sure if it was noisy inside you'd be able to hear better. Though it turns out I may have inadvertently bagged us an entire restaurant just for the two of us.'

'And there was me thinking you were flashing the cash, booking out a whole place.'

'Please, I am still my father's son.'

We both laugh.

'This is great,' I say. 'Thank you for thinking of the sound factor.'

A little candle in a jar sits on the table between us, adding to the golden glow. Under the warm lights, Levi looks sun-kissed.

'Don't thank me too early. I did bring you to a restaurant that predominantly serves garlic and fish.'

I giggle as the flush spreads over my cheeks. 'It doesn't matter, if we're both eating it.'

'True. We can both be disgusting.'

'Or delicious? Unless you brought me to a bad restaurant.'

'Ah, no, it's great here. And you're right, I like your optimistic thinking.'

'And yet you're the one who's already thinking about what happens after dinner.'

'Ah, now,' he says, his face going serious for a second. As though he wants to concentrate on his words, he drops his eyes, focusing on the empty table setting in front of him. Slowly, he says, 'I want to be clear that whatever this is, we can go as slow as you like and I never want you to feel pressured or –'

'Levi.'

'Yes?' He doesn't look up yet.

'While your thoughts on consent are very important, I think the waiter just wants to hear your order,' I say.

He looks up with the brightest, reddest face. And when he realises that I've just tricked him, he breaks into the biggest smile and tries to flick me across the table. 'Oh, well, now I feel like a total muppet.'

I laugh so hard I have to gasp for air. 'Sorry, that was too easy.'

'I was being serious!'

'I know, I know. But that's why it was *especially* fun for me.'

Levi pretends to get out of his seat. 'I'll be off, then.'

'Stop!' I squeal.

'I'll get you back for that, you know,' he promises.

'Sorry. But I appreciate it, what you were saying.'

'Oh, you do now?'

Levi shakes his head as he picks up his menu, but he can't hide the hint of a smile. As if to make it doubly clear, he reaches his hand across the table and takes mine, threading our fingers together. My heart flutters and I try my hardest to read what's on the menu, but the heat in his electric touch is mesmerising.

When the waiter does finally arrive, I'm still so garbled from the surge of hormones racing through my body at the idea of kissing him later that I have almost no idea what to order. The waiter tells us that they have some fresh fish caught that afternoon, to be cooked slowly and simply in olive oil. It sounds so good that we both order that.

'I don't think I've ever eaten a fresh fish like that before,' I say. 'Please don't judge me if I throw fish bones everywhere.'

'Just drop them through the crack in the wood and you'll be fine. Like you're returning it to the sea.'

'That's like making a tiny graveyard.'

'True. A warning sign for other fishes to stay clear.'

'Do not enter, or you'll get eaten.'

'The plot of *Finding Nemo III* is going to be very dark at this rate.'

We cheers our glasses of prosecco – another suggestion from the waiter, who periodically appears to top up our ice-cold water or leave us a new item of cutlery.

'This is like having a personal staff,' I say. 'Are you sure this isn't how you always live?'

'Sadly, no,' he laughs. 'I don't think I could though. I keep feeling self-conscious, like I ought to get up and help him fill the saltshakers.'

'Can I ask you something?' I say.

'About the saltshakers?'

'Surprisingly, no.'

'That is a surprise. But go on.'

'Did I upset you by not telling you about Mason straight away?'

He gazes out to sea. 'I wouldn't say *upset*. I was disappointed that you were with someone, but like, when I said I just wanted to get to know you because I liked hanging out with you, I meant that.'

'I still should have told you. Though, I don't know, I just

thought it was all an unreciprocated crush on my part. I think I was in denial about it all.'

'And now?'

'You're obviously obsessed with me.' I could never imagine saying this to anyone else, but he makes me feel so confident, so *me*.

He laughs loudly. 'That's true. I did take you on a full-day non-date. I tried to keep it subtle, but I'm not sure I managed so well. I just didn't want it to cloud our friendship, and if things were going to happen, I wanted it to happen with us both on the same page.'

I know what I need to ask, but the question lodges in my throat for a few seconds. 'What do you want, Levi?'

'Can we narrow the scope of the question a little? Do you mean right now or for my future?'

'Both, I suppose. I know it feels a bit . . . intense, but I want to know that we have that compatibility, before we get too deep. I spent a year with Mason not knowing where I stood or where our relationship was going, and I just don't want to put myself through that again.'

He gives me a soft look. 'That's still a very big question. But I suppose, to be happy. To have a life that feels full of love. I want to travel and do things I enjoy. Preferably with the person I love.' He looks at me meaningfully. 'You?'

I take a deep breath, because what I want to say feels so huge and important to me, something I've only just started to believe in, that I'm worried his response could be the end of this before it even begins. But I have to be honest about where I'm at in my life and what matters to me, or

I'm going to be in another relationship that ultimately does nothing for me.

'I think . . . I think that now I've got my foot in the door, I really want to keep going with my dancing. I never thought I'd have the opportunity to have a job like this, so I think I'm still kind of catching up to myself. But it really matters to me, and I think I'm good at it. Plus there's not many deaf dancers out there, so that feels important. It might not go anywhere beyond this job, and if so that's fine. I still had the experience. But it would be wrong to squander the chance to keep going.'

'I completely agree,' Levi says. 'Whatever you want to do, you should do it. The opportunities that could come your way are there for the taking, Cassie. All I hear from the staff who aren't dancers is how hard a worker you are, and how much you respect everyone. People notice that, and remember.'

'And you wouldn't mind that?'

'Mind what?'

'Me working wherever, whenever. Sorry to quote Shakira,' I say, laughing a little nervously. He can't possibly be saying what I think he is, can he? 'If I go for this and start building up my portfolio and references, I'll have a lot less choice about *where* I get to work, so . . .'

'We'd be apart a lot, is what you're saying.'

'Yeah.'

I feel guilty for throwing this at him already.

'I think that's fine, Cassie.'

'Really?'

'Yeah, like, sure, any distance will be hard, I'm not

doubting that. But I want you to take any opportunity that presents itself to you. I'll likely be doing the same.'

I nod.

'I just see it as possible that we could do that and *still* be a partnership, of whatever kind.'

'A partnership?' I ask, raising my eyebrow.

'Well, all right, that does sound a little like we're opening a law firm. What do *you* want, Cassie? I want you to be able to tell me these things.'

'A relationship,' I say, feeling light, like I can breathe out. I could never have imagined saying this to Mason. 'For us to be boyfriend and girlfriend. This seems kind of wild to say on a first date, but . . . it's really important for me to know where we stand from the off.'

He nods. 'That's what I want too. And I want us to grow together, and that means working through life logistics. That's part of the whole deal.'

I finally breathe out. 'I just wanted to make that clear before we, you know, got further into this.'

'Cassie,' Levi says, his eyes soft. 'Look at me. I'm all in already.'

I squeeze his hand even though mine is shaking. 'Me too.'

'Good. Then we're in agreement.'

A few more people have entered the restaurant, so it's not just us any more, but the waiter sits us all far apart enough that it still feels special, and I don't have to fight to hear Levi.

'You know, you declared your undying all-in for me quite early on in the date. You've not seen me try to dismantle a whole fish yet. Perhaps you'll change your mind.'

'Oh, man, did we agree no backsies?'

'No backsies,' I say solemnly.

'Well, it's a good job that I don't think anything will turn me off you.'

The fish arrives and I'm relieved when the waiter neatly fillets them both for us at the table. They've been cooked in olive oil and salt and herbs, and the meat is so light and flaky that every mouthful is heaven.

'I am a little sad that I didn't get to watch you take that thing apart,' Levi says in between bites.

'I told you. I think you would have changed your mind.'

'Impossible.'

At this, he picks a tiny bone off his tongue.

'One for the graveyard?' I say as he puts it on the side of his plate.

'We'll inter them all later. Anyway, you could have been turned off by my fish carving too.'

'Carving?' I laugh. 'I don't think it's called that. Plus, you'd have attacked it with an engineer's laser focus while I'd have probably just had to use my hands.'

'Hot. How did you know I was into that specifically?'

I snort with laughter.

'*Double* hot.'

'Oh no, my snort is embarrassing.'

'It's not. It means I've tickled you, which pleases me.'

There's something about those words. Tickle. Please. I feel a heat gather in my body.

I want him. I really want him.

When the waiter takes our plates, Levi asks, 'Do you want dessert?'

That heat is still pulsing through me, so I say, 'Do you have anything at home?'

'I'm sure there's a half-melted KitKat Chunky in my carry-on.'

'How romantic.'

'Only the best for you,' he says.

Just as he says that, out of seemingly nowhere, music strikes up from a string quartet. I feel the deep thrumming of the cello through my body. I can't believe it. Live music by the water, while we're under the stars. It's too romantic.

An older couple get up and start to dance, and to my surprise, I realise it's the people I saw on the beach the day Levi found me. Maybe it's a sign that I made the right choice. Choosing myself *and* Levi and us together.

'Come on, let's dance,' I say, getting to my feet.

'Oh no.' Despite his protests, he still stands. He's too much of a gentleman to leave me hanging.

'No?'

'I will if you want me to, but I need to warn you that I really cannot dance.'

'Everyone can dance.'

'That's what they said before they saw me.'

I take his hand. 'Let me show you.'

'Right here?'

'Where else?'

'OK, then.' He leads me to the boardwalk, just so we're out of the way of the tables and the other patrons. I place his other hand on the small of my back, and I step us close together.

'You're supposed to lead,' I say.

'Oh, you don't want that. And that's not me being polite. I just genuinely do not know how.'

'I'll show you.'

I teach him how to step forward, forward, back, back, in a simple little square and the poor boy was not kidding. He lifts each foot too high, as though it's the first time he's moved them this way, and when I giggle he starts to exaggerate it for effect and we have to stop because I'm laughing too much.

'OK, no footwork for a minute. Let's just sway.'

'Sway I can do,' he laughs, and pulls me tight against him.

'Feel the music. Follow the way it moves.'

I can feel his heart thudding in his chest, as I nuzzle my head in against the dip under his chin. I want to plant a kiss right there above his Adam's apple, and I make a note to do it later if I get the opportunity.

The song changes to something a little livelier, and we return to our gentle not-quite-waltzing. Levi gets braver, and tries the footwork again. I want to praise him, but I'm lost in his eyes, which haven't left my face once. Lost in this moment. And what I hope will be the first of many, many more moments of dancing on boardwalks I want us to have.

He steps away from me, throwing his arm to spin me out and back to him.

'Hi,' I say.

'Hi.'

Slowly, he dips me, one hand cradling the back of my

head. We're so close and I want to kiss him. We lock eyes, and I see it in him too. Not just the chemical want and desire. But everything else. The longing. The pull that exists between us, written all over his face.

When he rights us, I fall into his arms and kiss him softly. I don't even notice if we taste like fish or garlic or anything we joked about, because who cares. He tastes like Levi.

'This is perfect,' I say.

'It's easy when you've got the right partner.'

'Partner, is it?'

'Hush now. No teasing, only kissing.'

So I kiss him again, and it's so natural that I feel like it could be the hundredth, thousandth kiss we've had. There's promise in it too. It's every kiss that we're yet to have. I hope there are so many more.

Above us, the stars shine brightly, as though they came out just to watch us dance.

Chapter Twenty-two

We go back to his flat instead of mine.

Together, we engage in a gentle kind of fiction. I'm just coming back for coffee, after all. That's what we said. It's the kind of fiction that doesn't hold up under scrutiny because after all there's coffee at the restaurant that's probably better than whatever Levi has at home, and also I don't really drink coffee, especially not at 11 p.m. or I'd never fall asleep.

But in the end, we don't even go through the motions of trying to make any, because the moment we close his front door, I take his face in my hands and kiss him deeply.

'Good evening,' he says, and I can taste the smile on him.

'Hi.'

'We're not drinking coffee, are we?'

'No.'

'All right, then,' he says, and he wraps an arm around my waist, dragging me tight against him.

I walk him backwards, and press him against the door. A little smile bursts out as he kisses me.

The tiny, delighted moan that escapes his lips when I nip at that place on his neck that I've been thinking about this whole time thrills me. His Adam's apple bobs, and I place a slow kiss next to it, just like I promised myself I would.

He melts under my touch, and against me I feel his hardness.

I want him so much. He wants me too. There's nothing to stop us now.

I kiss him deeply, pressing myself against him, like I can't possibly get close enough. I really can't with all these clothes on. He seems to feel the same way too, as he reaches for my thigh, bare where the slit in the dress falls open, and grabs at it with his hands.

This time, I moan and grind my hips against his. He feels so good.

I've never been like this with a man before. With Mason it was all second-guessing and, if I'm honest, a bit manual. More going about the motions than taking time for pleasure, which I always knew wasn't satisfying me quite enough but didn't have the voice to say it. I was too busy trying to keep him happy to ever stop and think about what I wanted.

With Levi, I feel taken over by something. Not *just* desire, but the confidence to ask for it, to demand what I want. I want to explore every inch of him, and I'm greedy for it.

I break the kiss, leaving him still drunk on it, and skip away to the couch. It's right next to the bed, but still, there's time for that. No need to rush things.

'Come sit,' I say, patting the cushion next to me.

Instead, he kneels in front of me, like he's praying. A gasp gathers in my chest as he runs his hands down my leg, and slips off my shoes. The heat between my legs gathers like a storm.

I imagine what would happen if he stayed down there, if he buried his face deep in the most sensitive part of me, and by God, I want that.

I think he knows, because the grin on his face turns sharp. Hungry.

Before I can get carried away, I take the collar of his shirt in my hand and drag him back up to my mouth. Our shared kiss is aflame with desire. Heat flares through my body as he presses up against me, tracing his fingers up the bare skin of my thigh, where the slit of my dress has fallen away. Kneeling this way, he towers over me and I want to surrender to him.

Gasps build in my throat, and he kisses there too. It's so much at once, that I cry out and I'm too wrapped up in the sheer sensation of it all to care how I sound.

I run my fingers down his shoulders to his collarbone, and start to unbutton his shirt.

'Hi,' he says, leaning back a little to look at me.

'Hi,' I say. 'Is this OK?'

He nods. 'Yes.'

'I'm going to keep my implant in, so I can hear you.'

'I'll be mindful of it.' He reaches forward, and then looks down to me again, asking for permission. I nod. Levi touches my cochlear implant gently with his finger, as though he's making sure of its construction, where it sits. He's gentle. Normally I hate other people touching my implant, but I know that he's just being safe, making sure he knows how to be careful with me so he doesn't nuke it.

'We should be careful,' he says. 'We're still getting to know each other.'

Heat rushes through my body, and I bleat out, 'I'm on the pill.'

'I have condoms.'

'Me too.'

'Good.'

'Good.'

We both break out into nervous giggles.

'Can we please go back to the kissing?' I say. 'Seeing as you're still straddling me.'

'It seems only right.'

He swoops my hair back, kissing down my neck and the straps of my dress fall away.

The muscles of his back are tense under my fingertips. I dig my nails in slightly, lightly scratching his skin, and he groans into my collarbone. My nipples harden as he peels my dress down. I ache for him to touch them, take one into his mouth, and when he runs his thumb over one, it's pure electricity searing through my body.

I can't hold on any more. Somehow, I push him so he's on the couch on his back, and I clamber on top of him, losing my dress in the process. It pools on the floor, and I see his eyes widen as he takes me in. All I have left on are my knickers.

Underneath me, he's scorching hot, and when I lace my fingers through his, I feel a beat of him that echoes in me.

I drop kisses across his chest and neck and face, returning all he gave me, before unlacing one hand from his to undo his belt. He helps me, tugging the leather away. When his flies fall open, I run my fingers along the waistband of his underwear, so deeply aware of how close I am. I can feel the heat radiating off him as he gasps my name.

Between us, it's a game of to and fro, one of us always taking turns to lead. After I tug off his trousers, he leans me back on the couch while delicately making sure my implant doesn't get knocked. As he rests alongside me, his fingers trail into my knickers. I gasp 'Please,' and his fingers find the hottest part of me immediately. He trails kisses down my body, stopping between my legs, where he pulls down my knickers, and goes down on me. My whole body bucks from the pleasure of him, and it doesn't take long before I'm grabbing at his hair as I shudder with orgasm.

He carries me to the bed, and I'm drunk on him. And he on me.

When he lies me back, the speed changes. We go slowly, eyes locked on each other, a silent unbroken communication. That itself feels like the most intimate part of it all, in some ways.

We meet, and slowly in tiny increments we glide together, all the time breathing in sync. All the time gazing at each other.

It's cliché to say, but it's a dance. A duet. And one that we were made to do together. I come first as his thumb strokes me, and then he follows.

After, we lie wrapped in each other and his bedsheets, as though we're still trying to press together into one creature. I can't believe this is my life or that he is in it. That we could make this kind of magic together.

I feel so safe, that I decide I should ask him for what I want. 'Levi?'

'Yeah?' he says sleepily.

My heart is about to leap out of my chest. 'Will you be my boyfriend?'

He turns my face towards him and kisses me deeply. 'Always.'

Chapter Twenty-three

We wake up early, too high on each other to sleep deeply. I roll over to spoon him, and bury my face in his hair. He smells so good, even after sleep. And, well, all the rest of it.

He squeezes my hand, and I can feel the deep vibrations of him speaking against my body. I took my implant out when I did actually sleep, as usual, so I reach over to the bedside table to put it back on, before resuming my spot spooning him.

'Morning,' I say. 'What did you say?'

'Just good morning.'

'Well. Good morning, then.'

'Did you sleep OK?'

'The best.' I stretch out my body, taking up all the space on my side of the bed.

'Ooh, big stretch,' he says, like I'm a cat. I stay stretched out, and he lies on my chest, looking up at me. He looks so cute. 'What's the plan for today?'

I'm about to be rumbled. I flash him a cheeky smile. 'Well . . . I didn't plan anything beyond the date, just in case it all went very well.'

'Oh yeah?' His chest rises and falls with a rumbling laugh. 'Very tactical of you.'

'I'm just very smart. And I know what I want.'

It's so cute that when I say this, he wiggles backwards a bit so that he's pressed up against me. It turns out that cuddling him in bed might be one of my favourite things, especially because he lets me be the big spoon.

'What do you want to do?' he asks.

My stomach rumbles loudly. 'Eat, apparently.'

'How about we go out for breakfast? I know a place that does a good brunch.'

'Now, am I going to go out for breakfast dressed in my evening gown or totally naked?'

'Either works for me.'

'Can we stop at mine first? Then I can have a shower and get changed.'

'That sounds good. We've got time, after all. But I'm going to get in the shower now.'

'Noooo,' I protest, squeezing him with a slung-over leg. 'Stay here.'

'I thought you were hungry.'

I think about this for a second. 'Fine. Go get clean, then.'

He rolls over and kisses me softly.

'What was that for?'

'Just happy,' he says, getting up.

I let myself doze while he showers, but I'm wide awake the moment he comes back. He smells so good. What do they put in men's shower stuff to make them smell so delicious when all the packaging is always so aggy in tone? I stand up, and slip back into my dress which is quite wrinkled from being on the floor all night, but I look passable. Even if I am a dirty stopout, as Vics would say. I'm kind of revelling in it.

Levi slips a black T-shirt over his head, and I creep up behind him to kiss him on the back of the neck. His damp hair smells like liquorice and tickles my nose.

He spins round and growls, 'Cassie, are you trying to lure me back to bed by any chance?'

'Nope, just teasing you.'

I pat him on the bum, and continue grabbing my things from where they're strewn all over the flat. It doesn't take long, though one shoe has got pretty wedged under the coffee table so I have to get Levi to lift it up. A good excuse for me to stare at his arms.

God, I feel so lucky.

We drive to my flat in the glorious morning sun, and I can't help but look over at my boyfriend. My boyfriend! I glance at the glove box and wonder if he'll write songs about last night.

I flick on the radio and it's playing 'Time After Time', and it's so corny but I love it when both of us sing along. Neither of us sound particularly good, but that's part of the charm, isn't it?

'We should be quiet, just in case the others are still asleep,' I say, when we pull up at the apartment block and walk up to the flat. I unlock the door as quietly as I can.

All plans of being quiet are thrown out of the window the moment we get inside though, because the first thing I see is Pen running from the kitchen in just a T-shirt and pants.

And the room they go into is . . . Tyra's?

I don't think they saw me at all, so I just stand there unmoving.

What is going on?

'Well. I didn't expect to see Pen in their undies this morning,' says Levi, way too casually. 'Shall I put some coffee on?'

'Why are you not freaking out about this?' I ask, as he roots around in the cupboard.

He pops his head back out with a confused look on his face. 'The coffee?'

I furiously point in the direction Pen scuttled off in.

'Why would I freak out?' he asks.

I don't know how to answer this because there's too many things brewing on my tongue and all of them sound ridiculous.

Maybe this is all a misunderstanding. It doesn't mean they're sleeping together, right? I mean, people have perfectly innocent sleepovers all the time. Pen and I do. But do Tyra and Pen?

'I'm going to knock.'

'What? No, Cass, leave them alone,' Levi hisses and comes round the counter towards me.

I narrow my eyes at him. 'Did you . . . Did you know about this?'

'About what?'

I once again point furiously at the door.

'Yeah, they've not been quiet about it, have they? They've been making eyes at each other as much as I've been at you.'

'What?'

'Hey, good morning, guys,' shouts Tyra a little too loudly, emerging from her room. She's wrapped in a silky lemon dressing gown that I've never seen her wear before. 'Are you making coffee? Levi, can I get some? Oh, do you guys want some breakfast? I can get cooking if you help me?' She starts rooting in the fridge. 'Cassie, come look at this. Do you think this avocado is OK? I can never tell when they're overripe.'

I decide to look like I'm taking the bait so I walk over to her, but keep one eye on the door, which is how I catch Pen unsuccessfully trying to sneak out. They creep like someone in a pantomime, overexaggerated high steps and going at a really weird shuffling pace.

'AHA!' I shout, causing Pen to drop everything they're holding, which seems to be their car keys, some clothes, sunglasses, even their shoes.

I rush over to the front door, spreading myself across it so they can't escape.

'Morning,' they say, ignoring all the stuff they've dropped at their feet. They've got a pair of shorts on that I'm almost positive are actually Tyra's.

'Explain.'

The flush that creeps over their face means they know there's no way of getting out of this. They sigh. 'Cassie.'

'Are you and Tyra a thing?'

In the kitchen, Tyra gasps so loudly that she confirms it for me. If they weren't, someone would just say it, right? They'd say 'No, we aren't a thing,' and we'd all laugh and go about our day.

'How long?'

'I –'

'Pen? Why didn't you tell me?' I whine.

'I've just been working a bunch of stuff out.'

'OK, but I didn't know that? We *always* tell each other stuff.'

'Yeah, and you've been going through more than enough. And I didn't want to complicate things for you even more.'

'What are you going on about? I still want to hear about what's up with you, you total . . . total . . . dildo!'

A snort sounds from the corridor. 'Well, I walked in at the wrong time,' says Veena. 'What's going on?'

To my further mortification, Sorrel appears from the balcony with an empty glass and an open book between her fingers so she doesn't lose her place. 'Cassie's being codependent.'

'No, I'm not.'

Everyone, including Levi, gives me a kind of look that makes me want to shrivel up and die.

Oh God, am I? Am I being weird?

'I'm just processing!' I shout so that everyone can hear me.

'Hey, look, maybe let's go have this conversation somewhere it's just us two?' suggests Pen. 'And maybe you can change out of the ballgown? This argument is weird enough without you looking like you're about to walk a red carpet while I'm wearing Tyra's cast-offs.'

'Hey, those shorts are my good shorts. You look after them,' says Tyra from the kitchen.

'Fine,' I say, all the heat draining out of me. 'I'll be back in a minute.'

I don't think I've ever had such a quick or such an angry

shower. Why didn't they tell me? Why were they hiding it from me? Why am I so upset about it?

When I come back, Levi hands me a mug of coffee. 'I added some sugar to keep you sweet. Are you all right?'

'Yeah . . . I dunno. I just feel weird. Am I being weird?'

'A bit, but not beyond the bounds of you as a person.'

'Oh, great.'

'I just mean, you're passionate about the people around you. That's something we like about you. Just go easy on them.'

'Urgh,' I groan. 'Don't be so reasonable when I'm acting like a dickhead.'

'Go tell them that. They're out on the balcony waiting. Go on, we can do breakfast once you've talked it out.'

'Thanks. Sorry about this. We were all set to have a nice morning.'

'And we still will, once you've sorted things out with Pen. Veena and Sorrel are insistent I sit down and watch *The Great American Barbecue* with them.'

'OK.'

I take a deep breath and go out to the balcony, where Pen is curled up on one of the sun loungers picking at their fingernails. I've not seen them do that for years. It's a nervous habit that they had when we met, but have trained themselves out of because the sterilising hand lotions in their care jobs always make the little nicks in their skin sting terribly.

I sit down in the lounger next to them, put my cup down on the table, and put my hands in theirs instead.

'Sorry for being weird. Just tell me what's going on,' I say.

And to my relief, they actually do. 'I liked Tyra from the moment we met. Like, I've had a bit of a crush on her since I watched her when we were all teenagers.'

'Wait? How did you find her?'

They look at me with complete confusion. 'Your YouTube. When I'd stay over, if I was too wired to sleep I'd just watch stuff on your laptop, and the algorithm always recommended me her videos. I guess the newer ones you hadn't watched.'

'That explains why I kept getting so many videos of people making those tiny food kits, like the Japanese sweets.'

'Oh, yeah, that was me.'

'Well, that's one mystery solved at least. When did it go from you liking Tyra to you and Tyra being a thing?'

'Remember when everyone went out after the 'Damask' day?'

'You mean . . . when the girls I work with were making fun of me for being deaf?'

'No, it didn't *happen* then, Cassie. I'm just giving you context. She said that comment about dating people of different genders, and I wasn't sure if it was a hint, but the next morning she texted me to say it was.'

'Wow. Fair dos, that's pretty forward.'

'Yeah.'

'So, then what?'

'The day you went out with Levi on your non-date, she and I ended up hanging out, just us. We went up to that cave that I'd told everyone about, because she knew no one else really wanted to hike it.'

'I would have gone,' I insist.

'I know, if I'd asked you properly I know you would. But she was just doing a nice thing for me, is my point.'

I nod, and let them continue.

'We just got on really well and one thing led to another.'

'In the cave?!'

'Yeah,' they say, blushing. 'There's a bit you can jump into the water and swim around in. It was all sparkly and dark and so blue. She just pulled me across the water, and we kissed.'

'OK, aside from whatever we've got going on in this conversation – I need to say that's really hot.'

'It was.'

I see it now. The starriness in their eyes. They're in love with her. This isn't a fling or anything.

'And so you've been seeing each other since then?' I prompt.

'Pretty much. She's been so busy, just like you, so we've not had much time together. Last night was my first stay over here. But, err, she has been at mine before.'

'OK, then,' I say, laughing a little awkwardly as I realise that despite everything else we've talked about, we've never really talked about sex. Mostly because Mason was a kind of no-go conversation area.

'Do you want to keep seeing her?' I ask.

'Yeah,' they say. 'I do. I think . . . I think this might be important. I'm not sure I believe in The One, but I definitely believe in Big Loves, whether we get one or several in our lifetimes. I think she could be one.'

'Have you told her that?'

'I was working up to it.'

'Wow. I'm genuinely happy for you, Pen. I mean that.'

'Thanks, Cass. I'm sorry I didn't tell you but we both agreed we should keep it quiet while we worked out what it was. Like we didn't want to upset the applecart for no reason, just in case it was just us both being horny or something.'

'I get that.'

'Plus,' they say with a wince, 'I'm just really conscious of how much Vics stuff you had to put up with, and I didn't want you to feel like this was just another awful pining situation.'

'You weren't awful. It was kind of cute.'

'I'm sure I was both.'

I shrug. 'It's not like you and Vics ever did anything about it.'

A blush spreads across their cheeks.

'Oh my God?!' I shriek. 'What?!'

'I know, I know. You have full rights to be upset about this.'

'When did this happen?'

They bury their head in their hands. 'Please don't make me say it.'

'Err, well, now you *have* to actually.'

Pen blows air out of their cheeks and lies back. 'OK, but I can't look at you when I say it.'

'Fine.'

'Remember last summer when we went out to dinner with Vics in Leeds? It was that little taco place she likes, where they do the spicy margaritas? We bumped into Mason with some of his work friends, and he joined us for a drink.'

'Yeah, I do,' I say. 'It's like . . . the only time he's ever hung

316

out with you properly. The only time he met anyone from my family really.'

'Do you remember that you went home with him? And I said that I was staying in Leeds to meet up with a work friend?'

'Did you –'

'I mean, I really was supposed to meet Pete for a drink but he cancelled just after you'd left. So Vics said we should stay for one more, and defrag about Mason.'

'Defrag?'

'Like, talk about it.'

'What was there to talk about?'

They press their lips together. 'Vics didn't like him, and she wanted to interrogate me about it. Like, how did you guys meet and was he being nice to you? Is he just a dick or a dick we had to watch out for? Big sister stuff.'

'And what, you went from gossiping about me to snogging her?'

'It wasn't that quick. She saw me to the train, and I got a little stupid when we were saying goodbye. Like yes, we did kiss, but she stopped it right away. Nothing more mortifying than someone you've fancied for your whole life telling you they see you as a little sibling.'

'Ouch,' I say.

'Too right. Anyway, I ran away onto the train and we didn't speak about that again.'

'But why didn't you tell me any of this?'

'I didn't know how I could tell you about Vics without admitting that we both didn't like Mason. Especially when she made me swear not to tell you.'

'What do you mean?'

'Once she was fairly certain that he was just regular-level bad, she said you needed the time to work it out yourself or you might get upset with us, or distance yourself. Neither of us wanted that, so we just hoped you'd work it out in the long run. And you did.'

'So that's why you've never told me you didn't like him outright. It was kind of obvious, Pen. You should have just said.'

'Would it have changed things? I know we're codependent but I don't dictate your life, I hope.'

'Other than the whole reason we're in Ibiza.'

'That was just . . . a nudge.'

'More like a shove, but yeah, I take your point. I probably would have just made excuses for him, like I always did.'

I'm thankful that they just nod in agreement, rather than go into it any further. Maybe we need to leave Mason in the past once and for all.

'My head is spinning. So what you've just told me is that you're in love with Tyra, you and Vics had a rejected kiss, and you both hated Mason? Is that everything?'

'Pretty much. And I didn't hate the guy, I just hated the way he treated you like you weren't a priority and made you feel bad for wanting to be.'

It hits me like a punch to the chest. 'You're right,' I say. 'It was exactly like that.'

'Which is why – and to be clear I didn't meddle in this – I was so pleased when Levi was so into you, because he's a good guy.'

'He is,' I agree.

'And, given you came in last night's dress, I'm guessing that went well?'

My turn to blush furiously. 'Yes, it did.'

'Good. I'm really happy for you both.'

'Thanks. And, even though I didn't act like it, I am glad about you and Tyra, whatever it turns out to be.'

'Thanks.'

My eyes start to sting. 'But does this mean you'll go off to Texas to live with her?'

'Cass, I don't know. I don't know what it means yet. And I don't know where I'm going to be anyway.'

'What do you mean?'

Their eyes soften, and it's their turn to take my hands in theirs. 'Cassie, you're not going back to Yorkshire. Not right now, anyway. Look at this life. In hardly any time, you'll be in Paris, on the first tour stop. I know you're going to get another dance job right off the back of this, and it'll be amazing. Part of the reason I came with you is because I needed to think about what my life could look like without you in it every day.'

'That seems a little backwards when you see me every day here.'

'I know, but I found a new job. Maybe a new career in production. Michael is keen to recommend me to stay on in Rosa's team, potentially even off-tour times, and he's said he'd love to take me along with him as an assistant for any future jobs. There's doors opening for me too, ones I couldn't have imagined or found without you.'

319

The tears that have been threatening to fall spill over. 'Why do I feel like the band is breaking up?'

'We're not. There's these things called phones, which means we can still speak every day, even if we're far apart. But who knows, we might end up both still working for Rosa at this rate. Plus, we'll always be best friends.'

'Just maybe not quite so codependent.'

'I think that might be good for both of us.'

'You're probably right, but I'm not happy about it.' I lift up the bottom of my T-shirt to dry my eyes with, and seem to make more of a mess, somehow.

'It's honestly so impressive how much snot you produce when you cry,' they say. 'It's probably my favourite thing about you.'

'That's disgusting.'

'That's love.'

Snot aside, we wrap our arms around each other. 'I love you too,' I say. 'I'm sorry for acting like a weirdo.'

'It's OK. I *did* kiss your sister.'

'Don't remind me. Should we go tell everyone else things are OK, so they don't worry we've pushed each other off the balcony or something?'

'That seems . . . like a little too dramatic of a conclusion to leap to.'

'I think you underestimate how much reality TV has been watched in this flat the last few weeks. Anyway, come on. Let's all go out to breakfast, and you two can tell us all about how in love you are.'

It's the right end to it all, and to my relief, Levi doesn't mind that I invited everyone along. The breakfast place he suggested seats us all on one big round table. Me, my friends, and my new boyfriend. He's going to be one of those big loves. I can tell.

And it's clear that Tyra and Pen are too. The gooey look they give her is mirrored back, so much that Sorrel keeps teasing the pair of them.

There's so much more about to happen for all six of us. The tour itself is drawing closer, and it's not long before we start dress rehearsals. After that comes Paris, the first show on the new leg. And then the rest of the tour.

It almost doesn't feel real. I'll be sad when we leave this little bubble of love and friendship and support and happiness that we've built, the six of us.

It feels right to be here, and it feels like the start of something. For all of us.

Chapter Twenty-four

I could never have dreamed that I'd be working and (temporarily) living in Paris, and yet somehow, I'm here. Not that I'd necessarily know, because boy are we busy. I've barely seen the Paris beyond our flat and the studio we've moved to while the production team install the sets at Paris La Défense Arena.

For so long, it felt like we were so far from the tour part of this job, and now suddenly it's here.

The main cast of dancers arrived ahead of us. I'm excited to meet them but nervous too. They're the people we have to match up to, to stand in for at a moment's notice. I just have to hope that after weeks of training I'm up to the task.

Deep breaths.

Levi already flew over a couple of weeks ago. We're right in the middle of that adorable, can't-stop-touching-each-other phase, so it was kind of excruciating to be apart from him. But we've been video calling every night, even if it ends up being us just falling asleep as we're both so tired. He's been working on his songs though, and he even played me a little bit of something new over the phone. I'm so proud of him for chasing his dreams too.

It was sad saying goodbye to our flat in Ibiza. Sorrel insisted we do something called *a packing party* which meant making a playlist of bangers and dancing our way through packing. Veena complained that this made it even more of a job given what we do for a living, but it still kind of worked. We got hyped and it didn't feel quite so sad any more. We went out for a last margarita at the little tapas bar down the road that we went to on our first night, and bravely went to sleep early.

The flight was quick at least, and we pretty much just dropped our things and went straight to work. That was a few days ago – we've been hardcore running the full set every day since we got here. I've not seen Pen and Levi yet as they've been both extremely busy, but I know they're here and excited to catch up at the weekend when we all get a bit of a breather, though I suspect we'll mostly just be sleeping.

Today, Michael's insisted that we're going to run the set, but we'll all be dancing different positions. We've been doing this over time, making sure we know each other's parts and the routine as a whole thing, but still. This close to the actual tour kicking off means that every misstep is a problem for all of us.

Even though we're in a different country, the new studio reminds me of the one we just left. The big mirror, the decent sound system, the brightly painted walls and floor ready to be scuffed by our trainers. Maybe they're the same all over?

'Salut, understudies,' Michael calls as he saunters into the studio trailed by Pen, who blows a kiss at me. I catch it out of midair and pretend to shove it in my mouth.

Typically, Michael spots that exchange. 'Honey, if that's how you're doing it, let me tell you, you're doing it wrong.'

Everyone breaks into giggles, including me, and I feel some of the tension in the room lift. I guess everyone else was just as nervous as I was. Well, if me being a total dork helps that, then good.

'I've got a bit of an announcement,' he says, and all that nervous energy floods right back in. 'As you know, the former understudies are now main cast. Yesterday, they had assessments with the doctors on staff to make sure everyone was ready, but two of the main cast did not pass medical.'

'Oh no. That's so sad for them,' gasps Sorrel.

Veena shakes her head. 'After all this time and work. Poor guys.'

'I feel awful for them, but also if you're too sick, you have to rest. There's no getting round it,' says Tyra. 'You can't work on nothing.'

'Correct,' Michael says. 'Which is why, after discussions with Rosa, we've decided that we're going to pick two of you to graduate up to the main cast for this entire leg of the tour.'

The room rumbles with shock.

The *entire* run? I thought he was going to say just for the next couple of weeks. It's awful that they're not well enough to dance the whole run but . . . wow, what an opportunity for two of us. There has been no guarantee that any of us would make it to actually performing despite all this hard work, and we knew that when we took the job. But now? The opportunity is right there.

I glance at the flatmates, and all of us have the same look on our faces – hopeful but sad that only two people will get the gig. But I'm determined that at least one of us needs to get it.

'The two people picked will be working with the main cast for the rest of the rehearsals, and I'll be grouping you understudies into more roles to cover those gaps being left as we don't have time to recruit anyone else. I know, it's a lot of work. But you're all good enough to do this or you wouldn't still be here,' Michael insists. 'We'll be choosing today –' The sound of shock rises up again, until Michael holds a hand up to silence everyone. 'We'll be choosing today. I'm going to split you all into two smaller casts that will be assessed from. And it won't just be me assessing you. Rosa will be joining us.'

Rosa? She's here?

And she's going to watch me dance *today*?

I want to be sick.

'I know plenty of you are wondering about more notice, but hey, that's the life of an understudy, guys. You've got to be prepared for anything.'

He's right. I know he's right, and yet the thudding in my chest won't calm down.

'In fact, let's just split the room down here,' Michael says, pointing directly between Veena and me. I spin round to see who I'm with, and while I have Seojin and Kam, I am also with Giselle, Tori and Natalie. Not necessarily the people I'd choose to be with for such a huge moment, but there we go. That's my lot, and I need to be a grown-up and get the job done.

Michael points to the other group first. 'Group one, you'll go first. I want all of you back here in an hour. Go get warmed up.'

The gym attached to this studio is much smaller and more basic than the one that Rosa had built for us, so as soon as half the room has sprinted off I know that there'll be no more machines or weights available. Floor work it is.

Luckily, there's a decent cluster of rolled-up yoga mats, so I take one and lay it out in front of the mirror. I'm about to beckon my flatmates over, when I spot Veena staring into space.

'Veena?' I ask. I prod her, and she doesn't move. 'Veena?'

Tyra frowns. 'Do I need to get someone, Veena?'

'No, sorry,' she says, blinking. 'I'm here. I'm just . . . you know, freaking out.'

Sorrel takes her hands. 'Talk to us.'

Veena presses her lips together, and I see tears form in her eyes, threatening to spill. 'I think the nerves finally got to me.' She laughs awkwardly as one spills down her cheek. 'I just want to impress Michael. Mortifying!'

'Sweets, they're getting to us all. You do not want to see what I did in the bathroom earlier. It was really not ladylike,' says Tyra, shaking her head.

We all fall apart laughing.

'OK, I'll be all right,' Veena says.

'And let's just agree, if any of us get it, that's a win for all of us,' says Sorrel. 'But if we don't, that's fine too!'

I nod eagerly. 'Whatever happens, we're good.'

'We're good,' agrees Tyra.

'Your bowels apparently aren't,' says Veena.

Tyra rolls her eyes. 'OK, enough of that. We've got warming-up to do.'

An hour might be long enough for me to warm up my muscles, but it's not enough for me to feel remotely mentally ready to meet Rosa Cordova, let alone dance in front of her. I know it's silly, like obviously we were going to meet eventually, but still. I didn't think it would be today.

Everyone files back in just before our hour is up, determined not to be late, which means that the room is full of buzzing nerves radiating off each other.

We got this, I tell myself. *We've got this. Just do your best.*

We all jump when Pen arrives first, thinking it's Rosa, but they just set out some chairs for Rosa and her team.

When Rosa finally walks in after Michael, it's like seeing someone unreal. Like, I've watched so much of her concert footage, interviews and music videos that she almost isn't real as a person, but she is. She's right *here*.

Her hair is somehow glossier and thicker than I imagined. I would kill to have hair like that. She wears a silk rose-pink shirt tucked into high-waisted ecru trousers with a sharp line down the front. A pair of assistants follow behind, one carrying her enormous handbag in the same rose pink, while the other is typing something on her phone without looking up.

Despite Rosa's small stature, she commands a huge presence. Everyone is silent.

'Understudies, please meet Rosa,' announces Michael.

'Buen dia,' she says, smiling at us all as she takes her seat. 'It's lovely to meet you. I hear that you have risen to the challenge set to you, and I'm proud to watch you dance today. I know there's pressure on you because we're choosing some dancers today, but please remember that I'm just excited to watch you perform. The thing about being a performer is that I'm not often granted that pleasure. So please, enjoy it.'

Michael announces that we'll be performing 'Diamonds Under My Eyes', which is a signature group number, but doesn't require any of the lifting or breaking into other groups that the other songs do. It makes sense. I reach up to my cochlear implant and feel for the tit tape, and it feels secure enough. I can do this.

Our group stand at the side against the wall while group one prepare to dance. I give my friends a thumbs up.

All of them nail it, doing arguably one of the best performances of their lives. But Sorrel, in particular, dances like wildfire. She's magnetic, alive, creating something new inside the choreography. When you're dancing together, it's harder to appreciate what everyone else is doing because you're all so focused on your own work and moving with the team. Now I get to appreciate what she's been serving this whole time. Her attitude, her playfulness, leaps out in her performance. The joy of dancing is all over her face, and it's infectious. I want to dance *with* her, and I've been dancing with her for weeks.

Michael said they wouldn't announce who got the gig until they've seen all of us dance, but I know that she's got it. Rosa

328

can't take her eyes off her, and even starts clapping along happily as she watches.

'Bravo, bravo!' she shouts, and we all applaud their work. I want to run to them all, squeal about how amazing they are, but I can't. I have to stay focused.

'Our turn,' says Natalie next to me.

'Let's give it our all,' I say, and she gives me a nod.

Right at that moment, everyone turns to the doorway, clearly hearing something I'm not picking up. And then there's a huge crash from outside, which I do hear.

To my mortification the person who walks in bearing a huge bouquet is . . . Mason?

'Oh, good God,' I moan, drawing Veena, Sorrel and Tyra's attention to me.

As if in confirmation, Pen races towards Mason, and puts one hand on his chest. 'Dude, you have to go,' they say firmly.

But then he spots me, still frozen against the wall. 'Cassie! Cassie, please. I need to speak to you! Forgive me!'

Please kill me, I think.

I stalk across the room, and drag him out of the studio, followed quickly by Pen, who closes the door behind them.

'Mason, what are you doing here? How did you even find me?' I hiss.

'Cassie, I've made a horrible mistake,' he says, practically shoving the bouquet at me. 'We were so good together, and I didn't show up for you. So I'm here! I'm here to support you.'

I take the flowers so that I can actually pay attention to what the hell is happening without petals in my eyes, and drop it to the floor. Unfortunately, this seems to be some kind of cue for him to pull me into a bear hug. His arms wrap around my head, and I step back, trying to reset my hair and my implant.

'Mason, get off me,' I growl, and he drops his arms, freeing me.

The door to the studio unfortunately has a glass window built into it, and I can see people peering through.

'Just please hear me out, Cassie. I've felt so terrible since you left, and since you got so angry at my texts. I've realised that I blew it, and that I really want to be with you.'

My stomach sours. *Now* he wants to commit to me?

The door opens and Michael comes out. 'Are you OK, Cassie? Do I need to call security?'

I hesitate long enough for Pen to nod, and Michael walks off to fetch someone.

'I'm just here to get my girlfriend back. You don't need to call security.'

Girlfriend? He literally never called me his girlfriend in the entire stretch of our 'relationship'.

'Oh, I think I definitely do!' yells Michael.

God, did it have to be now? In front of Rosa? This is my big break and it's being obliterated by a drama I did not need.

I growl with frustration. 'Mason, you can't just do this!'

'You really need to go,' Pen adds. 'You're trespassing. Probably. Come on, I'll take you out.'

'I'm not going anywhere without her,' he protests.

And this is when I see it. All that stuff I felt about how everything was on his terms, all about whether he wanted to support me. It's right there. I can see it so clearly that I

330

don't know how I didn't before now.

'Cass, do you want me to get Levi?' Pen asks.

'No, I can handle this myself,' I say to Pen before taking a deep breath.

There's so much I want to say.

'Mason. What was the plan here?' I snap. 'Show up with flowers and say everything is OK and expect me to just agree with you?'

'Well . . .' He looks down at the flowers on the floor. 'That was the first part.'

'And what, you thought I was going to leap at the chance to talk to you when I'm at work just because you finally showed up to support me, which you haven't done before, like, ever, even though I very clearly broke up with you and told you not to contact me? We are not together. We will not be together again. I need you to understand that.'

'Cassie, come on.'

'No, Mason, I've moved on.'

Something flashes across his face, but it doesn't look like hurt. 'You're seeing someone else?'

'It doesn't matter if I am or I'm not. You're not privy to that information. The point is I've moved on from *you*,' I hiss. 'I don't have time for this. You need to go.'

'I'm sure you've got the time to just talk to me. I know you're busy but it's not like you're saving lives here.'

'Oh, and you do? I was always expected to drop everything for you. But you couldn't even support me a little bit, not even when I was offered the job. You spent so long undermining me that I didn't even think that was abnormal until I got away from you and realised how fucking brilliant I am. And you're still doing it now!'

'I –'

'No, you don't get to speak. I don't need you, Mason. I don't need your negging or your conditional support. I'm different now. I know that I deserve way more than that, and I was sacrificing parts of myself just to keep you happy. That's not me. You should be able to understand that I've found something that matters to me, and I'm going for it. But you couldn't when I was at home. You couldn't bear the thought of me doing something for myself. Well, I've changed for the better, and there's no way in hell I'm going back.'

To my surprise, my colleagues on the other side of the door are cheering and clapping.

It's clear that he didn't think it was going to go this way. I *almost* feel bad when I see the flush cross his face, and the tears well in his eyes, but I don't. I didn't want to hurt him, even though he hurt me so much, but this was just ridiculous and emblematic of everything wrong with us.

Two enormous, beefy security guards who I'm sure are part of Rosa's personal team show up in matching black suits. 'Sir, you have to come with us.'

'Mason, you're embarrassing yourself. Go,' Pen says.

And for once, he listens.

He leaves.

'Also, you suck!' Pen shouts after him. 'Man, I've been wanting to say that for ages.'

'He really did suck,' agrees Michael, who came back with the security guards. 'Everything OK?'

I want to be sick, but what I need to do is be a professional, and go back inside.

Except what actually happens is I break into huge, racking sobs. I can't catch my breath and I know that I'm on the edge of a full-blown panic attack if I don't get some deeper breaths in me. God, how could this day get any worse?

'Come, come,' says Michael, dragging me away from the view of the door into the empty workout room next door.

I start slowing my breathing, and he joins me, so we breathe together. The racing in my body slows down.

'Sorry,' I say, wiping tears away. 'Fuck. Sorry.'

'Hey, it's OK. Who among us hasn't had a bad boyfriend show up at the worst possible time?'

'Really?'

'Oh, the stories I could tell you. Stages stormed, dressing rooms staked out. I've seen it all. And so has Rosa.'

'Oh God, I wish she hadn't been here.'

He shakes his head. 'Never repeat this, but she's a messy bitch who loves the drama, so she's probably eating this up.'

I burst out laughing.

'That's better. Now, come on. Don't blow this.'

'I think I already did.'

'Extenuating circumstances.'

'Michael.'

'Yes?'

'Why are you being so nice to me?'

He fixes me with a tired look, one perfectly coiffed eyebrow raised. 'Girl, you know you're one of the top contenders for this gig. You're reliable, hardworking, and adaptable under all kinds of circumstances, including your terrible boyfriend –'

'Ex,' I interrupt, not quite believing what he's saying to me.

'Terrible ex-boyfriend showing up for a love declaration. Capiche? Get dancing and show Rosa what you've been showing me for weeks.'

He thinks I'm good? I can't keep up with what is happening, but it lights something in me when he says, 'It's time to get to work.'

He's right. I've come too far to let Mason ruin this for me. This whole journey has been about me putting myself first, believing in myself. And I do believe in myself. It helps to know that Michael does too, I'll admit. But that fire has to come from within. I find it, and stoke it, and I know I can do this.

I'm not going to blow it. I roll my shoulders, and my head on my neck, getting back in tune with my body.

'I'm ready,' I tell him, and he gives me a rare warm smile.

When I walk back into the studio, everyone, and I mean, everyone is staring at me.

'Good for you,' says Tori, and I stand a little taller.

'Thanks. I'm really sorry, everyone. That was incredibly unprofessional and it won't happen again.'

'Call it the half-time entertainment,' says Rosa with a chuckle. 'Are we ready to dance, group two?'

Everyone is still looking at me, so I answer for us all. 'Yes. Let's go.'

The song pulses through me. It feels like a full-circle moment as 'Diamonds Under My Eyes' starts and I leap into the choreography. I'm comfortable, I'm confident, and thinking of Sorrel, I throw everything into it. All of me. The part of me that makes me a great dancer. A great performer.

I've never really thought of myself like that until right now, as Rosa locks eyes with me and gives me a nod.

I can do this. I *am* doing this.

And then, right on the same move that caused me all that trouble when I first danced this routine, the world goes silent. I know that means my cochlear implant has fallen out, just like it did before. When Mason hugged me, he must have knocked my head enough to unstick the tape a little.

But this time, I keep dancing.

I know these steps. I know this dance. And I'm here for me. I'm fighting for me, and hang everyone else who has stood in my way or said I was only here because I'm deaf or made me feel that I was less than I was.

I feel the vibrations through my body, all the cue I need.

I'm a butterfly, opening her wings.

Nothing can hold me back. I'm ready to fly.

And I nail every step, without hearing any of the music.

Chapter Twenty-five

The moment the choreography ends and everyone begins to clap, I look for my cochlear implant.

To my relief, Michael has picked it up, and now holds it out to me.

I check it over, making sure there's no obvious damage and it's all still intact. When I reattach it and test the batteries, there's a reassuring beep to tell me it's working but everything is quiet. I realise it's because, once again, everyone is looking at me.

'All working?' Michael asks, and I breathe a sigh of relief that the silence was because everyone was holding their breath.

'It's working fine,' I say. 'Thanks for grabbing it.'

He smiles at me and mouths *well done*.

'What a show,' Rosa cries. 'You're all such incredible dancers. I'm so glad to have you as part of my team for this tour. I really am in awe.'

'Everyone, Rosa and I will now discuss who her pick for dancers will be,' says Michael. 'Please wait here.'

The moment they leave trailed by Pen, the roommates and

I all rush together, wrapping our arms around each other.

'You're a fucking rock star, Cassie,' says Veena, gently grabbing me by the cheeks.

'I'm so proud of you,' says Tyra, on the verge of tears.

'None of that,' I say, laughing. 'Or you'll set me off.'

'No, come on. That was huge. You've come so far since that first week,' insists Sorrel. 'We're all so proud of you.'

'I'm proud of all of us.'

Sorrel shakes her head a little. 'OK, but also you can take this moment and be proud of what you just did too. You don't always have to turn it back to all of us.'

'Agreed,' sobs Tyra, who is being propped up by Veena who is now also crying.

I feel the tears catching and laugh. 'We all need to get a grip.'

Luckily, we manage to stop before Michael and Rosa return. It feels like the air is sucked out of the room. We all want it so much. Though if I'm honest with myself, I hadn't considered it as an actual possibility until Michael's pep talk and until I showed everyone that I can dance without my implant in.

'I'll keep it short. We will –'

'Michael,' Rosa laughs his name throatily. 'Let us first tell them they did a good job.'

'They know by now that no criticism from me means they did a great job. Plus, they don't need me to tell them that. Do you?'

We all nod and it's clear that a huge change has come over us all. We're so far from the people we were that first day in the studio – nervous and unsure and trying desperately to impress everyone.

'Well, in that case, I'm pleased to announce that I will be adding the following two dancers to the main cast,' Rosa begins. 'First, Sorrel.'

No one is surprised except for Sorrel, who takes a deep gasp that I know she's desperate to release as a scream, but holds it in while hopping from foot to foot with excitement. 'Thank you!'

'And second will be Cassie.'

I look at the others, worried I imagined what she said. But she said it. I heard it. I read it on her lips. My name.

Me.

I got it.

I'm not an understudy any more. I'm a performer. I'm main cast. I'm going to be on stage . . . from *next week*. I can't believe this.

I grab for Sorrel, and we are wrapped in hugs from not just Veena and Tyra, but Demi, Seojin and so many of the others. It feels lovely, and I feel loved. It's bittersweet, because this is the last time I'll be in the practice room with them. I have a whole new team of dancers to meet. I can't help it, but the tears start again.

When I'm freed from the cuddle pile, we all turn back to Rosa who is standing waiting for us to finish.

'Thank you, everyone, again. Cassie, could I please have a word with you outside? Sorrel, come chat to me after.'

'Me?' I ask, still not really sure I believe what's happening. But Rosa is already out of the door, beckoning me to follow, so I race after her. She leads me down the hall to the kitchenette, sitting down at one of the tables and signalling for me to sit next to her.

This is so weird. Yes, I knew I was taking a job to work for her, but I never imagined talking to her while sitting on slightly sticky IKEA basics kitchen furniture.

'Can I first apologise –'

'No,' she says, stopping me in my tracks. 'If I apologised for every bad boyfriend I or someone on my team had causing a scene, we'd never get any work done.' She laughs throatily again, and I join in. God, this is so weird. 'I called you in here because I wanted to tell you how excited I am to have someone so diligent and talented on my team.'

'Thank you,' I say.

'No, thank you. This show wouldn't exist without all the work of hundreds of talented people, including yourself. I may be the name in lights, but I'm just the queen in the hive. There's plenty more of you who build the show far more than I could.' She rubs at her hands, cracking the knuckles a little under her touch. A wince crosses her lips. 'What I wanted to tell you, away from everyone else, is that I know what it's like to be different, to be disabled, and to do it anyway.'

I realise what she's telling me. 'You are . . . ?'

'I'm not deaf, like yourself, but I've got a body that works on its own beat, if you'll pardon the pun. That's why I was so keen for Michael to find dancers from different walks of life, different experiences, who would understand what it's like to have to work harder to keep up. You're a great dancer, just like I'm a great singer. And I wanted to create an opportunity that removed the obstacles and helped you flourish. It's why there was no second thought about firing Fenella.'

I blush. 'Thank you.'

'And I'm glad to have a group of dancers working for me who know that her behaviour was wrong. Plenty of your colleagues came to Michael on your behalf. We don't tolerate that in any society, but especially in this team where I'm trying to make something different.

'I know that fighting to keep up in an ableist world changes you. It's made me scrappier, and I can see that in you, that hunger to prove yourself. Michael thinks so too. I want to take that, and nourish it. Beyond just this tour too. I want you to know that. If you need anything else to help you keep doing this job, you just say. I'm all here for taking the underdogs and growing them into killers.'

At this, she laughs again. I fully believe her.

'Then,' I say, the words on my lips before I can stop them. 'There's someone working in your production team, Levi McHugh. He's a songwriter, and I know that if you read his work, you'd be keen to –'

She cuts me off and my stomach plummets. 'Levi? Excellent, I will meet with him, and he can show me. Have him speak to my assistant, Clara. He's a good man.'

'He is,' I say, my voice shaking. She's really going to look at his work? 'Thank you,' I say, getting to my feet. 'I won't take any more of your time, but know I'm going to work so hard for you.'

'I know you will.'

As I leave, I'm pretty sure I hear her say, 'I'm so glad they finally worked it out.'

Thankfully, Michael lets Sorrel and me do what we want for the rest of the morning, as we have to come back to meet the main cast later with Rosa, once their training session is done.

'I have to go tell Levi,' I say, bouncing up and down. About my job. About what I just did for him. I hope he takes it better than I did.

Pen grabs me by the hand and we run out onto the street, hailing a cab. They've been working between here and the studio for the last week, so they take me right to backstage. I gasp when I see the size of the stadium from here. It's enormous. And backstage, so many of the sets are being finalised, ordered ready to be brought on and off. I know Levi said that the production team have been running drills for that the last few days.

It's really happening.

And I'm going to be on stage, here, next week.

Pen walks over to the sound guy backstage, grabbing one of the walkie talkies on the wall to call for Levi to come down and meet us.

'Hey!' I look up and see him waving down from the scaffolding above us. 'Give me five. It's time for my break anyway.'

'Do you wanna go stand on the stage?' Pen asks, and I nod silently. I can't speak as they lead me out into the arena. It's enormous.

I take their hand and squeeze. 'Thank you,' I say. When

they don't react, I squeeze their hand again. 'Pen, I'm thanking you.'

'Oh, sorry, I thought you were, like, thanking yourself. Why are you thanking me?'

'If you hadn't done that application for me, I wouldn't be here. This is all because of you.'

'No, Cass, it isn't,' they say. 'It's because of *you*. It's because of who *you* are and how hard *you* worked for it. I just gave you the first shove out of the nest.'

'Best shove of my life.'

'Oo-er.'

I wonder how far our giggles echo round the stadium.

'What are you two giggling about?' Levi says, slinging his arms round both of us.

'I'll leave you to it,' Pen says, slinking away with a smile on their face.

'I have some news,' I say, bouncing on my toes and turning to face him.

'Tell me!'

'I got promoted. I'm main cast. For the whole tour.'

He yells with excitement and I jump into his arms, my legs wrapped around his waist. He spins us round, and all I see is the arena. My future around us, and in my arms too.

'I knew you'd get it,' he says, leaning back to look up at me. 'I'm so proud of you.'

'There's something else, and you should put me down so I can tell you.'

'Worried I'm going to drop you?'

'Well, you might want to . . .'

He sets me down gently. 'Lay it on me.'

'OK, so stick with me on this. Mason showed up right before my audition with Rosa.'

Levi's thick eyebrows shoot right up into his forehead. 'The prick!'

'That's what Pen said,' I say. 'Don't worry, I got rid of him.'

'Well, look at you.'

'Only after you chewed him out so beautifully,' shouts Pen from across the stage. They do a chef's kiss, smacking their lips together loudly. 'Perfection.'

'Anyway, the point is, I then performed in front of Rosa and I was thinking of, like, everything that held me back, and the things that pushed me forward. Well, not things. You. Pen. My flatmates too. Michael. The people who got me here. And so, when I spoke to Rosa, I told her about your music.'

He goes very pale. 'My music? To Rosa?'

'Yeah. And she wants to meet with you. Ask Pen to put you in touch with Clara, her assistant.' I hand him the card Rosa gave me.

'Cass, I'm not ready for this. I'm still so raw.'

'Good,' I insist. 'She wants to nurture talent. She told me. And she's shown me from all this. I trust her with you, or I wouldn't have said.'

He looks down at the card, and back up at me. To my relief, he nods. 'OK. I can be brave too.' I scoop him into a hug, as he laughs with disbelief. 'What a world. Thank you, Cassie.'

'Thank Pen for starting the shove train.'

Levi puts me down gently and runs across the stage to grab Pen into a hug. I follow, throwing my arms around them both. 'Does that mean we go back in a circle and I have to shove you?'

'Not on stage, please,' they say. 'I'm too beautiful to fall off.'

'Guys,' I say. 'Look at us, we're *doing* it.'

'Doing what?'

I squeeze them both tight, two of the most important people in my life. Pen as my past and future. Levi joining us on the journey, loving us both. I'm overwhelmed with love. 'Following our dreams, together. For ourselves, and for each other.'

Chapter Twenty-six

Naturally, Levi takes it upon himself to ensure we go out to celebrate. The first few days working with the main cast passed in a really intense blur, and I definitely would not have remembered to take a moment to stop and breathe and celebrate it if it weren't for him.

So at the weekend, the two of us spend an afternoon walking through Montmartre, taking the steps all the way up to Sacré-Cœur. It's the end of August, the last gasp of a city in summer, which we survey from the dome as we catch our breath. He holds my hand the whole way.

It's my first time in Paris, and it feels so right to be here in love.

As the sky begins to darken, we cross the city, and he leads me towards a park with a huge lake. On one of the islands in the centre, we find Le Chalet des Îles, a sloped wooden building lit with fairy lights and hanging plants. A waiter leads us to a table by the water, and we sip red wine, watching the lights of the city play out across the water.

'Will all our dates be water themed?' I joke, after we cheers our glasses.

'Well, on that note.' He reaches into the inside pocket of his blazer, and pulls out a little pouch which he holds out to me.

Inside is the piece of sea-glass we found on the beach, threaded onto a delicate silver chain.

'You kept this,' I gasp. 'I thought I lost it.'

'Sorry to be sneaky. I had it in my pocket for weeks, and I just thought now was the right time to make something of it.'

'Did you do this?'

He blushes. 'Yeah. I'm sorry if it's a bit rough.'

'No, no! I love it,' I say, putting it on. It hangs just below my collarbone. 'I really love it.'

'It suits you.'

'You suit me.'

'Well, naturally. I'm very suitable.'

We giggle because, wow, we are such dorks but we can be dorks together.

'And our dates can be whatever you want them to be, Cassie,' he says. 'We've got a lifetime for them.'

And I believe him.

I really do.

'My incredible daughter!'

We're backstage in the dancers' dressing room when my parents wrap me into a huge hug.

'Thanks for coming,' I say, though it's muffled by their embrace.

Vics waves from the doorway where she leans, looking effortlessly cool.

The moment I got home after I got the job, I called to tell

them and they immediately booked flights out to see me in Paris on opening night. Thankfully, Pen was able to pull some strings and get them some of the friends and family tickets – I was too busy working my butt off with a whole new group of dancers to be able to think about anything else.

Until now, my last week has been eat, sleep, dance, befriend everyone I can, repeat. Luckily the main cast are all legends, and Sorrel and I fit in with them easily. It's such a privilege to be dancing with people who've been doing this for a while. There's so much we can learn from them, and they're all eager to share.

'Well, this is a bit fancy,' Mum says, looking around with one hand over her heart. 'This must be what it's like on the West End.'

'Do you want a tour?' asks Pen who stands looking a little nervously at Vics.

'*Yes!*' shrieks my mother, as Vics wraps Pen in a very platonic hug.

'Thanks for sorting all this out,' says Vics.

'No problem. It is quite literally part of my job.'

Pen's been so useful that they've had a kind of promotion from just helping out Michael, to essentially project managing the whole tour. They run from team to team, fighting fires and sorting communication issues, all with a smile and a joke. Everyone loves them. They've become the lifeblood of this tour, and that makes so much sense. It's like they were born for this.

'Not had to throw out any errant ex-boyfriends recently?' Vics asks.

'Thankfully, no.'

'Good. He's such a turd.'

Turns out Mason had found out where we were because he'd worked out what company was hiring staff on behalf of Rosa's tour, and had been setting up meetings to get to know the team on the premise that he would be able to use his non-existent contacts to find suitable candidates. He lied and cheated and thankfully, got in a lot of trouble.

'I need to start getting ready,' I say apologetically but Dad cuts me off.

'No apologising. We're just proud we get to come see you. My little girl, on stage.'

Everyone starts crying then, including me, but Pen manages to rally them out of the door, just in time for the other dancers to arrive. We've got hair and makeup to get into, and warm-ups to do, and then . . . we'll be dancing.

When Sorrel comes in, she wraps me in a huge hug. 'We did it, sweets,' she says.

'We did it.'

She took to the main cast like a duck to water. I swear she's got some besties in the making here, especially in the other trans girl on the team, Karina. They've been giggling and texting all the time, and it makes me so happy. In the past, when I was a teenager with my one friend, I'd have been so frightened of them making new ones, as though there was only so much love to go around. But Sorrel and the others have shown me that's not the case at all. There's enough love for all of us.

I don't know what she and Rosa talked about in the

kitchenette the day we were offered the job, but she came back beaming, bright eyed. I'm glad that Rosa made her feel as good as I did. This industry and Rosa especially are making a home for us, two girls who didn't fit in easily elsewhere.

'Also, I have this from Tyra and Veena for us.'

From her bag, she takes out two envelopes. We're still sharing a flat as a foursome, but I've barely seen the other two all week. Our hours only overlap a little, and then when we get home all of us are totally zonked or already asleep.

Inside, are two cards, one from each of them. Tyra's is a pretty picture of the Seine, Veena's is some inexplicable joke in French that we don't really understand even when we both Google Translate it.

In the end, Veena didn't need the shove that I did. After she performed for Rosa, she seemed to have experienced every possible moment of anxiety ever in one go, and walked right up to Michael and told him she wanted to be a choreographer. He's put her in touch with Katie Woo, and is training her up himself, so that she's ready for her first job after this, if she wants that. Adam was overjoyed, of course.

And for Tyra it's turned out that Hart really was the start of something new. They reached out to her and offered her the kind of long-term brand deal that she dreamed of. More campaigns, more content, all to begin once she's finished being an understudy. Tyra has decided that she's going to try and do a mix of both, so that she can share her life as a professional dancer on tour with the world on screen and on stage, while also making sure she gets the downtime between jobs that she needs. I really admire her decision to carve out a path that feels right for her.

Once I'm dressed, I make my way backstage, and find Levi running through a list on his clipboard. When he looks up, I say, 'Good luck tonight.'

He looks at me and gives me that grin I've come to love. 'You look so beautiful in that outfit.'

'I know,' I giggle, twirling for him.

'You ready to kill it out there?'

'We'll see.'

'You will.'

'You too.'

He wraps his arm around my waist, dips me slightly like he did on the boardwalk, and kisses me.

We've got two shows this weekend, and then two more next weekend, so in the mid-week, he and Rosa are going to meet to talk about his songwriting. I'm so excited for him. Since he agreed to the meeting, he's been sending me videos of him hard at work. The other night, he even played a few things for me. He's really talented, and I know she's going to love his work.

My boyfriend. We're end game. It's a wild thing to say, but it feels true to me.

I feel like I'm changed for the better.

This weird thing has been growing inside me that I think might be called confidence, though it feels alien. It makes me think that I'm good at my job and that I can handle anything life throws at me. I don't know, it's unfamiliar and weird but I'm learning to sit with it and not be afraid of it.

I spent so long being afraid of myself, my power as a dancer, my deafness. The amount of effort I'd put into making sure my hair covered my cochlear implant, and for what? I don't want to waste any more time. And I've got enough good people in my life now to feel like I'm getting there.

Learning to love yourself and love what you can do takes time, and I'm not going to lie to myself and say I've nailed it at the age of twenty.

But I know where I'm going, finally.

I know who I am, and who I want to be.

And when the lights go up, I dance.

A Note From Tasha

Dear reader,

I'm so proud to share *Hits Different* with you, my debut novel co-written with Lizzie Huxley-Jones. It's a spicy summer romance set in Ibiza, but it's also about embracing our differences, surrounding ourselves with people who value us and learning to put ourselves first.

I wanted to incorporate some of my own personal experiences into Cassie's story, and so she's deaf, wears a cochlear implant and dreams of becoming a professional dancer. Sounds familiar, right? There are lots of elements of me in Cassie, but she is also completely her own character, and this book is about her journey to find herself and self-love; I always believe you can't love somebody else unless you love yourself first. Cassie overcomes many obstacles along the way, including kissing some frogs who don't fully appreciate her or bother to learn about her disability. But with the support of her friends, including her non-binary bestie Pen, and Levi, who truly loves her for her, she's able to achieve her dreams. She has to make some hard choices, but she realises she has to because her happiness comes first.

It's been amazing to work with Lizzie, who I share so many similar experiences with, and who has made the process of publishing my first book so special. We had the same vision of what we wanted to achieve with Cassie's story and it's been incredible to bring it to life together. First and foremost, *Hits Different* is a romance, but perhaps you'll find that it's taught you something too – about cochlear implants and how to approach people with disabilities, about pronouns and being a good ally, and maybe even about how to love yourself for who you are.

I hope you've enjoyed reading it!

Lots of love,

Tasha

xxx

Acknowledgements

Huge thanks, first and foremost, to my incredibly talented co-author Lizzie Huxley-Jones, who has made this experience so fun and enjoyable. I've loved getting to know you and crafting this story together. Thank you for helping me bring my vision to life and understanding what I wanted to represent.

I'm also grateful to my publishing team at Hot Key Books, including: Ella Whiddett, Ruth Bennett, Amber Ivatt, Pippa Poole, Jas Bansal, Emma Quick, Talya Baker, Jenny Richards, Jessica Webb, Stephanie Bramwell-Lawes, Kate Dewey, Kate Griffiths, Holly Potter, Charlotte Brown and everyone else who has helped bring this book to readers. Thanks also to our amazing cover designers Beth Free and Studio Nic&Lou, and Abbi from NDCS, our lovely early reader.

Thanks also to my management team at Off Limits, and to David Riding at MBA Literary for helping connect me with the right publishing team.

Thank you, Andrew, my soul mate, for being with me every step of the way. You've shown me what true love is and I'm so lucky to experience that every day with you.

My parents and brother, you're all amazing, thank you for

believing in me and my crazy dreams!

My friends, you all really are the best of friends I could ever ask for!

And finally, thank you to all the readers out there, especially those with a disability, this is for you.

Tasha

First thanks must go to my co-author, Tasha. Writing *Hits Different* with you has been such an amazing creative experience, and I knew from our first meeting where we talked about our love of romance and shared aim of representation in literature that we were cooking up something special. Thank you for trusting me with this adventure. We did it!

This book is absolutely born out of love for our community. Thank you to the other disabled and queer people kicking open doors in their respective industries, making this world a much more interesting, vivid and honest place. This one's for all of you.

My agent Abi Fellows deserves the world and more! Thank you for keeping me moving forward while juggling three very different books. Cake's on me.

Thank you to everyone at Hot Key Books who has supported Tasha and me through the creation and development of *Hits Different*. Ruth Bennett and Ella Whiddett, our extraordinary editors, ensured that this ambitious book hit the ground running, and Anna Bowles, Felicity Alexander and Talya Baker polished it up perfectly after the most whirlwind year! Thank you to Jasveen Bansal and Pippa Poole for taking us out on Valentine's Day proof drops, and to Amber Ivatt and Emma Quick for all your hard work on getting *Hits Different* out there. Thanks also to the brilliant sales and production teams for getting the book onto shelves. We have the most gorgeous cover, with Cassie wearing her cochlear implant front-and-centre, thanks to Beth Free and NicandLou. Thank you as well to Abbi at NDCS for the extra pair of hands in making sure Cassie's deafness felt authentic.

Thank you to all the friends I've neglected but have continued to support me through this wild year and more broadly my career so far. Sorry I keep saying I'll be less busy soon, because that seems to be a total lie. I can't possibly name you all because I'm blessed with so many of you, but if you've ever had me last minute cancel our plans because of a disability flare-up and stuck around, then this is for you. I love you all; thank you for loving me right back.

Thanks also to all my family for their love and support and enthusiasm since I announced, while concussed, that I was going to be an author. I did it! Sorry there's so many of them.

My sister deserves a line of thanks all her own because she has been and continues to be an absolute rock in my life. I'm so glad we are two.

Nerys, sorry I continue to ignore you and keep staring at the computer. There's dog biscuits in the cupboard. Final thanks always go to my partner Tim, who has been both metaphorically and literally picking me up off the floor for a decade. Thanks for always making the tea.

Hux

About the Authors

Tasha Ghouri is a television personality, activist, model and social media influencer. She is a brand ambassador for eBay, Ann Summers and L'Oréal Paris, and recently launched her own podcast, *Superpowers with Tasha Ghouri*, which focuses on normalising disabilities by embracing them as superpowers. As a proud cochlear implant wearer, she is also a global ambassador for DeafKidsUK, and works with the National Deaf Children's Society and RNID to help those with hearing impairments.

Lizzie Huxley-Jones is an autistic author and editor based in London. They are the author of the queer holiday rom-com *Make You Mine This Christmas* and the Vivi Conway series – middle-grade, fantasy adventure starting with *Vivi Conway and the Sword of Legend*. They write joyful stories that centre queerness and disability. In their past career lives they have been a research diver, a children's bookseller and a digital communications specialist.

HOT
KEY
BOOKS

Thank you for choosing a Hot Key book!

For all the latest bookish news, freebies and exclusive

content, sign up to the Hot Key newsletter – scan the

QR code or visit lnk.to/HotKeyBooks

Follow us on social media:

bonnierbooks.co.uk/HotKeyBooks